THE FORGOTTEN WIFE

ALEX SIGMORE

Storm

Ebook ISBN: 978-1-83700-261-0
Paperback ISBN: 978-1-83700-262-7

Cover design: Blacksheep
Cover images: Deposit Photos, Shutterstock

Published by Storm Publishing.
For further information, visit:
www.stormpublishing.co

Oak Creek Thriller

The Darkest Game

Never Strike Twice

Emily Slate FBI Mystery Thriller

His Perfect Crime

The Collection Girls

Smoke and Ashes

Her Final Words

Can't Miss Her

The Lost Daughter

The Secret Seven

A Liar's Grave

The Girl In The Wall

His Final Act

The Vanishing Eyes

Edge of the Woods

Ties That Bind

The Missing Bones

Blood in the Sand

The Passage

Fire in the Sky

Oh What Fun

Ivy Bishop Mystery Thriller

Her Dark Secret

The Girl Without A Clue

The Buried Faces

Her Hidden Lies

PROLOGUE

She sits at her desk, facing away from me as she types on her computer. Her dark hair falls in locks over her exposed shoulders. She's typing frantically, like she can't wait to get it all out; like she'll die if she doesn't finish it.

I approach slowly as not to startle her. This is what's best. Maybe she doesn't see it now, but I want to help her. *Have* to help her. She's all alone and no one else is coming. If I don't, she'll be trapped forever.

As I step closer, I notice the fresh bruise on her arm, and it sends a rage through me. It only proves what I'm doing is the best for everyone.

Even though my steps are silent, she must sense me as she turns in her chair. Her eyes go wide with confusion at first, then with fear as she spots the gloves I'm wearing. I lunge forward, any hopes of making this clean having evaporated into the evening air. My hands lock around her throat, and I squeeze as hard as I can as she tries to scream, but with the pressure on her larynx, nothing comes out. I see the betrayal in her eyes, the pleading. But she has to know this is the only way, right? This will be better for her.

My hands tangle in her hair as we struggle about. She's almost the same height as me, but she's been caught unawares, and despite the adrenaline that must be flooding her system, she doesn't have a plan. She flails, trying everything she can to get me to release my grasp. I avoid most of her attempts to break my hold, though she manages to land a few punches.

But to me, pain is an old friend and I don't flinch when her fist makes contact with my face. I'm numb to it, and I don't quit squeezing. I only have one chance at this; if I let go now, it all falls apart.

Finally, after what seems like an eternity, the fight begins to go out of her as she struggles for breath. Her eyes roll back and her arms go slack, still attempting to grasp at my hands and pull them from her throat. Deep purple bruises have begun to form around her neck and will never leave. A permanent mark of my actions.

There is something like a gurgling sound deep from within her and finally her body goes limp. I gently lower her to the ground, but don't remove my hands... not yet. I have to make sure. But it doesn't stop tears from filling my eyes and dripping onto her cheeks. As soon as I'm confident it's over, I remove my hands; impressions in the shape of my fingers remain around her neck.

She's so beautiful, frozen in time now, never needing to experience the humiliation of the days passing anymore. It's over. I've done it. I've saved her.

I wipe my eyes. Her green ones stare back up at me. I gently pull her eyelids down, closing them forever.

I love you.

ONE

WINTER

At almost five o'clock the doorbell rings.

I glance up from my book, momentarily annoyed at the intrusion. It's probably another person out to sell me something I don't need, but I swear, if I have to tell one more contractor I don't want the trees around my house trimmed, I think I might scream.

All I wanted was a few minutes to myself after a harrowing day at work. The Williamson project hadn't gone very well and I doubt we'll land the contract. And I put in more hours on that job than any other. Not to mention I have two more contracts this week which are going to take any remaining free time.

I just wanted to come home, throw on my comfies and settle in with my book before Fenton got home.

I suppose I better go tell whoever it is that if they keep harassing us, I will file a restraining order against their company. I wonder if anyone has ever done that. Or if it has ever worked. It's at times like this when I wish Fenton would finally cave in and let us buy outdoor cameras, then I could tell someone to go away from the comfort of my couch. But *no*, they clash with the architecture, or so he says.

I sigh. At least while I'm up, I might as well grab the mail. And who knows, maybe it's not a salesman but instead one of the neighbors coming by to say hello, though, *God*, I hope not. Not that I wouldn't be happy to meet more of the neighbors now that I'm living here full time, but not today. And not tomorrow either. And not for a few days, in fact. Just give me enough time to mentally prepare for their arrival... like a month.

I slip on Fenton's old sneakers he'd left haphazardly by the door, unable to keep a smile from forming across my face. These are my *fiancé's* sneakers, no longer my boyfriend's. I wouldn't call myself a sentimental person, but I am a bit of a romantic, so I notice the little things. He proposed two weeks ago, during a romantic weekend at Powder Ridge Mountain. We've been together for three years, so I knew it had to be coming, but I was still surprised. I was even *more* surprised when I saw the announcement in the local papers. I guess I just need to get used to being in the public eye more.

But none of that matters. And soon enough I'll be putting on my *husband's* shoes at the last minute when I need to meet someone unexpected at the door.

I take a deep breath to reset myself, plaster a fake smile across my lips and open the door, praying this interaction doesn't take long. But instead of someone standing on our doorstep, there's nothing but a small brown package leaning up against the timber. Left by the mailman no doubt. *Oh, thank God.*

I can't help but notice he left it leaning on to the more "traditional" side of the house. I'm not an architect, I'm an engineer, so my concern lies in the practical. Fenton... he's the artist out of the two of us. And he calls this house an architectural "dream." His words. If I recall correctly, it's *"classic English Tudor merged with post-modern impressionism."* I had to memorize that in the beginning because I understood exactly zero words in that sentence. But now I've become a little more cultured, at least according to him. The door itself is set into a small alcove with cross timber over wattle on one side and glass on the other, the entrance sitting between them at the end of a short path winding down from the driveway. He told me when he first found this house, it didn't even have an indoor bathroom and had fallen into neglect and disrepair. But slowly, over the course of two years, he'd managed to transform it into the magnificent swan it is today, the pride of the local community and the recipient of the AIA Connecticut Design Award for best single-family residence in the state three years running. The award had made him something of a minor celebrity in our little town and, oddly enough, was what first brought him to my attention. So you could say, in a way, this house was what brought us together. So then it's appropriate this is where we'll start the rest of our lives together.

Ignoring the package, I walk down the long driveway to the mailbox itself, where I retrieve a small stack of flyers, advertisements, and what I suspect are at least two bills. The freezing air whips across my exposed face and I shiver as I make my way back up, the wind blowing in short, but powerful gusts. A cold front moved in last night in the middle of what had been a very pleasant start to spring, bringing with it the chance of snow on all the newly opened flower and tree buds.

I take a deep breath, bend down and grab the small brown package leaning up against the entryway, and make my way back inside. The security system beeps twice as I open and close the door again. I kick Fenton's sneakers off and immediately trash the junk mail, setting the two bills aside to leave in Fenton's—wait, no —*our* home office later. I'm about to leave the package as well since it's addressed to him, but I can't help but notice the stylish calligraphy on the front. Perhaps *calligraphy* is too generous a word, but the writing is almost certainly that of a woman and, it seems to me, contains a personal touch to it. Maybe it's in the way the end of the *F* in Fenton's name almost forms a heart. How often is it you get a piece of mail that's been hand-addressed anymore? And a package at that. But as I examine it further, I realize there is no stamp on the package... no label and no return address.

That's odd. Could someone have hand-delivered this?

I'm being ridiculous. I toss the package on top of the rest of the mail, annoyed with myself for being so paranoid. I don't do that, not anymore. Cammie would have called me on it if she'd been here. I can't forget all the progress I've made and the glowing endorsement Dr. Hobart gave me on our last session. He said I'd come far and that as long as I made intentional decisions, I could live whatever kind of life I wished. One free from what caused me so much trouble in the past.

Still, it's hard to deny the possibility some woman sent my fiancé a personal package. Even after three years, I still don't know all of his friends. Could this be a prank by an old college acquaintance?

Or maybe someone closer?

I pick up the package again and shake it, feeling its heft. It's dense, like a book. But not like one of those coffee table books he's always going on about; this is shaped like a regular-sized book. He doesn't even read books. So why would someone "mail" him one?

Winter. Stop it. You're better than this. It's Fenton's package, he'll deal with it when he gets home and then you won't have to worry about it anymore. You're being paranoid.

I gently set the package down, resigned not to think about it anymore until he comes home. But as I walk away, I can feel it *watching* me, tempting me to unwrap its secrets. The packaging isn't held together by more than a couple of pieces of Scotch tape. I could...

I rush back over and, before I can stop myself, peel the top edge open, allowing me to see into the package itself. It is indeed a book. My heart does a little flutter at the confirmation, and I manage to slip the paperback out of the brown wrapping without ripping the packaging.

"Oh." I didn't expect this.

"*The Last Man I'd Marry*," I say, reading the title, which takes up most of the cover. "By Miranda Meriwether."

I flip the book over, reading the blurb on the back.

Some secrets can't be kept forever. Dean has a dark past, one that he's neglected to tell his new wife, Abbie, about. But when Abbie accidentally stumbles upon a letter from his former life, her world comes crashing down around her. Suddenly, there's no one she can trust. And the more she learns, the more dangerous Dean becomes.

Will Abbie find a way out of this labyrinth of secrets? Or will it swallow her whole, burying her forever?

"Huh," I say, flipping it back over. It's not a book I've ever seen before, but I can't deny it's right up my alley. In fact, it's not so different to the book I'm currently reading. I wonder who could have sent it? I'm sure Fenton won't mind me borrowing it, since the odds of him actually opening it are about one in a hundred thousand.

I flip through the pages, for no other reason than I like the feel. But I'm also looking for maybe a note, or some explanation as to why this book has all of a sudden shown up on my doorstep for free. But there's nothing. No letter or note tucked inside. Though when I get to the dedication page, my eyes go wide.

To: F.
No matter what, you'll never get rid of me.
Love you forever.

Well, that's... *ominous.*

F.

F for Fenton? It has to be; why else address the book to him?

I stop to take a few deep breaths. *Think.* Who could have sent this? A fan? Someone who saw Fenton's name in relation to the award? Maybe some crazed person out there looking for attention? But there's something about the dedication that doesn't sit well with me. It's personal and yet, foreboding.

Oh, Dr. Hobart would not like this. This is exactly what I'm *not* supposed to be doing, but it's not my fault I found a book dedicated to my *future* husband. Obviously, we were going to open this package and—

He. *He* was going to open this package. If I hadn't gone snooping, I might have never known about this secret admirer.

Winter, remember you're not to make any assumptions. You have to communicate with those you love, not assume.

Right, right, I know. He's right, of course. But the damage is done now. I might as well keep going. It isn't like this could get much worse. I turn a few pages to the first chapter, intrigued about what could have convinced Ms. Meriwether to dedicate an *entire book* to my fiancé.

"There are only two constants in life. Death and love. And right now, I'm staring both in the face at the same time."

I don't even feel myself sink into the couch as I continue reading. Before I know it, half an hour has passed and I'm *glued* to this book. I realize with a start that Fenton will be home soon, and I can't be caught with it in my hand. I'm sure there is a reasonable explanation for all of this... even though that little voice in the back of my head is screaming otherwise.

I scramble up off the couch and do my best to re-wrap the book just as it came, gingerly folding the ends of the packaging back up. Fenton shouldn't be able to tell. But I can't leave it like this.

In the corner of the large room, lined by windows on the north side, sits a crate full of shipping tubes for Fenton's designs. It takes me a second to dig through everything, but after a moment I retrieve the small roll of packing tape wedged into a corner of one cabinet. I place the tape right back on top of the piece I'd cut, making it virtually indistinguishable from before. And he won't look that carefully, I'm sure.

I place the package back with the rest of the mail, though I can't help but stare at it for a few moments. Whoever Miranda Meriwether is, she's not a half-bad writer. Part of me wants to keep reading just for the sake of it. Once Fenton has explained himself, I plan on finishing it.

Careful, Winter.

I swallow and turn away from the mail. Only good habits. I head into the kitchen where I retrieve a bottle of pinot noir from the fridge and a glass. He'll be home soon. We can discuss it then.

But as I'm pouring the wine into the glass, movement at the edge of the driveway catches my eye. And then I see it. A shadowy figure stepping across the drive between the bushes.

I scream, dropping my glass, which shatters in the sink.

TWO

WINTER

My first instinct is to run.

My second is to call 911.

But as I get my phone in my hand, ready to dial, I realize the figure isn't there anymore. I squint, looking closer, but whoever was there is gone. The kitchen has windows on both sides, which means it looks out on the woods in the backyard and all the way down the driveway out the front. The streetlights at the end of the drive illuminate the road beyond, but the path lighting along the driveway is the only light coming up to the house. And it was there that I saw him. I *know* it was a him because of how big he looked. Unfortunately, the neighbors are just a little too far to see from here. We're all on our own little lots, cut off and secluded from each other. It's one of the things I thought I liked best about this place, but now I'm not so sure. Could it have been one of the neighbors out on an evening walk?

It isn't like there are any additional lights I can turn on out there. And I'm sure as hell not going back outside by myself again. I've seen enough horror movies to know how that ends.

You're being extra paranoid today.

Shut up. *Where is Fenton?*

Ugh, what am I doing? Cowering by myself in this big house?

I'm better than this. I open the drawer beside the sink, revealing a small notepad with a series of numbers scrawled across it. I run my finger over the first one and dial on my cell.

It rings three times before she picks up. "Hello?"

"Hi, uh, Janet? It's Winter from next door."

"Oh, hello," the voice echoes on the other end. "How are you, dear? Is everything all right?"

"Good, good. Are you at home?" I ask, still straining to see the figure. But whoever was there has vanished as if they were nothing more than a puff of smoke.

"I'm just fixing myself some dinner," she says.

"Can you do me a favor and look out towards our place? Do you see... someone standing at the end of our driveway?"

"You saw someone? What were they doing?" Janet asks, her voice cracking a bit. Janet is pretty tough, but still. It's not like I expect her to just head on out and ask this person what they're doing on our property. This is what I get for not making time to meet all the neighbors. Thankfully, Janet and I have similar schedules and have run into each other more than half a dozen times since I moved in with Fenton. And I don't want to be one of those people who lives twenty yards from four other families and doesn't know any of their names. From what few interactions we've had, I know Janet is single, recently divorced from her husband of almost thirty years, and sharp as a whip. She's also in her early seventies. If someone is being a Peeping Tom or something similar, I'm pretty damn sure she would go out there and beat them with her own shoes if she had to.

"I don't know, but it looked like they might be watching the house. Though... I might have imagined it."

"Nonsense," she says. "Hang on." I hear rustling in the background. "I had to get my binoculars," Janet says, her voice slightly muffled. I assume she's holding the phone between her shoulder and ear while looking through the binoculars. "Where was he again?"

I squint out the window, but small halos are forming in my

vision from looking at the bright driveway lights. "He was right there, at the end of our drive, by one of the pillars. I don't see him anymore. I don't even know if it was a him." *Yes, you do.*

"It was definitely a him. No woman would be standing out there looking at you in that glass box you live in. Probably some pervert."

"But you don't see anyone?"

"Not yet, hon, but I'll keep a sharp eye out."

"That's okay. You're probably right, just some nut. Or maybe someone admiring the house. We've had a few of those since the articles came out," I lie, trying to make myself feel better. No one has come out to see the house, despite all the press about it. But it doesn't mean someone couldn't, though it is late in the day for a viewing.

"I'll keep checking anyway. It'll give me something to do other than watch game shows all night."

"Thanks, I appreciate it. I'll talk to you later."

"I'll call back if I spot the bastard."

I hang up, slip the phone into my pocket and cross my arms. A cold shiver runs down my back. Could it have been my imagination? It has been a long day.

Looking down into the sink, I sigh. It takes me a few minutes to pick out all the pieces of glass and dispose of them. I need to get a hold of myself. I can't be so jumpy all the time.

It was a coincidence. Or I didn't see what I thought I saw. Or some other reasonable explanation. Just like the book. Something explains that dedication page in there—I just don't know what yet.

I pull my phone out again and google the name *Miranda Meriwether*. But nothing comes up. I look up the book on all the normal retailers and there are a few with the same title, but they're not by the same author and don't have the same description. Whoever Miranda is, it doesn't look like she's doing a very good job publishing her work. I can't even figure out how to get a copy of this book if I didn't already have one.

Pen name. It has to be.

I google the name in the area, but again, nothing comes up. No book signings, no author events. Not even a mention in the local writers' club. Instead of making me feel better, this has all just made me feel worse.

I rub my temples, trying to get my limbic system to calm down. Maybe there never was a person at the end of the driveway. Maybe it's just my imagination. But what if it's the person who left the book? Are they waiting for Fenton to get home? Is something else coming? Something worse?

I take a deep breath. Dr. Hobart would be so disappointed in me if he saw me this way. Wasn't I supposed to be confronting my anxiety? Wasn't I supposed to be free of it? His words echo in my head. *You can't be free of your fear until you confront it.*

I shake the shivers out of my body and stomp over to the closet, slip my feet into boots, grab my overcoat and pull it on over my clothes. I'm not going to live my life like this. Not when I have a wonderful future ahead of me. All that crap that happened before... it's over now. I have an opportunity for a good life. And if someone wants to try to scare me out of it, I'm not going to take it lying down.

Life isn't a horror movie, and I'm not the victim.

I walk out into the cold, the wind blowing my coat up against my silhouette and I hitch my breath. It's dropped more than a couple of degrees since I was last out here and that wasn't more than an hour ago. Regardless, I trudge on down the driveway again, sliding my eyes from side to side, keeping an eye out for any movement in the darkness beyond the driveway. I don't know exactly what I'm going to *do*, but I'm not just going to wait for whoever is out here to come to me.

When I finally reach the end of the drive, I pull my cell phone out and turn on the flashlight, scanning the area with the weak beam. Janet's house is visible from here and I see the older woman in her window, the binoculars still glued to her face. I smile and wave, and Janet waves right back but doesn't take her eyes off the area. She's keeping an eye out for me, which I appreciate more than she probably knows.

I scan the road again, looking for any trace of the person who could have been out here, finding nothing. No dark figures lurking in the shadows, no footprints, nothing the person may have dropped or disturbed in any way. Part of me is disappointed. But another part of me is relieved. It must have just been in my imagination after all.

The wind is blistering, and I'm already chilled down to the bone. Taking one last look around, I finally head back to the house for the second time this evening. I'm about halfway up the drive when bright lights illuminate my shadow on the house. Behind me, Fenton's car rumbles up the driveway, the loose gravel crunching under the tires. I move to the side to let him pass, but he slows and rolls down his window.

"Hey, hon? What are you doing out here? Aren't you cold?"

My first instinct is to ask him about the book. I want to throw a thousand questions at him, get my explanation and find out just who the hell is sending books to my future husband.

But instead, I just bend down and kiss him through the window.

"Hi, sweetie, welcome home."

THREE

WINTER

"Why were you outside again?" Fenton asks, shrugging off his satchel and hooking it over the end of the kitchen counter stool. I came back through the front door while he'd pulled into the garage. I couldn't help but sneak a cursory look into the office as I passed just to make sure the package was still there and hadn't magically disappeared like my ghost outside.

"Just admiring our beautiful house with all that uplighting," I say, smirking, trying to remain playful.

"But, babe, it's like thirty degrees out there. Good way to catch something." He makes his way around the counter to wash his hands; a peculiar little habit he'd had ever since I've known him. Whenever he gets back home from somewhere, he always takes a few minutes to wash his hands, as if he's scrubbing off the dirt of the world. As if dirt wasn't allowed in this place.

Almost like the house is responding to his commands, the heat kicks on automatically, and a low hum reverberates throughout the room. I've still got my coat on, trying to warm the chill from outside. But I don't want him to know that. While he's got his back to the sink, I pull the coat off and rub my arms before returning it to the closet.

"I wanted to get the mail. You got a package," I say. He's given me the perfect excuse. Maybe now he can just open the book, he can explain, and all of this can be over before we sit down for dinner. Nothing but a nice, relaxing evening ahead. I'm not going to tell him about the guy out at the end of the drive, not until I'm sure it was real and not a figment of my imagination. He could blow things out of proportion—something we have in common—and I'm not about to ruin his night by telling him there might be a prowler around. If someone does try anything, our security system will scare them off. If that doesn't work, I'm a decent shot, and the gun is right in the back bedroom.

"I could have grabbed it," he replies, drying his hands. He comes over and gives me a deeper kiss than the one we shared outside. Now that he's back home and situated, he's much more comfortable. He pulls away. "Thank you, though."

I'm struck by his earnestness. The mention of a package doesn't faze him; which means he isn't expecting it. He's not trying to hide it. That makes me feel a bit better, but also a little worse because now it's a totally unknown element. *Some*one sent that thing to him and I'm *going* to find out who it was.

"It's kind of heavy," I say, trying to steer the conversation in the right way without overshowing my hand. But he's not moving. Just standing there staring right into my eyes.

"Hmm? Oh, the package." He snaps his gaze away. "Maybe it's an early wedding present. That was quite the write-up."

"Yeah. You'll have to thank your mother again," I say, keeping my voice light. He obviously doesn't expect it to be anything nefarious, yet I did. What does that say about me? "I left it in the office."

He turns back and gathers me into his arms, pulling us together. "How about we skip dinner?" He buries his face into my neck, sending a different kind of tingle through my body.

But I tense up a second later. I can't relax until I get some answers. This is one of the things I've been working on so hard with Dr. Hobart about. Unfinished business. Closing the loops.

Just let him explain it, then you can both have a nice night.

"I'm really hungry," I say, pulling my palms up and placing

them on his chest. My brand-new, three-carat engagement ring catches my eye as I say it. "Playtime after."

Fenton laughs. "Want to fuel up, huh? I gotcha." He gives me that near-irresistible smirk and pulls away.

"Why don't I get it started?" I ask, hoping he'll find his way into the office.

"Then I," he says, loosening his tie, "will go find something more comfortable myself."

I turn towards the refrigerator and grind my teeth together. At this rate he won't look at it until the morning. "I think I saw something else in the mail too, something from AIA maybe? I'm not sure," I lie. That should do it. He won't be able to resist the possibility of another award nomination.

Good job, Winter. Lie to your future husband.

"Oh?" He perks up and turns from his path towards the bedrooms, swinging around the large partition wall and descending the two stairs into the office.

Finally. This will all be over in a few minutes. I pull out the pinot noir I'd opened earlier as well as a fresh glass. Maybe I can actually enjoy this one. I nab a second glass for Fenton.

To busy myself while trying not to listen in on him unwrapping the package, I begin retrieving ingredients from different places around the kitchen. Tonight will be a good night for taco bowls, sans tacos. No need to add all those extra carbs into our diet when the bowls have plenty of nutrients in them.

A sound catches my ear: the rustling of paper being torn away. He's opening it. I can already breathe easier knowing that, one way or another, this package business is about to be concluded.

He doesn't return immediately, and no other sounds reach me from the office while I prepare the meal. Maybe he's just processing it, trying to figure it out himself. Or maybe he's trying to decide what to tell me. I return to chopping peppers, trying to put it out of my mind.

Nearly ten minutes pass. Enough time for me to completely finish fixing everything. The bowls sit on the counter, a small bit of steam rising from each. Our glasses of wine remain rooted on the counter, untouched.

This is ridiculous. What is taking him so long? I take a deep breath and head to the office, poking my head around the partition without actually descending the stairs. "Hey," I say, keeping my voice soft.

He's hunched over his computer, but from this angle I can't see the screen. I *can* see the tension in his shoulders. He jumps at my words and stares at me a minute, like he's coming out of a trance. But then his eyes relax. "Hey."

"Dinner's ready," I say, my heart picking up speed. This is not the reaction I was hoping for, and as I scan the office, there is no trace of the book anywhere.

"Great, I'll be in there in a second."

"What are you doing in here?"

"Hm?" he asks, looking up again. "Oh, just some work stuff. A couple of emails I had to follow up on from the office."

My heart is hammering now. "So," I say, trying to keep the myriad of images and possibilities from running wild through my mind, "do we have a new knife set or something?"

He looks at me as if my head is screwed on backwards.

"The package?"

"Oh," he says, pausing. His eyes flicker away, then back again. "No, it was just junk mail, one of those promotional things."

Even if I hadn't already opened it, I would have recognized the lie. "Promotional thing from whom?" I try to keep my voice from shaking. He is unapologetically lying right to my face.

He shrugs. "Just one of those small no-name societies, probably wanting me to join just to give them some prestige. Junk mail." He returns his attention to the screen, all his former warmth gone.

This is not happening. Not after I put this ring on my finger. I have to push. There's no other way, not if we're going to build a life together. I won't do that again; I won't live in a relationship built on secrets. "It looked like something personal. It didn't have an official label or anything."

Fenton stops typing for a split second, then resumes. "They must have interns doing some grunt work, probably think it will make things more personal."

Oh my God. He's not going to stop. I struggle to keep breathing. Not only is he lying, but he's doing it without hesitation. Should I call him out right now? If I do, there is a one hundred percent chance we'll have a fight about it. He was supposed to come home and explain this thing, not cover it up! This isn't the man I agreed to marry. For the entire three years we've been together, he's been nothing but honest and upfront about everything... right? Maybe I've missed something. He can obviously lie without compunction; what else hasn't he been telling me? I recognize the spiral beginning and pull it back. Focus on the problem, not the emotion, like Dr. Hobart says. We can deal with the rest later.

I'm going to have a hell of a session coming up.

"Fenton?" I ask, steeling myself for the confrontation we're about to have.

He glances up again.

"Where's the book?"

FOUR
WINTER

His eyes flash and recognition dawns on him. I see it all over his face before he has time to wipe it away. If I hadn't surprised him, he might have been able to hide it. And now it is all out in the open.

Why couldn't he have just told me? Was it really so bad he had to lie about it? I hold his gaze while using considerable strength to resist looking down at my ring finger, as if to say, *You promised you'd never lie, you made a promise, and here's the physical proof.*

"You opened it," he says, his eyes falling.

"Yes." No sense in denying it. I'm not the liar here.

He sits at the computer a moment longer, then taps the power button and stands, crossing the room to one of the suspended cabinets on the far wall. He removes the package with its torn wrapping.

Part of me is confused. If he'd been trying to hide it, there are far better places than inside the cabinets we both use on a regular basis.

"Here," he says, tossing it to me with no warning, hurt in his eyes. "Happy?"

It isn't a hard toss, just an awkward one. I fumble the catch but manage to grab it before it hits the floor, though my grasp only reaches the outer wrapping. As I pull at it, the wrapping tears even further, producing an audible *rip* that echoes through the room.

"Why did you lie about it?" I ask, staring at the thing, the tear having revealed the bold cover plastered with her name.

"Why did *you* open it?"

He's accusing me? I take a deep breath. "Because when a package comes hand-addressed to you in what looks to be a woman's handwriting, I find that strange."

"Why?" he asks. "I wouldn't care if a package came addressed to you by a man."

Is he seriously doing this? "Do you really not know?"

He comes over to take me by the shoulders, but I shrug him off. "Is this because of Thomas?"

"You know what it's about," I say, my eyes downcast. "You're supposed to understand. Not defend your secret admirer."

"Secret admirer?" He frowns, but his brow is creased in confusion.

I huff and tear the wrapping away from the book and toss the brown paper with the feminine writing on the ground. He's playing dumb and I've almost reached my limit. I angrily flip to the dedication page and shove the book back at him.

He scans the page, and for a split second I see something in his eyes: sadness, maybe? Regret? It's so quick that it's gone by the time I realize I'd seen anything at all.

"F," I say, not wanting to let go of my anger. "That's you, right?"

"Yeah, maybe." He swallows hard, still looking at the page. That's not a good sign. Is this even worse than I'd imagined?

"Okay, so who is Miranda Meriwether? And how does she know you?"

"I knew her in school," he says softly. I'm almost surprised by the admission. Part of me thought he'd just keep denying it. He turns to the first page and scans the words. As he begins reading, I catch the faint upturn of one corner of his lips.

"In college? You never said—"

"No, younger. Back in high school, a long time ago. That's who I was looking for on the computer. I haven't talked to... Miranda in probably twenty years."

"Why would she dedicate a book to you?"

He shrugs again and closes the book, seemingly unconcerned. "She used to have a thing for me way back when. That's the only reason I can think of. I swear I haven't talked to her in a long time." It's like he's run out of energy, like something zapped the fight out of him, and I can't help but pity him, cursing myself as I do so. Why does he get all the sympathy and I get all the hardship? *Because you let people walk over you*, Dr. Hobart says in my head.

Should I take this high-school-sweetheart idea at face value? I don't want to make this any harder either, but he needs to give me more.

"Why didn't you just tell me that from the beginning?"

He glances up and purses his lips. "I *was* going to tell you, but I wanted to find out about Miranda first, so I could give you the whole story all at once. I didn't think you'd come in here and start browbeating me. Had you given me time to research, I probably could have found out tonight."

"But instead, you lied to me."

"I'm sorry, I shouldn't have done that." No excuse. I have a hard time accepting it. "You caught me off guard. I know what you've been through, and I wanted to wait until I could tell you everything. I thought you'd drop it, but you're just so damn persistent... I should have known better."

I stare at him, not sure what to say.

"Oh, and by the way, there's no AIA letter in here. Obviously." He glares at me, his gaze teasing.

"That's different," I say. I wasn't trying to hide anything; my lie was to expose the truth. They're two different things.

"Be honest. If I'd come back into the kitchen and told you I'd received a strange book from someone I used to know back in high school, what would you have done?" Before I can answer, he continues. "You would have started asking me questions. Who is she? Why is she sending me a book? Why now? Where does she live? When was the last time you saw her?" He closes the distance between us. I want to back up but remain resolute. "I know how things get for you sometimes. I know you hate not knowing what's going on and you want all your questions answered immediately. That's all I was trying to do. Why didn't you just tell me you'd opened it when I got home? We could have avoided this whole song and dance."

Dammit. Now I'm not as upset with him as I am with myself. He's right, I should have confronted him immediately. Normally, I would have. But this just... felt *different*. Like I needed to hide it for some reason, or at least make him come to me with it instead of the other way around. I'd wanted him to prove himself to me, which he shouldn't have to do and now I feel like shit. That's not how I want this marriage to start. This is the man I love, not one of those others. He isn't Thomas, because he actually loves me back, and here I am grilling him over a stupid package that neither of us knows anything about. Love means he shouldn't have to prove anything to me.

But... what if I hadn't opened it? Would he have even mentioned it to me? Or would he have just tossed it and never told me about it? I don't like the implications of that thought. This is my chance to do what I should have done from the beginning.

"Maybe it wasn't right," I say, "but I saw the writing on the front and I couldn't help myself. Tell me, would you have told me the truth about it if I hadn't known? Or would you have kept it secret?"

He stares directly into my eyes. "I would have told you. I don't want to screw up something so perfect." He smiles. "I would have gathered all the information I could find and then presented it to you. Maybe even set up a whole PowerPoint presentation."

Okay. Now he's just rubbing it in. "Smart-ass." I stifle my own smile. "You would tell me, right? If there was something going on. You know I can't—"

"Winter," he says, in that way that always means he knows this is important and he wouldn't hurt me. "I promise on my grandmother's grave I am not having an affair or seeing anyone else. There is no one but you, okay? I swear to it."

His voice doesn't waver, and his eyes don't shift. He is dead serious. Even if I don't completely buy the high school thing, it doesn't matter, because this is real.

"Did you find her yet?" I ask, attempting to shift the attention away from me now that I've made a complete butt out of myself.

He shakes his head.

"She's... she's a decent writer."

One of his eyebrows goes up. "You read it?"

I shrug. "Just the first few chapters."

He picks it up. "I'm guessing now that you know where it's from, you probably don't want anything else to do with it."

"Actually," I say. "Keep it. Knowing that you knew her... I'm interested to see what happens." After basking in the warmth of his comfort for a second, I pull back. "But if you do find her, would you please tell her to stop sending my future husband books telling him she loves him?"

He chuckles, clearly relieved that the danger is over. "Yeah, I don't know *what* that's about. I assume the *F* is for me, but it could very well be a Freddie or a Franklin or a Ferdinand."

"Did you have any of those in your class back then?"

"Probably. But I'm not sure she's working with a full deck, if you know what I mean."

I place my hand on his chest. "What *are* you going to say when you find her?"

"To not send me anything else and suggest she never contact me again. If she does have some kind of infatuation, I think it's best not to encourage it."

I smile. The perfect answer. "I'm sorry I opened your package."

"I'm sorry I didn't tell you." He pauses. "Or maybe I'm just sorry you're too damn impatient for your own good."

I move to smack him again, but before I can, his lips are on mine. For the first time since it arrived, I don't give a damn about that book anymore.

FIVE

WINTER

I awake with an uneasy feeling in my stomach. Which doesn't make sense. Everything has been resolved, Fenton told me everything and we'd had some great makeup sex. So why do I feel like something is off? Am I just being paranoid about finding him in the office last night?

I woke up to a cold spot beside me, which isn't the norm. Sometimes Fenton uses the bathroom in the middle of the night, but he's never gone so long that his side of the bed grows cold. After the strange night I couldn't get back to sleep without him there, and finding him hadn't taken long. Despite the fact he was trying to be quiet, in a house as cavernous as this, sound travels, though I hadn't been able to tell what he'd been saying. But he'd definitely been talking. I tell myself he'd just been muttering to himself over his latest project, as he sometimes did when he got excited.

I also tell myself the fact that his cell phone wasn't on the nightstand either doesn't mean anything.

I've already made more than a few wrong assumptions in the last twelve hours. I don't need to continue down that path.

But when I found him he'd been staring out into the dark woods beyond the house. Had he seen someone out there too? The computer was on, but the chair was still under the desk and something about the whole scene didn't feel right to me. Did I ignore my instincts and ask him back to bed instead of pressing the issue? Yes, on both counts. Mainly because I didn't want to get into it again. And maybe it was another test... to see if he's still lying. Because if there is one thing this has already taught me, he's scary good at it.

And maybe that's the source of my uneasy feeling.

I get up and shower, leaving him in the bed. By the time I'm dressed and ready for work, he's already in the kitchen, coffee in hand. But he wears dark bags under his eyes and he hasn't bothered to shave yet. I would have commented that he looked homeless, but I don't want to be cruel, so I let it drop.

"Did you get any sleep last night?" I ask while I pull a bottled water from the fridge.

It doesn't escape my notice that his hand tightens around his coffee cup. "Yeah." He pauses. "Yeah, I think I'm just frazzled by this project."

"What is it?"

He glances up like he didn't hear me. "Hmm?"

"Your project. What is it?"

"Oh," he replies, taking a sip from his coffee. "Angel's firm wants four new designs for one of those subdivisions down south. But he wants them to be modular so he can get six or eight variations out of them. You know the type. Sprawl."

He says it with such disdain. Why does he keep accepting these jobs for subdivision work if he hates it so much?

"Sounds about like my day. I have to meet with the city planners for two new bridge overhauls. At least you have a budget to work with." I smile, taking a few sips from my bottled water.

He tips his cup in my direction. "Don't let them screw you over."

"I never do." Obviously, he's not in a talking mood this morning, which doesn't make me feel any better. I grab my coat and pull it on over my suit jacket. With as cold as it was yesterday, I'll need the extra warmth. Especially if I'm expected on-site.

Site visits are my favorite part about being a civil engineer. I love seeing the structures up close, or the areas that will soon be transformed by my designs. It's like seeing into the future, watching the landscape change before my eyes to accommodate these gleaming structures. I love the simplicity of it. After all, how complex is a bridge? The answer is *very*, but only if you look closely. Most people will never know everything that goes into something that just gets you from one side to the other. And I love the uncomplicated beauty in that. I haven't won any design awards yet like my soon-to-be husband, but I suspect I'm close. The rumor mill is going strong.

"Well, have a good day," I say, leaning in to kiss him on the forehead.

"No breakfast?" he asks.

"I'll grab something on the way. I may be home late."

"Okay. Love you."

"Love you too." I wave to him, that unease only growing. As I pass the office on my way out, I can't help but notice neither the book nor the wrapping are anywhere in sight.

Almost five hours and nothing but an unsatisfying croissant later, I finally find the time to hop in the car and go look for my lunch. I spent all morning on both sites and the odds we'll get one of them to start from scratch look promising. Maybe both if we're lucky. I always do better under pressure, even when there's plenty that could be distracting me. On the way to work, I'd been worried I'd be thinking about either the book or the ghost all morning, but as soon as I walked into the office, all thoughts of home life fell to the back of my mind as I was smacked in the face with the work I'd left yesterday. The situation revolving around the book is over and done with. Now, if I could just manage to keep my mind from running wild, I'd be in good shape.

For these jobs our firm wasn't hired directly by the city, instead we were hired by a general contractor bidding for the job. I origi-nally formed a loose partnership with a couple of other engineers right out of college, and over the past ten years, we've built our firm to substantial reputation. GWH is my pride and joy, and I love the work of not only designing, but implementing those designs so they become reality. It's not unusual for me to be on-site for the final surveys; it gives us the edge over the competitors. And if we land this contract, there's a good chance we'll be hiring a few extra people to help with the workload. But Henry and Sidhara can wait until I get back to their office before delivering the good news. I want to see their faces in person.

But as soon as I start thinking about faces, Fenton's gaunt visage from this morning pops into my head and won't leave. What *was* he doing last night?

This is ridiculous. I'm going to keep going in circles unless I talk with someone. And my next session with Dr. Hobart isn't for another two weeks. Still, I need another perspective. I'm too close to the situation to be objective anymore.

I pull over into the parking lot of a small café and dig my phone out of my purse. There's only one person I can trust with this, who will keep it quiet if I ask her to.

"Hello?"

"Hey, Cams?" I say. I love hearing her voice. She's always so chipper.

"Winter! Hey!"

"Are you free this afternoon?"

"Why, what's wrong?"

"Nothing. I just thought we could catch up."

There was a snicker on the other end of the line. "You do realize this is me you're talking to, right? You typically don't call unless something big is going on."

No, that isn't true, is it? "I call."

"Yeah, when you need something." Cammie's voice is still light and playful, but it makes me feel bad. Do I only call when I need something? Okay, maybe I'm not the most social of people. Why is that? Why don't I ever call for fun? It's the thing with the neighbors all over again. I always tell myself I will go out there and meet them... one day. And then I never do it. I will call Cammie to catch up... one day.

"You're right. I'm sorry, I shouldn't do that. Not to you."

"You're fine," Cammie says, drawing out the word *fine*. "It doesn't bother me. I know you're super busy and you like your privacy. So what's up?"

"Something might have happened. Something at home."

"You're pregnant," Cammie replies, the excitement building in her voice.

I almost drop the phone. "No! *No*. It's... it's about Fenton. Something is going on. Can we meet somewhere?"

There's a pause. "Oh, I'm sorry, Winter. I thought things were going good between you two."

"They were, I mean... they are. I just need another set of ears."

"I don't have an appointment between four and five thirty, wanna meet then? You'll have to come to my side of town; all my clients are over here today."

"Sure, I can make that." I can pop back into the office and deliver the promising news, then slip out early to meet Cammie.

"Anything I should know beforehand?"

"It's easier if I explain it when I get there."

"Okay. See ya then!" Cammie ends the call abruptly. I can't help but wonder if maybe she does harbor some hidden animosity towards me for only calling when I need something. I need to make a better effort of staying connected with her, but with work and the engagement and everything else, I've fallen behind on so many things.

It doesn't matter, Cammie is here now and once I explain everything, I'll at least have another opinion on the subject. Ever since college Cammie has always kept me in check. I hadn't realized how much I'd missed that until I started seeing Fenton. And then it was like I just dropped off the planet into my own little world. There had been a time when we had been inseparable. And if Cammie had been there last night, she never would have let me open that package. She would have reminded me about my triggers, would have kept me from overthinking it.

I sigh. Not much I can do about it now. I glance up at the sign hanging from the small building whose parking lot I've occupied. It reads, *The Stone Inn Deli*. I scan the area but see no trace of an inn, just the little café that probably couldn't hold more than twenty people at a time. Strange. But I'm famished and I'm not above supporting some local businesses with my lunch order.

I step out of the car and, in the corner of my eye, catch movement a few hundred feet away. But when I look around I don't see anyone. Thoughts of last night linger in my memory, but I dismiss them. I went out, I looked. I faced my fear. There's nothing else I can do about it.

But as I walk across the parking lot, I notice just how quiet it is out here. There's only a few other cars in the lot and none driving by, probably because the site I just came from is way out on Route Six. Part of the reason the job has sat neglected so long is because there isn't normally a lot of traffic out here. But the city has put it off for a lot longer than they should have. If we get it, Route Six will have a brand-new bridge for the handful of people that drive over it per day. Which is fine by me.

I pull my coat tighter as the wind begins to pick up and make my way into the café, all my thoughts having returned to work, and nothing else.

Nothing else at all.

SIX

WINTER

The line inside the café is only a few people long, which doesn't give me much time to pick out what I want. Their menu is larger than I would have expected for such a small shop. Do I go with the Reuben or the BLT? Or maybe a Cobb salad instead? But then wait, were there sides? What about a sunshine burrito? Crap. Now I'm next and there is already someone else behind me. Why is it things like this stress me out like crazy?

"I can never decide what I want when I come here," a voice behind me says. I turn to see a brown-haired woman, maybe a little older than me with black-rimmed cat-eye glasses. Her hair is done up in a bun and she's wearing an oversized, fur-lined black coat as she stares at the specials board.

I'm not used to strangers striking up conversations with me, but I don't want to be rude. "Do you come here a lot?" I ask.

Her eyes find mine for just a second before returning to the menu board. She smiles. "I don't know why I do. Perusing this menu is worse than scrolling through Netflix."

I can't help but smile in return. "This is my first time, and I have no clue what to get. Any suggestions?"

"For your initiation?" She presses her lips together and lifts her chin slightly, apparently considering the matter carefully.

Initiation?

The man in front of me finished up and now it's my turn. The cashier doesn't say a word, just stares at me like me being here is an inconvenience to him. I've already forgotten everything on the menu and this guy's blank stare isn't helping matters any.

"I... Uhhh." I scan the menu again, seeing none of it, hoping to spot some familiar word or ingredient I can fall back on. I like chicken, right? What has chicken?

"She would like the Rachel sandwich. Chips on the side."

I turn back to the woman behind me, somewhat stunned. Did this stranger just order for me?

"In fact, make that two," the woman adds, smiling at Winter. "And a couple of bottled waters." She pulls a credit card out of her wallet.

What is happening here? "Wait, um, you don't—"

"Nonsense," the woman says, cutting me off. "It's my pleasure for a first-timer. And you aided in my decision as well, so I owe you."

"I aided?" I ask as the woman hands her card over to the cashier.

"Nothing like making the decision for someone else to help you realize what you really want." The woman retrieves her card, the cashier still looking like he couldn't care less about the transaction. "As far as lunch is concerned, anyway."

"That's very kind, but I can't—"

"Of course you can," she says, placing her hand on my arm. Her eyes widen in horror. "Wait, you're not a vegetarian, are you?"

I'm still fumbling over what just happened as the woman leads us away from the counter so the next person in line can order. "No, nothing like... I... Please let me pay you back."

The woman waves her hand dismissively. "Don't be so quick to repay me. You may not even like it."

I glance at the menu board again. What the hell is a Rachel? "I've never heard of that kind of sandwich before."

"It's like a Reuben, only with turkey instead of corned beef."

Oh. My stomach grumbles in response. "That does sound pretty good." Should I introduce myself? I'm so awkward in these situations. It's only polite, right? What had I just been complaining about? The fact that I don't reach out enough to people. This is the perfect opportunity to fix that.

I stick out my hand. "I don't think I thanked you. I'm Winter."

The woman smiles again and takes my hand without really shaking it, more just holding on to it in the way a grandmother might. "Laura Blackwell. And you're very welcome."

"Do you live around here? Or work? If you come here a lot?" I ask.

"Work. What about you? New to the area?"

"Oh, no. I live on the other side of town. I'm just over here because I was on a site visit. But if my firm gets this new project, I'll be over here a lot more, so maybe I'll stop in here more often." I glance at the cooks in the back, working furiously. "If it turns out to be good."

"What sort of work do you do?" Laura asks, watching me intently. Is that normal? Maybe this woman is just really friendly.

"Oh, I'm an engineer. We're bidding to rebuild that bridge down on Route Six."

Laura's lips set into a line. "The reservoir bridge?" I nod. "Well, shit. I guess I'll be finding a new way to work soon. Though I don't disagree it needs some work."

That's an understatement. If the general public actually knew the true condition of the local bridges, I doubt anyone would ever drive over one again. But that's why I'm here. "What about you? Where's work?"

"Order up!" the cook at the end of the counter yells.

"That's us," Laura says, leading me to the counter where two bags wait for us. We grab our bags and bottles of water and head out of the café.

"It was certainly nice meeting you," Laura says, pausing a minute. "Maybe I'll see you here again sometime and you can tell me about how you got that interesting name of yours."

I chuckle because I get this a lot. "It's not really that interesting. Just my mom thinking she was being original." I raise my bottle of water in a cheers gesture. "Next time."

Laura waves as she heads off towards her car parked a few spaces away.

"And thanks again!" I add, thinking of it too late as the woman slides inside her vehicle. I should have thanked her *first*. Shoot.

I can't believe it; there were still some decent people left in this world. The woman wasn't mean or petty or rude, and she'd even paid for my lunch. How often does that happen? Sure, she was a little quirky, but who wasn't these days? I make a mental note that if I ever see Laura again, *I'll* be the one paying for lunch.

I check my watch. I'll have to eat on the road if I want to swing by the office and get over to Cammie's house in time. But I feel lighter after this whole encounter, like it's lifted some of the darkness from last night away. I'm excited about the possibility of securing the contract again, and maybe this whole deal about the book isn't as big as I'm making it out to be. No matter what Cams says, I'll drop everything regarding the book after today. It's not worth dwelling over and life is too short. Not *everything* is sinister or duplicitous in some way.

As I pull out of the restaurant's parking lot, I unwrap the sandwich and the smell of turkey and sauerkraut reach my nostrils. And as the sublime bite hits my tongue, I find myself grateful for having met Laura Blackwell.

SEVEN
FENTON

"What am I going to do?"

Fenton paced his small one-person office. He'd rented it from a local guy back when he branched out on his own. Back before his notoriety and success, before he was anything other than a *Byrnes*. He honestly didn't even need the space anymore with work on the house finished and the giant office there, but he'd kept his little office because it seemed more trouble than it was worth to get rid of it. Plus, sometimes there could be so many distractions at home, and here it was easier to think.

A couple of art prints and a few high-quality photographs were all that adorned the walls, an attempt at decorating that had never gotten off the ground. And a couple of boxes stood in the corner, full of things he'd never finished unpacking. Other than his desk and his drafting table, there was no other furniture. A half partition stood between the front part of the room and the back, a holdover from the previous tenant. And he had access to a bathroom through the back door; the only problem was it was accessible to the other tenants in the strip and often not very clean. The unit was a tiny place in the middle of strip mall facing a burger joint and a nail salon across the way. To his left a local pizza place and his right a cell phone repair shop. But it didn't matter; it was his.

He stopped pacing to glance out the window. His new Mercedes looked out of place here, as if the moment he'd bought it, he'd outgrown this part of town.

"You're going to keep your mouth shut," Brian replied. He'd already been there when Fenton arrived thirty minutes later than he'd meant to and was sitting in his Range Rover just stewing. He'd practically rushed Fenton inside, like someone was out there looking to take a shot at him from a hundred yards. And considering Brian had a good sixty pounds of muscle on his little brother, Fenton had had little recourse but to comply.

After Winter left for work, Fenton had been almost too paralyzed to move. Someone was out there. Someone knew his secrets and they knew how to expose him. And there was literally nothing he could do about it. It was all Fenton could do to keep his hands from shaking in the shower and he'd had to take a Prozac to calm himself down before driving over here.

Brian flipped the book over in his hands, examining it. He wore latex gloves, careful not to press down on any flat surface.

"You saw the dedication, right?" Fenton asked, noticing the gloves for the first time. He'd been so distracted that he hadn't even seen them when he handed Brian the book. It was understandable; he was doing all he could to keep from hyperventilating at the moment.

"Of course I saw it," Brian said.

"Well? What the hell? *You'll never get rid of me?* What am I supposed to do with that?"

"It's someone trying to shake us down," Brian said. "We just need to figure out who."

Brian set the book down on the desk and lifted up the small case he'd brought with him, laying it on the table and popping the latches. Inside were a couple of containers, a brush, scissors, tape and a few other things Fenton couldn't identify.

"What is that for?"

"Fingerprints. Let's see if whoever sent this was stupid enough to leave something for me."

"Where did you even get something like that?" Fenton asked.

Brian glanced up. "The kit? You can get them on eBay."

"And you know what you're doing?"

Brian rolled his eyes and returned to the book. He opened one of the small containers and dipped the brush in, using it to lightly dust the front of the book. "You and Winter may have touched it too much already, but there might still be something here. Did she get a really good look at it?"

Fenton shrugged. "She said she read the first few chapters."

"Fuck," Brian said under his breath.

Fenton could relate. Why couldn't the book have come on a Saturday, when he'd been home to intercept it? And why had she been so nosy? He knew why; because she was a reader at heart and when a book shows up for the taking, it was unlikely she wasn't going to read at least part of it.

Brian finished dusting and pulled out a roll of tape, placing it on certain areas of the book, then lifting it off gently.

"Did you get anything?"

Brian didn't respond, only placed the tape on a small card, pressing down hard. He repeated the process a few times.

"How are you going to even find out who those belong to?" Fenton asked. "You're not a cop."

Brian carefully placed the card back in the kit. "If you really have to ask that question, you're not thinking like a Byrnes. This is why Dad doesn't trust you to take care of this on your own."

Fenton slumped down into his chair. The only chair in the office. "I really wish you hadn't told him. Does Mom know?"

Brian shrugged, pulling another piece of tape from the book. "If he told her, I guess. I didn't say anything."

"This is bad. We're screwed, you know that, right?" Fenton ran his hands down his face. "This was all supposed to be over and finished. Things were finally good!"

"Aw, what's wrong? Baby's perfect little life hit a road bump?" Brian chuckled. "You have it so good, you don't even know. Nice car, by the way."

"Yeah, well, at least I bought it with my own money."

Brian shook his head. "Put a down payment, you mean. How long are your payments? Fifty years?"

"Maybe I bought it outright."

Brian grinned, staring at him. "Be careful who you lie to. Don't forget I know you better than anyone."

"I don't need you and Dad keeping tabs on me all the time. That's the whole reason I'm not doing what you do. It's the whole reason I never got into the family business."

"Don't remind me." Brian waved his hand dismissively. "I'm the one who has to hear about it all the time."

Fenton sighed. "What do we do if the prints are hers?"

Brian packed up his kit again. "They won't be. Odds are I won't get anything except for you and Winter. But I need to eliminate the possibility."

"And then what? What happens if you don't find anything?"

Brian smiled. "We'll handle it. But don't you worry your pretty little head about it."

"You don't need to keep me in the dark. I'm part of this family too."

Brian walked over to him, placed his hand on Fenton's cheek and tapped it a few times. "Not since you walked out on Dad. Plus, plausible deniability, little brother. Look it up."

Brian gathered the book and the wrapping in his arms and strode out the door.

"I know what it means!" Fenton called after him. He watched as Brian climbed into his gleaming black Range Rover and drove off.

Fenton shot straight up in his seat. He glanced around; he was still in his office, the sun threatening to set over the other buildings on the opposite side of the strip mall. How long had he been asleep?

He checked his watch and saw it had been at least three hours since Brian left. He didn't remember falling asleep, but then again he couldn't remember a lot of what happened today. An unfortunate side effect of the Prozac he'd taken. But the dream stuck in his memory. It had been her. The room was dark, and he'd been so afraid she'd turn on the light. Afraid of what she really might look like. He'd realized it was a dream at the last second, like the ones he used to have all the time. And now, one day after that book showed up, he'd lost eight years of progress. All that therapy, hypnotism, power of positive thinking he'd worked so hard on, gone in a matter of hours. He hadn't been prepared to see her anymore, but it was her. The voice was too unmistakable.

He hit his forehand repeatedly with the heel of his hand.

"Get... out... of... there."

He stood and gathered his things; another day of work wasted. He'd already been somewhat useless the past few weeks, encouraged by the promise of another award but also put off that no matter what he did he might never reach the same high. He hadn't wanted to let go of that notoriety. He didn't want to be Connecticut's next one-hit wonder. It almost seemed preferable to languish in indecision, never having to move on or take the chance to improve. Because no matter what, after each great success in Fenton's life had come crushing disappointment.

Back in high school, his biggest worry had been qualifying for the golf team. And after two years of tryouts, he finally made it. That was, until a new kid moved into his district and bumped him off the team—*There's only so many spots, Byrnes, and you're not one of them*—despite the fact he was doing okay. But this new kid had some sort of gift, and the school wasn't about to let him slip by. Then, in college, when he'd finally gotten a date with Allison McIntosh, he found out two weeks later she was pregnant from her old, long-time boyfriend, and Fenton just couldn't deal with it. He was a sophomore and he was supposed to help raise a baby? He walked away, despite the fact that Allison was the only person he'd been interested in that entire year. He laughed. Imagine... giving Dad that little nugget of news. It was better for everyone involved

that he just walk away. And then of course there had been her...
Miranda.

He shook his head. He couldn't think about her at the moment. Everything kept coming back to that damn book. He just hoped Winter was over it and didn't ask him any more questions. He really didn't want to lie to her again.

He locked the door to his office and got back into his new car. Twenty-four minutes later he pulled out of the spot and headed home.

EIGHT
WINTER

"Charlie! Charlie, get back here!"

I pull up to the scene, smiling. A thin blonde woman wearing jean shorts and an oversized jacket runs across her yard, chasing down a very wet and somewhat soapy basset hound who is moving impressively fast despite being as low to the ground as he is.

Cammie looks up and relief washes over her face as I step out of the car. "Win! Help me wrangle him! It's too cold for him to be running around out here!"

I cut the engine and run over, hopping the low chain-link fence without even thinking about it, landing right in front of the charging basset hound. "Hey, Charlie," I coo, "come to Win-win."

Charlie stares at me a split second, then by some sixth sense feels Cammie creeping up behind him and takes off to my right, barreling through the yard.

"Dammit!" Cammie yells, traipsing after him.

"How did he get out?" I ask, doing my best to keep from laughing.

Cammie, out of breath, points at the soapy bullet now running circles in the yard. "He was my three o'clock, but his owner was late dropping him off and then I forgot to lock down the doggie door in the back, so when he slipped out of my hands, he bolted.

It's a good thing he's not a taller dog because I have no doubt with that much energy he could scale the fence."

"He's definitely the most hyper dog I've seen that wasn't a chihuahua."

"I know." Cammie exhales. "He's sweet, but damn, he's fast."

"He just needs proper motivation." I scale the fence again and run back to the car, grabbing the remnants of my Rachel sandwich. I had planned on maybe saving the rest of it for dinner, but it seems Charlie might need it more than I do.

"Charlie! Treats!" I yell, waving the bag at him. The dog stops mid-run and locks his eyes on me, before taking off in what I can only describe as a sprint directly for my shins. He slams on the brakes just before reaching the fence and jumps up, his tiny little legs only launching him so far.

"Gotcha!" Cammie grabs him in a bear hug from behind, pulling him from the fence.

"Good boy," I say, pulling a slice of turkey from the sandwich and watching it disappear down the canine's maw as if it were a black hole.

"Get the door for me, would you?" Cammie asks. "He's a handful."

I trot ahead of them, opening the side door to the house. Once we're inside, I close it back *and* the doggie door protector. Cammie sets Charlie down on the kitchen floor, but his wide eyes haven't left my bag.

"Here you go," I say, giving him a larger bite, which he takes with enough enthusiasm I'm scared for my hand.

Cammie draws a deep breath. "Sorry, I know I said between four and five thirty, but this is going to take me a few more minutes. I'll probably have to wash him again with all the dirt he picked up outside. Then he needs a good blow dry."

"No problem." I hold up another piece of turkey. "Maybe if I can keep him distracted, he'll be more inclined to cooperate. Plus, he's a cutie."

Cammie shoves me playfully with one hand. "I knew there was a reason I liked you."

There aren't many people in this world that I trust. But Cams is one of them. She's outgoing, friendly and always in good spirits, much in contrast to me most of the time. And for some reason she puts up with me, though half the time I can't figure out why. She's also a savvy businessperson who was determined to start her own business after we graduated college. And now, not only has she started her own dog grooming company out of her home, but she's also bought a mobile grooming van so she can reach more customers. She's told me about it maybe half a dozen times, but this is the first time I'm seeing the equipment in person.

"Does all this stuff go in the van?" I ask, pointing to the variety of hoses, pumps and accessories Cammie has strewn around the room.

"Yep, it's finally happening. We bought the van two weeks ago and Mike is working with a guy to convert it to fit my needs. I want to carry my own water supply, so they have to do something to the suspension so it can hold all that extra weight. But you watch, it's gonna be awesome."

Charlie grunts as she starts scrubbing him down in the mobile tub.

"How long until it's up and running?"

"Maybe tomorrow."

"Tomorrow? That soon?"

"Yep," she says, "I've still got some equipment coming. Mike should be back with it later today. And then I'll be able to lock this guy inside so he can't run around." She scrubs his head as I feed him another part of my sandwich. Upon seeing the food, Charlie's butt immediately hits the water, splashing us both.

"Well." I giggle, trying to wipe my face. "At least you know how to get him to sit."

"Okay, so tell me what's happening in *Winter's wonderland*."

I grimace. "Don't call it that."

"Why not? Fancy, well-to-do fiancé, living in a gorgeous custom-built home and nothing but good things on the horizon. Who could complain?"

A pit opens in my stomach. The conversation with the woman at the café had made everything seem so trivial, but now that I have to talk about it again, it feels a lot more real.

"It's not that simple. Something... came up."

Cammie stops washing Charlie for a moment. "What kind of something?"

I try to explain the situation the best I can, leaving out the part about seeing someone at the end of the driveway. I don't need Cammie thinking I'm seeing things in addition to my paranoia and obsessiveness about this book.

"Jeez, Win. I'm sorry," she says. "That's really weird, though. Are you sure he hasn't had any contact with this Miranda woman lately? I mean... to just come out of the blue like this..."

I feed Charlie the last bit of my sandwich and he licks his lips profusely. "I guess I just have to trust him. I don't have any real way of knowing."

"Sure you do."

I look up, surprised at her candor.

"Look at his accounts... his phone. Whatever you need."

No. Out of the question. "I can't do that. He told me the reason, and I need to trust him."

"I'm sure he's telling the truth," Cammie says, wiping her hands down and grabbing the hair dryer. "It's just for your peace of mind. After what you've been through, I think anyone would understand. Especially Fenton. He knows everything, right?"

I nod.

"Then he probably wouldn't blame you for going through this stuff. I mean, you'll be sharing everything in a few months anyway."

Before I can respond, Cammie turns on the blow dryer, waving it over Charlie.

Maybe she's right. It would help my peace of mind if I double-check everything. But what about the next time something like this comes up? Will I have to check again? Or is this one time enough? If I definitely know he's telling the truth this time, then I'd never have to check again.

Right?

As soon as Cammie finishes drying Charlie, I pipe back up. "Is that what you and Mike do? Check each other's phones and accounts and stuff?"

Cammie shrugs. "I mean not purposely, but sometimes I'll get on the computer and he'll still be logged in, and I can't help but look through messages and stuff. Or when my phone dies, I'll borrow his and I might sneak a look."

"And you'd have no problem with him looking at your stuff?"

"He can look at whatever he wants. If he sees something he doesn't like, I'm sure I'll hear about it." She winks at me. "But there's been no complaints so far."

"I just don't know," I say, looking down. "We keep our boundaries. Even though I don't have anything to hide, I don't like the idea of anyone going through my... things."

"You're a private person. The point is, how does Fenton feel about it? And, more importantly, if you don't do it, how long is this going to gnaw at you?"

"It's just all so stupid. Maybe I should just let it go."

"Yeah, that's probably the healthier option." Cammie chuckles, lifting Charlie out of the drying area and wrapping a thin scarf around his neck. "There you go, buddy. All pretty for your mama."

Charlie looks up, wagging his tail. As I stare into those big brown eyes of his, I'm reminded about how many times in the past few months I've tried to convince Fenton we should get a dog. But he likes the house as it is; he doesn't want to be cleaning up after a dog all the time.

I just... wish he'd reconsider.

Cammie rubs my shoulder. "You do whatever you think is right. But if this bothers you that much, and you don't talk to him about it or do anything about it, is that really any different than him hiding something from you?"

The pit is growing deeper, forcing me to rethink everything. What is he really hiding? And just how bad is it?

"How did he seem when he told you the truth about it?"

Charlie marches around the kitchen, in search of another sandwich. Crossing my arms, I lean up against the counter. "Sorry. I guess. But the problem is he lied so effortlessly to me. Had I not *known* he wasn't telling the truth, I would have just accepted it."

"Maybe he's like one of those savants who can lie without having the tells. Like someone who would pass a lie detector test, no problem."

"Great. So where does that leave me? He was doing something in the office last night, I know it. Despite his promise that it had all just been for work."

"Win," she says, losing that trademark smirk of hers. "I'm worried about you. If you can't trust him... what does that mean?"

"It means I think you're right."

Her eyes go wide. "Wait, you're gonna look in his stuff? I was only kidding about that. Kinda."

I shake my head. "I don't think I have a choice."

NINE
WINTER

When I arrive home, Fenton is already there. He's passed out on the couch, still in his work clothes, looking as if he'd come in the front door, barely taken his shoes and jacket off, then collapsed.

Not surprising, considering he was up half the night.

I slip my shoes and jacket off, placing them in their designated places, and tiptoe past him to the kitchen, doing my best not to make any kind of sound. He's been working so hard lately, and all this extra attention from his design award has pushed a type-A personality into the stratosphere. Before any of this happened, he was already under a lot of stress. After the award came through, he's been bombarded with calls for interviews, not to mention all his regular work and new incoming clients. It's a lot for him to balance on his own, which is why I keep insisting he hire an assistant.

But he keeps insisting he can do it on his own, and that after the fervor around the award dies down, things will go back to normal. Still... I'm not so sure.

I remove the half-consumed bottle of pinot noir from the refrigerator, silently cursing myself. The guy at the wine store said to put it in an hour before drinking, then remove when done. As someone who didn't grow up with a lot of money, I'm still trying to learn all the ins and outs of living what some might consider a "privileged life." Fenton and his family come from money. I've been doing everything I can to try to fit in. It's intimidating when your fiancé's family has millions of dollars and they look at you like you just walked out of the gutter. Fenton has never said anything directly, but I can feel that judgement sometimes. I don't want to disappoint or embarrass him, and at the same time, I'm not sure it's who I am at my core.

Then again, it's just wine. I'll remember next time.

I pull the cork and pour half a glass, not even paying attention to the taste as I drink. Thoughts of the wedding invade my mind. Of course I want to marry Fenton; I love him. But the thought of going through *another* ceremony is almost too much. The first time had been such a spectacle, all of my and Thomas's families there, a huge venue, four-tiered cake, photographer, videographer; the whole works. It was supposed to be a once-in-a-lifetime event. Little did I know not more than four years later, I'd be recanting all those vows I'd made in solemn oath. And the worst part of it was Thomas had passed a pretty rigorous *smell test*. Enough so that I'd had no reservations about entering a lifetime of commitment with him. Thomas's problem was he *changed*.

As I stand there, watching my soon-to-be husband's chest rise and fall, I can't help but wonder if Fenton will change too. Would he one day decide maybe I'm not enough for him and start looking for his emotional needs elsewhere just as Thomas had?

Or is he already doing it?

Cammie's voice plays through my head like a stuck record.

Look at his accounts.

Look at his phone.

Do whatever you have to do.

I drain the wine glass and move across the hardwoods, none of them creaking under the pressure. Where does he keep his phone? Still inside his jacket pocket? Or in his pants? I pat the pockets of his jacket hanging on the hook by the door—right beside mine—

and find the small black device nestled in the upper-right breast pocket.

My heart rate picks up. I've never looked into his personal devices before. But this is just a one-time thing. Once I confirm he was telling the truth, then this will all be over. This is the last hurdle. And maybe it's a little farther than I want to go, but I can't live with the uncertainty. Otherwise I'll be obsessing over it every day. Look how much mental energy I've already invested, and that stupid book arrived barely twenty-four hours ago.

I tap the screen. The image that greets me is a picture of the two of us when we were in St. John last year. My heart pangs. I can't do this. Fenton is a good guy; he isn't hiding anything. He isn't Thomas. I slip the phone back into the coat pocket and return to the kitchen.

I'm a coward.

No, I just happen to trust my partner. What's so wrong with that? The real question is, can I live with never knowing for sure? As I pour the remainder of the bottle in my glass, I think maybe I can. Is this growth? Is this what people in normal, healthy relationships do?

In fact, I should just rid us of the entire problem. Letting Fenton continue to sleep, I make my way into the office. Keeping it is a mistake... no matter how good it is. And if I really want to, I can download it from somewhere... probably. But if we keep it in this house, it'll be nothing but a constant reminder of his deception. To move past it, we need a clean start.

I reach in and open the cabinet where I'd seen him place the book last night, but it isn't there. That's odd. I check the small office trashcan to see if he's beat me to the punch, but it's empty. What has he done with it? There's no trace of the wrapping it came in either. Could he have thrown it in the big trash can outside? I glance around the rest of the office to make sure I'm not missing it then make my way out to the garage. The can in there only has the one bag of kitchen waste I'd put there myself the day before. If he didn't throw it away, what did he do with it?

I remind myself to take a deep breath before I get too worked up. There's a reasonable explanation for all this. I return to the living room and check Fenton's satchel he carries to work every day. No trace of it in there either. Damn. Was that what he was doing last night? Getting rid of it somehow? Did he throw it outside in the middle of the woods? Bury it? Or did he do something with it after I left for work this morning?

Either way, I don't like this feeling. Now I really have no choice. I pull his phone out of the jacket pocket again, ignore the splash screen and unlock it easily. He uses my birthday as his code; I've seen him enter it enough times. He never made a big deal of hiding it, as a gesture of trust perhaps, after knowing what I've been through. Which means it's unlikely there is anything on here that might incriminate him. I'll probably have to check his other accounts on the computer to make sure. But there's no harm in checking this off the list.

The first thing to eliminate as a possibility are the texts. I open the app to find his latest conversation with Brian. No big deal, he talks to his brother all the time. Except when I see the time stamp from their most recent chat. It was from 2:28 a.m. The exact time Fenton had been out of bed. I open the conversation and have to stop myself from audibly gasping.

FENTON:

Are you up?

BRIAN:

What do you need at this ungodly hour?

FENTON:

IMG attached.

BRIAN:

Is this a joke?

FENTON:

I wish. It showed up in the mail today.

The image is of the book. My hands go numb, but somehow I

manage to keep tapping away. There's nothing left of the conversation, but I check his previous calls and see Brian had called him at exactly 2:30 a.m. Brian knows about the book. And it worried them both enough to discuss it in the middle of the night. It couldn't even wait until the next day.

"I can't believe this," I say aloud.

Fenton groans and turns over on the couch. He still isn't awake, but he's not a heavy sleeper.

My first thought is to just pack up and go. He's obviously lied to me again, twice now about the same thing. Which means something serious is going on. How is this possible? Am I such a bad judge of character that I missed the signs *again*? We've been dating for three years and not once, *not once*, in any of that time had he ever given me an opportunity to doubt him. Not until this damn book showed up. And in less than a day, it's all fallen apart.

I glare at him, my fury blooming.

Breathe, Winter. You're not supposed to do this, remember?

Fenton was supposed to be different. Mostly because *I'm* supposed to be different. Instead of running away from things, I'm supposed to confront them head on, work through the problems instead of just saying *screw it* and moving on. Dr. Hobart said people were never going to be perfect, and they were going to screw up, and it was worth working through the problems.

But the betrayal. Fenton *knows*. He knows what I've been through, and my triggers, and knowing all that, he decided to lie to me about this. I'm so mad I almost throw the phone to the floor, hoping to smash it to a million pieces.

Instead, I walk around to the other side of the couch, and phone in hand, draw my arm back, holding it like a baseball and chuck it as hard as I can at Fenton.

Damn the consequences.

TEN
WINTER

A corner of the phone hits Fenton square in the stomach but, due to the angle, skips off him like a stone across a pond and over the couch, landing somewhere behind him with a *thump*.

"What the hell?" His eyes flutter open and his hand immediately goes to his stomach, missing the phone by milliseconds. "Winter?" He looks at me with a confused expression. "What was that?"

"Your phone, dickhead."

His eyes snap open. He looks over the couch for it, as if finding the device might erase the last fifteen minutes. It's like he wasn't even trying to hide the panic on his face.

"I'll give you one chance," I say, putting up a finger through heaving breaths, "one chance to tell me the truth or I am out that door right now. And I promise you will never see me again." I swear I'm about to hyperventilate, but I don't care. He's cheating, I know it. What else can he be hiding?

Fenton sits up, holding his stomach, as if to consider the offer, which tells me all I need to know.

That's it. I'm done.

I turn and head towards the bedroom. It's time to pack up and start over. Again. I can't believe this.

"Winter, wait. Wait," he calls, right behind me. Too late.

I stop and turn. He's on his feet with a panicked look in his eyes.

"If I tell you, do you promise not to leave? At least not until I explain everything?"

I don't reply. He doesn't deserve it. But I deserve an explanation. If for no other reason than to hear whatever lie is about to come out of his mouth. Let's see how much deeper he can dig this grave. I cross my arms.

"Do you want to go sit back down?" he asks.

I don't move. He'll get nothing but the silent treatment until he starts explaining. It's what he deserves. I can't get the image of that book out of my mind. Brian knows. How many other people? Do his parents know too? Who *the fuck* is Miranda Meriwether?

"Okay, right. Then... just brace yourself. You saw the texts, yeah? When I told you yesterday that there was no one else but you, that was the truth. But what I didn't say, was that I've been married before."

My body feels like it's being squeezed in a vise. Married before? He'd said he hadn't been with anyone for five years when we met. Before that he'd explained he'd had some serious girl-friends, but none of them had gone anywhere permanent. It seems like *marriage* should have come up around then.

"When?" I demand.

"About ten years ago. We weren't married long, only about a year and a half."

"Miranda?" My anger starts to dissipate, but only slightly. I can't believe this. I should have known better. I should have known at the time it was a flat-out lie. He was too smart, too good-looking, had too many positive attributes for someone to pass him by. This explains so much.

But he still hasn't answered me.

"Was it Miranda?"

"It's complicated."

"How can it be complicated? It either was or it wasn't."

"Hon..." He reaches for me.

I pull back. "Don't."

"Win, please, I'm trying to explain here," he says.

"You had your chance to explain three years ago when we met." I say it with such disdain. "And you didn't. You didn't tell me about her. I specifically asked you if you'd ever had any other serious relationships. And you said *no*."

"I didn't know how to tell you. It was... it was a hard breakup. I didn't want to open that wound again, especially not after meeting you. You were just so... wonderful and caring. I just wanted a fresh start."

"That's an excuse and you know it."

Fenton lowers his head, returning to the couch. I watch him walk back, not believing what's transpiring in my own home.

It's not your home yet. It's his.

I silence that voice for what seems like the hundredth time in two days. This *is* my home, just as much as his. We're supposed to build a life together. We're supposed to grow old together. How are we going to do that now?

"How am I supposed to trust you ever again?" I ask. "It's been nothing but lies since this book showed up."

He shakes his head. "You don't know how many times I've tried to tell you. But then every time I'd worked up the courage, I'd think about what happened to you, with your divorce, and about all the pain you've been through, and I just couldn't do it. The longer it went on the worse it got. I kept thinking, *Tell her now, it's only going to be worse later*. Eventually, it just got to the point where too much time had passed and I knew telling you would result in... this." He makes a gesture with his hand.

"Would you have ever told me? Or would you have taken her to the grave with you?" It all feels like such a betrayal—not the fact he'd been married before, but that he'd kept it from me. If he could hide something like that, what else was he hiding?

"It's just... I know how sensitive you are about Thomas. I didn't want you to think I was like him... that I could hurt you in that way.

And I didn't want to lose you. I was too afraid. Afraid because of what you—"

"Stop making this my fault!" I yell. "It's *your* fault you didn't tell me, not mine. Don't pin that on me!"

He pauses. "You're right. It was my fault and my decision not to say anything. I should have trusted you could handle it. For what it's worth, I'm sorry."

For the first time I consider what would have happened if he *had* told me. Would I have overreacted? Or would I have been able to keep my cool, remembering my lessons from Dr. Hobart? The point is he didn't give me a chance to find out. And by not telling me, he's only made things worse.

I need time to process this. What am I supposed to do? I love him. And I know he loves me. But I can't live with a man who just keeps lying to me. I won't do that to myself again.

"Brian knows?" I ask.

He nods.

"Who else?"

"My family, a few friends. That's it."

"Great." His entire family has been lying to me too. I may have never asked them about his previous relationships, but a lie by omission is still a lie. On the other hand, his family is... well, they're something all right. It's not like I feel they're particularly trustworthy anyway. In fact, that's one of the things that brought us together—we're both trying to escape our pasts.

What if... what if his marriage to Miranda was a reminder of that life? He was so much younger then, much more under his father's iron fist—from what he's told me. Maybe all this comes from the same core wound. We've talked about wounds a lot in my therapy sessions. And it took me a long time to recognize and identify the causes of those wounds. Fenton... he's never been in therapy as far as I know. I have to remember he may not be as equipped to deal with these traumas as I am.

I walk back over and sit down across from him, pinning him with my gaze. "I know what it's like to not want to look back at your past." He doesn't reply, but I have his attention. "You need to know you can trust me, confide in me. *Especially* about stuff like this. Because if we can't talk about the hard stuff, I don't even know what we're doing."

He nods. "You're right."

"I think... maybe you need help. Would you be willing to talk to someone?"

"Like Dr. Hobart?"

"It doesn't have to be him," I say. "Just someone. Because I think you have a lot more going on than you think you do."

"I'll... think about it," he finally says. A noncommitment. I don't know if that's still his father talking or if he's actually considering it. "You're not going to leave, are you?"

"Let's just take it one day at a time, okay?" I say, reaching out for his hand. He takes it, though he's careful, almost like he expects me to slap him instead. Part of me wants to. But I'm not going to let my emotions run me all the time.

"I really am sorry," he says. "I should have told you."

"Yes, you should have."

"I just never expected... I never expected to hear from her again. Especially like this."

"Why is that?" I ask.

"Because the last time I saw that book, it was nothing but a loose set of typed pages," he said. "She never published anything."

"Well, it looks like she finally made it," I reply. "Maybe she sent it as a gift. So you'd know she finally made it."

He returns a tight smile. "Yeah, maybe."

"Are you at least... proud of her?" I ask. Writing a book seems like such a monumental task; I'm not sure it's something I could ever do. In a strange way, I respect her for it. As my anger cools, I realize I may have blown this whole thing out of proportion. He hasn't been unfaithful. But if he hadn't reacted so badly, like there was more he was trying to hide, it wouldn't have been a big deal.

"Um... yeah," he replied. "I mean, she wrote while we were

together. I guess I just never suspected... You know what? It doesn't matter."

Finally, my heart rate has come down. I already feel a little better. "So were you *Mr.* Meriwether then?"

"Oh," he says. "That was just a pen name."

I chuckle. "Yeah, I kinda figured that part out when I searched for her and nothing came up."

"You searched for her?" Is that worry in his voice?

"Why wouldn't I? Her book shows up on our doorstep. First thing I'm gonna do is look her up. It's just... I couldn't find anything. The book isn't for sale on any website."

"Huh," he replies, looking off into the distance.

"Fenton," I say, my heart rate picking up again. Is he being cagey again or is that just me?

"Yeah?"

"What was her name? Her *real* name."

He takes a deep breath, though I'm not sure he knows he's doing it. "Laura," he says. "Laura Blackwell."

ELEVEN
WINTER

It takes me a moment to realize I've been holding my breath. I'm not sure how long I sit there, stunned, but it's long enough to register pins and needles in my legs. He'd been married to the same woman who not more than four hours ago bought me lunch? Had she known who she was talking to? What were the odds of two Laura Blackwells in this town? And what were the odds it was nothing more than a coincidence?

"Win? Are you okay?"

I need to choose my next words very carefully.

"When... uh, when was the last time you had contact with Laura?" I ask with a measured breath.

Fenton's eyes are red-rimmed, like it pains him to talk about her. "Eight years ago."

Eight years. And I run into the woman today. That *can't* be a coincidence. Does he know she's here in town? Have they been seeing each other on the side this whole time?

Stop it. I need more information before I can make a decision. I need to understand *everything*.

"What happened between you two?" I manage the words without emotion. Good. Keep it straight.

He wipes his eyes with his sleeve. Fenton is not a pretty crier, and as if to send this point home, snot runs from his nose. Why is he so upset?

"Things... just didn't work out."

He's being intentionally obtuse. I'm the one who's supposed to be distraught here. But learning I've already met his first wife has focused my thoughts, sharpened me. It's obvious Laura sent the book, and then followed and befriended me. But why? To get to know me? Maybe find a way back to her lost love again? Was this all just a ploy to push me out of the picture? If so, Fenton didn't know about it, or he's good at pretending not to. Though I have to imagine if they concocted this plan together, he wouldn't keep telling me I'm the only woman in his life. We're not married yet; is he too afraid to back out himself and needs help? And who better to help than his ex-wife? The person who knew him before me, the person who maybe he believes knows him best?

I rub my temples. The only problem is none of that sounds like Fenton. Neither did lying about having a previous wife, but subterfuge on this level? It just isn't in his nature. Despite what he's done I know him, deep in his core. If he wants something, he doesn't have a difficult time telling me. He's always been very straightforward, something I admire and envy. I've always avoided confrontation if I can help it, after having so many of them blow up in my face. But Dr. Hobart said it was important to confront. It keeps things honest. Maybe I wasn't forceful enough with him yesterday when I first found the book. This couldn't be my fault... right?

"Tell me."

He sniffs. "It was just... an incompatibility. We weren't right for each other. We grew apart. After that... she was gone."

"You swear you haven't talked to her since you two broke up?"

He shakes his head. "I swear to God. I couldn't."

I watch his eyes, looking for any trace of deception and seeing none. But if the past twenty-four hours have proven anything, it was that he is an accomplished liar. And if he can do it, so can I.

There's no need to tell him about meeting Laura just yet; if he's still lying, I don't want to show my hand. I'm going to figure this situation out one way or another.

I pull my fingers out of his grasp. "Where's the book?"

"I gave it to Brian."

"Why?"

"So he could find out who sent it." He wipes his eyes again. "He's got all those connections. You know."

I do know. Unfortunately. "You don't think Laura herself sent it?"

"No." His voice is small. What, did he think Laura wouldn't intrude on his life so brazenly like that? Or was there another reason? Maybe I should get in touch with Brian, tell him what I know. Bypass Fenton altogether.

"Why not?"

"She has no way of contacting me. Of finding me."

So you think.

"Does that mean your dad knows about it by now?" I ask.

He nods.

He's being more open, but I have the sense I'm still not hearing the whole story. That's fine. If he wants to keep omitting the truth, I will find it elsewhere, either from Laura herself or by doing a little digging. Then I can decide how I want to proceed. There is something deeper going on here, and just like the book itself, I can't let it go until I know the whole truth.

The good news is I have some experience in this area. Thomas was sloppy; he got too confident and his frequent phone calls gave him away. Fenton is smarter, more careful. But there will still be evidence... somewhere.

"I'm going to bed," I say, standing up. "I think it's better if we take a little time apart. You good with the guest room?"

He nods.

I turn and head down the hall, utterly spent but my mind reeling with possibilities. Should I bring Cammie in on this? After all, Cammie was the one who suggested I get involved in the first place. Without that advice I might never have found out what was going on. And Cammie had been there when things went south with Thomas. But it means admitting I've been played yet again, and I'm not sure I want to face that embarrassment. Cammie and Mike have the perfect thing going for them, and if everything holds, Fenton is lining up to be just another disaster in the long string of failed relationships that's been my life. The stupid thing is I thought I'd found a way around this sort of thing. A series of tests and trials to qualify potential candidates and weed out the undesirables. Cammie had no such test, none that I've ever seen anyway, and she hit the jackpot on her first try.

I close the door behind me and press the button to lock it from the inside. Maybe I'm just not supposed to have a solid relationship. Maybe it's just supposed to be a series of partners that don't really matter. After all, I have my job, my friends, my family. I still have a lot going for me. Maybe all this isn't worth it. Will I really be any happier with a partner?

I think back to Cammie and Mike again. How they love each other, support each other. Right now, Mike's probably working through the night on Cammie's van so she can go out and wash more dogs tomorrow.

The stupid thing is Fenton is like that too, but in his own way. Even though he has no automotive experience whatsoever, if I asked him to go out and work on my car, to improve it in some way, he'd absolutely do it even if he had no clue how. It was very clear to me from the beginning that he was interested in making my life better. He's been the most balanced relationship I've ever had. Neither one of us ever has to do one thing all the time. If the trash needs to be taken out, he doesn't wait for me, he just does it. Or if he forgets to grab the mail, I'll go out and get it. We're a partnership; it's all about getting the job done and not about who isn't living up to their responsibilities. And it had been perfect. All up until yesterday.

I flop down on the bed, but the tears don't come. I'm burned out. Burned out from worrying about this, burned out from trying to find the perfect relationship. I just want answers. And that begins with finding Laura again, letting her think she can be my friend. Then, and only then, will I have enough information to find out what's really going on here.

It looks like I'll be having Rachel sandwiches all week.

TWELVE
FENTON

Fenton was on his hands and knees as he searched for his phone. He'd been in a deep sleep when Winter had woken him, thanks to the Prozac. At first, he'd thought he'd been shot, or punched really hard. That girl could throw. Even if he did find the phone, what were the chances it still worked?

He reached his hand under a refurbished credenza, picking up dust and debris until his hand touched something cold. Bingo. Fenton examined the phone. The screen had a hairline crack, but when he touched the power button, it sprang to life. He reviewed the texts again and cursed himself. Could he really blame her for wanting to leave him after this? For being suspicious?

The minute he laid eyes on that book, he should have come clean. But no, he'd panicked, thought up some lie and immediately tried to bury it all.

Why face the truth when a lie will do just as well?

God, he hated his dad for putting that nonsense in his head. That man, with all his secrets and all his machinations, who couldn't leave well enough alone, had somehow still managed to permeate his life despite the fact that Fenton had all but cut off communication. And now that he knew about this book—thanks to Brian, the snitch—it wouldn't be long before he'd find a way to become involved. If for no other reason than to hold it over Fenton's head as a penance for not following in the family footsteps.

Fenton sighed and glanced toward the other end of the house where Winter had sequestered herself. How could he have done this to her? He needed to make it right somehow. But first he needed to find out who really sent him this book and why. Because if their goal had been to disrupt the best thing he'd ever found in his life, they'd more than succeeded.

He shoved his phone into his pocket and made his way into the kitchen, drinking two full glasses of water before taking a breath. He should have been awake when Winter got home. Or at least, he should have changed the code on his phone. But the question was, what should he do now? Would they speak again at breakfast? Or would she give him the cold shoulder in the morning until she decided what she wanted to do?

There had to be something he could do. Some way to get her back on his side.

Just as he decided pushing her in *any* direction right now was a terrible idea, his phone vibrated in his pocket. His first thought was it was her, texting him that she was really leaving, or to tell him to go find a hotel. But when he pulled the phone out and looked at the caller ID, he winced.

"Hello?" he said.

"Son."

Fenton bit his lip. "Dad. What can I—"

"Cut the shit," Lazarus Byrnes replied, his voice hot. "We need to have a visit."

Right on cue. Fenton was actually surprised it had taken this long. But then perhaps Dad had been waiting for *him* to call for help. It put a smile on Fenton's face to know he hadn't caved. "I can come by tomorrow afternoon."

"Now."

"It's ten thirty at night."

"Then I'll see you in twenty minutes." Lazarus hung up.

Fenton glanced down the hall again. He couldn't leave now. What would Winter think when she heard him drive off? This was the worst possible timing. He could try to sneak out, open the garage door without the motor and maybe pull the car out quietly?

There was another possibility. He could just not go. He considered it for a moment, before the consequences of something like that caught up to him. Not going would only make things worse. When Lazarus Byrnes called you, you showed up. No ifs, ands or buts.

Maybe he could text Winter he was leaving, let her know Lazarus had called. She would still understand that much at least? Right?

He began to type out the message, then thought better of it and shoved his phone back in his pocket. He didn't need to bombard her with his every movement. Plus, this shouldn't take long. He would be back within the hour.

Yanking the kitchen drawer open, Fenton removed a small pad they used for grocery lists. He jotted a quick note:

Dad called, I'll be back soon. I love you.

Sweet, simple and to the point. He laid it right on the counter where she couldn't miss it, then went into the living room and slipped his coat back on. He'd been so tired from the pills he barely taken off his shoes when he got home. But after hearing from Dad, he doubted a dump truck full of Ambien could put him back to sleep.

Winter

I'd almost drifted off to sleep when the rumble of the garage door opening rattles me back awake. Moments later the low purr of Fenton's Mercedes filters through the walls, and then the space grows quiet again. Where is he going? Not that I'm complaining. I need a few minutes to myself without feeling like I'm under his microscope. Maybe he figured a drive would do him some good, and maybe it will. I'm tempted to drive around myself if it weren't so late. And, with him gone, I don't have to stay in the bedroom.

I unlock the door and head down the hallway, just catching the taillights of his car as he turns out of the long driveway. I hold my gaze for a moment, watching to see if my ghost appears again, but there's no one else out there. Maybe I *did* imagine it. Work has been stressful, and after finding that book I was on edge—more than usual. I probably scared poor Janet half to death.

I walk around the house, feeling its emptiness. It's solitude. In some ways it feels like a tomb, a cavernous mausoleum. A perfect blend of style and function without a bit of warmth a home should have. Why haven't I noticed it before now? Probably because I was too enamored or too distracted or some other excuse. But I think I'm finally seeing it with fresh eyes.

There's a specific corner of the living room where there's no furniture, where a vent sits right under one of the large glass windows looking out into the forest beyond. I imagine that's where the dog bed would go, where he or she would sleep the day away, waiting for us to come back home. I think being with Cams made me a little more sentimental than normal because I nearly tear up thinking about how we'll never have one.

It's just going to be me... and him.

And I'm not sure I can handle that.

I head into the office, really examining the place for the first time. Everything in here is so organized, so... *structural*. Fenton is meticulous about his records. He has tax documents going back fifteen years, *twice* the required time to keep documentation. He has files and files of all his designs, blueprints and floor plans and everything else. His entire life, boxed up and cataloged nicely.

Whereas most of my stuff is shoved in boxes that are in storage. A lot of my stuff doesn't fit the aesthetic of the house. It's not something I'm upset about because he's right. And we chose a lot of our décor together. Still, when I look around I see a lot of him and very little of me.

But as I'm trying to stay out of the pit of self-pity, a realization clicks on in my head like a pen light. All these records. There should be something of Laura here... somewhere.

Fenton said they were married ten years ago. But hadn't seen her in eight years. Which means there should be a solid one-to-two-year period where she was part of his life. Where there was evidence she was here.

I don't know why I go looking, nor do I know what I hope to find. All I know is I felt compelled to find it. Maybe it's because he's been acting so strange about this whole thing. It's not like I don't understand—I'm divorced too. But I was upfront about Thomas. I told Fenton immediately. I didn't hide him and pretend like he didn't exist. And I think that's what's bothering me about all of this. If we break up, is that how he'll treat me? Like I never existed in the first place?

In many ways, I feel sorry for Laura. But I also don't like being used. I don't know what her endgame is, or if it was just an innocent meeting. But my gut tells me something else is going on here. And I guess that's why I end up going through almost everything in his office.

Unfortunately, after a solid hour of looking, I've come up empty. It's nothing but business records and things related to his work. No personal notes. No photographs. No handwritten messages between the two of them telling each other to have a good day.

Not one. Single. Mention of her.

I look around at the mess I've made and vow to clean it up later. But I'm obviously not going to find anything here. Nothing useful, anyway.

As I head into the kitchen for some water, I catch sight of the note on the counter. Funny. I was just looking for handwritten notes, and here I have one of my own.

Lazarus has summoned him. Probably because Brian told him about what's been going on. As I grab a glass and get some filtered water from the refrigerator, my heart goes out to Fenton. Lazarus

Byrnes is a difficult man in the best of times. I know I wouldn't want to be facing him down right now. Even if he *is* sticking his nose in our business. It's very possible Fenton won't be back home tonight.

"Best of luck," I say, raising my glass to the empty driveway out the window. "You're gonna need it."

THIRTEEN
WINTER

I awake to a cold room. I'm sure I turned the heat on before going to bed, but it's possible I forgot. With everything that happened last night, I can't really blame myself. A cold snap has made its way down from Canada, and even though the house is insulated well, it's probably only sixty degrees in here.

I wrap the comforter around me and shuffle down the hallway to the thermostat, the wood floors like frozen concrete under my feet. Sure enough, the number fifty-nine glows bright green on the device mounted to the wall. I tap the heat button, then set it to a comfortable sixty-eight. When I turn, the door to the guest room stands open before me, the bed still made. Did he come back home at all last night? Or was he caught in Lazarus's clutches until the wee hours?

I return to the bedroom and retrieve my phone, noting it's almost seven. It's unlikely he left early for work. Unless he purposefully didn't want to see me. I move through the house, passing the office with all the papers strewn on the floor and head into the kitchen. Other than my wine glass and subsequent water glass on the table, nothing has been moved. Fenton's note is still in its place and the coffeemaker is off.

Nope, he didn't come back home last night.

I fix myself a quick breakfast before grabbing a shower and getting ready. I need to focus on something other than this Fenton-slash-Laura business for a while. Like my actual job, which I should probably be paying more attention to. I have a lot of work today, which means I need to get moving.

As I hurry drying my hair and getting dressed, I can't help but wonder what his father said to him last night. And what did Fenton say in return? The two of them have never had a good relationship. When Fenton went off on his own, Lazarus saw it as a slap in the face to the family business. Ever since I've known him, they've both been at each other's throats, with Fenton trying to remove himself completely from that sphere.

Of course, when you're born into a rich and powerful family, that's easier said than done.

As I'm making my way out of the house, my eye lands on the vent under the window again. Maybe it's better we don't have a dog. He'd be left alone most of the day. Unlike Cams I can't stay with him all the time, and he'd probably get lonely.

Still... that doesn't mean I want him any less.

I glance at my phone, weighing whether I should call Fenton or not. I'm not even sure what I want anymore. I know I don't want to fight anymore. But I need... something. I need to understand what happened ten years ago. On my way out I pass the office, still a haphazard mess from last night. He always kept things so organized... so *perfect*.

I pause.

The home office is only one half of the equation. Fenton still has his other office, the one he opened when he went off on his own. There have to be tons of things still there. And if I were looking to hide something from my significant other, where better to keep it?

Careful, Winter.

But I've already broken the seal, haven't I? Looking a bit more won't make any difference. And if he really *is* hiding something, then I'll know. And if he isn't, maybe we can put this whole mess behind us.

Yes, now *this* is progress. Humming a little tune, I head out into the cold.

I call Cams from the car.

"This is rare, twice in two days," she says on the other end. Her voice is light and I don't sense any animosity in the words, but they still sting a little. "How'd it go last night?"

"Well, I took your advice."

"Really? And?"

"And it kicked up a shitstorm of epic proportions."

Cammie gasps. "Nooo. What happened?"

"I can't explain it all right now, it's too much. But maybe over lunch?"

"Hey, you don't have to threaten me with a good time. Just tell me where and when."

I pause. "You're free? I thought you were starting the mobile service today."

"Van still needs a little work," she replies. "I only have two bookings today. Would one work for you?"

I think back to the day before. What time did I meet Laura? It was later because I'd been on-site all morning. Probably around two thirty. If the woman is stalking me, she'll probably show up no matter what time I get there, but if I want to make it look real, I'll need to pretend like I'm just trying to repay her favor. I could meet Cams early, then stick around for her to show up.

Then again I could be misreading this entire thing. I might never see Laura Blackwell ever again.

"Win? You've gone quiet, hon."

"Right, sorry," I say. "One works for me."

"Great. That'll slot nicely between my only two appointments. Got anywhere in mind?"

"Do you know the Stone Inn Deli?"

"That tiny place? On the *other* side of town?" she asks.

"You got it. Let's meet there."

"Ugh. I guess beggars can't be choosers. Okay, see ya then." Cammie hangs up, leaving me feeling like I haven't been very good to her. I really need to do something nice for her one of these days.

I pull off the highway and into a large strip mall. It's been around since I was little, and I even remember coming to the Ames that used to sit at the head of the mall way back when. But they ended up demolishing that and building a grocery store instead, which has also gone out of business. As a result, the largest part of the strip mall stands empty. The other tenants are small, one-door operations. It had been the perfect place for Fenton to set up his business and get out from under his father's feet. A place his family would never approve of and that wouldn't flaunt the Byrneses' social status.

I scan the parking lot, no sign of Fenton's car anywhere. It's almost eight thirty. He'll head home for a change of clothes and a shower before he comes here. Which means I should have at least thirty to forty minutes. I'll be a little late to work, but that's okay. Henry and Sidhara will understand. Plus, I've been putting in a lot of extra hours lately. I can afford thirty minutes.

The car rumbles to a stop in the space in front of his office. *Byrnes Architecture*, reads the small plastic sign affixed to the strip mall's overhang. I pull my keys out, and using the spare key I've never used in my life but was given "just in case," I unlock the front door and enter the small space.

I've only been here once, back when Fenton and I first started dating. It's just as I remember it, sparse and clean. A few pictures hang on the walls and a computer desk with a drafting desk sit off to the side. About three feet of stacked plans adorn the cubby under the main table, all rolled up and safe in their own containers. They're either plans he mails out to clients or vice versa, for those projects where he's picking up the slack after coming in following another architect. It's a cold space, not inviting and not particularly comfortable to work in. I need light, space and greenery if I hope to get something done. Something other than just bland gray walls and blinds covering the front floor-to-ceiling windows beside the door. I pull open the main blinds, flooding the space with light, and notice he hasn't even cleaned recently. A thin layer of dust coats the top of all his boxes.

"Now, if I were a secret wife, where would I hide?" I ask the room. Fenton keeps a series of filing cabinets tucked under his main desk. I go for those first.

An hour passes without any headway. It's taking longer because I have to put everything back as I find it. I don't care if he finds the house in a mess, but if he found out I was in here searching through his files, he might think I'm too obsessive. That I'm taking this too far. And maybe I am. I don't even want to hear what Dr. Hobart is going to say about all this.

Then again, they're not the ones who have been lied to, over and over. I deserve better. And if that means I have to dig through filing cabinet after filing cabinet, I'm gonna do it.

But... I'm short on time, and it's either come back later or take stacks and stacks of file folders with me, neither of which is an ideal option. I've already tried to leave half a dozen times but knowing I could just be on the cusp of finding out about Laura keeps me searching through just one more folder. I glance at my watch. If he's coming into the office today, he'll be here soon. He might have been distracted by the mess at home—Fenton can't stand it if things are out of order. And if he decided to put everything back it might buy me an extra thirty minutes, but I'm already pushing it. I need to leave, now.

Replacing the last file folder in its spot, I scan the room for anything I might have missed or moved. The advantage of having such a sparse space was I didn't need to worry about upsetting a delicate balance of materials. But I can practically feel him on the back of my neck. I gotta get out of here. Why did I wait so long?

I head back out, my hands fumbling with the lock as I try to get it closed and locked the way it was. Finally, the bolt slides and I sprint back to my car, throwing the door open and turning over the engine before I even close it behind me.

He's close. Move.

I pull out of the space, my tires squealing slightly and scan my rearview for any sign of him. Every second that ticks by seems to resound in my gut, as if he'll appear at any moment. I take the rear way out of the lot just to be sure, back behind the abandoned grocery store.

And just as I'm approaching the corner, Fenton's black Mercedes pulls into the lot from the other side.

I gun it, trying to get out of eyesight quickly. It's possible he didn't see me. As I disappear around the edge of the building, the last thing I see is Fenton getting out of the car, staring against the sun in my direction.

FOURTEEN
WINTER

"You don't know if he saw you or not?"

Cammie and I sit at one of the small, two-person tables at the far side of the Stone Inn Deli. I managed to explain everything that happened the previous night, in addition to how I met Laura here yesterday, and the mad dash out of the parking lot this morning. Laura wasn't here when I arrived, and I haven't seen her yet. In fact, there's no indication she'll show up at all. But I can't help but shoot glances at every person that comes through the door regardless.

"I don't know. I can't be sure." As I run through the events of the morning again, my heart practically stops.

"Win?"

"Oh my God. I forgot to close the blinds."

"What?"

"The blinds, in his office," I say. "I was in such a hurry I forgot to close them. He's going to know I was there. He's going—"

"Hang on," she says, holding up her hand. "Don't panic yet. Does he ever leave the blinds open?"

"You don't understand," I say. "Fenton is meticulous. If he leaves something one way, he expects it to be that way when he returns."

"Well, maybe a cleaner came in and opened it. Or maybe he'll think he did it. You said he's been more tired and stressed than normal lately."

That's true. I force my heart to stop thumping so hard.

"And he hasn't called you? Or texted?"

"No. I think he's afraid if he does, it will set me off. He left me a handwritten note last night."

Cammie leans forward on her elbows. "So just pretend like you don't know anything about it if he asks."

I nod, taking deep breaths. I don't know why I'm so on edge. Maybe because I've never been caught doing something I shouldn't... ever. Not even when I was little. Daisy was always the one who took the risks. And I, as the little sister, was happy to fade into the background.

"The real question is, what are you going to do? Stay? Or go?"

I just shake my head. Obviously, things can't go back to the way they were. But is there any possibility of moving forward? I turn to watch the deli chef at work. His hands move quickly, slicing and stacking, his total focus on nothing but the task ahead of him. Does he have a spouse who lied about prior relationships? What are his worries? His obstacles?

"I want to believe we can make it. That this is all some kind of messed-up test. But I just don't know," I finally say.

Cammie reaches out and pats my hand.

"God, it's just so cliché." "Loving" husband lies about his past to his future wife because he's doing something he shouldn't be doing. And he knows it.

"*You're* not a cliché."

I don't reply. Instead, I keep my eyes trained on the chef. His quick and precise movements soothe my mind. Why can't life be like that? Smooth, efficient, and without all this extra drama. How in the hell am I supposed to be this great engineer if I can't even get my own house in order?

Cammie tugs on my sleeve, bringing my attention back. "Fenton *isn't* not Tom. You know that."

"I thought he wasn't. But now I'm not so sure."

Cammie leans back, blowing her bangs out of her eyes. "Tell me again what this woman looks like. Who should I be looking for?"

I sigh, thankful not to think about Fenton for a damned minute. Better to focus on the other half of this equation.

"About as tall as you. Our age, maybe a smidge older. Dark, *dark* brown hair. And yesterday she had on glasses and was dressed smart. Like a lawyer."

"Someone who's got that 'don't fuck with me' look, huh?"

I smile. "That's what I thought too. I thought... why is this woman talking to me? Everything about her appearance was designed to be intimidating. I know if I wore something like that, it would be a clear signal for everyone to stay out of my way. But she couldn't have been friendlier."

"Do you think she knows who you are?" Cammie asks.

I grimace. Everything hinges on this one unknown. Laura had to have known who I was, which meant she'd targeted me for some unknown reason. An idea I don't relish one bit. "I hope not. I really, really hope not. Because if she did, there's no telling what she's planning."

"I hate to do this." Cammie glances at her phone. "But I have to get back. I wish I could stay longer, but I can't miss my next appointment. Mike says we should have the van up and running this evening. If you're free, you should come check it out for a tour."

"Yeah, that sounds great," I say. "Tell him hey for me. I haven't seen him in a while."

"We need to get together more often," she says, getting up. "Not just when there's a crisis. I miss seeing you."

"I miss you too. Both of you."

"Then let's make a date," she says. "You need some time away, especially now. Shoot me a few dates and we'll set it up. And if you need a place to stay out of that house, you know where to come."

I stand and give her a quick hug. "Thank you. This is more than I deserve."

She pulls back. "No, it isn't. The only reason I'm snarky with you is because I love you, Win. And I don't want to see you get hurt."

I nod; thankful I have someone in my corner. "Tonight?"

She grins. "Tonight. Good luck today."

As soon as she's gone, I turn back in the general direction of the deli chef again without really watching him. Have I been foolish for looking for some evidence of Laura? If Fenton hadn't wanted me to know that badly, wouldn't he have destroyed or gotten rid of everything that might show a prior relationship with someone? If so, the fact that he'd done so was sort of impressive, especially if it was all for my benefit. In its own way it was sweet, while at the same time incredibly deceptive. I have the urge to be just as deceptive with him. To finally unleash that part of myself I've kept inside for so long, that little kid who just wanted to open herself up and do a few not-so-nice things. But I don't want to hurt anyone. Just... ugh. I don't even have a word for it. It's as if I'm sitting on a pile of dynamite and the fuse just burned out. I want to find out what happens when that lit fuse reaches the pile. I've been blowing it out my entire life.

I sit in the café with a cooling cup of coffee for another hour before finally giving up and leaving. I've already missed a crucial meeting this afternoon, and given my tardiness this morning, I'm already in the hot seat with my partners.

As I reach for the car, I hear the crunch of gravel behind me.

"Winter?"

I turn, coming face-to-face with the woman I'd spent the afternoon looking for and I'm not prepared for it. I mentally fumble for a moment.

Do something. Say *something.*

"Oh, hi. Umm, Laura, right?" I say, feigning ignorance, as if I hadn't been thinking about this woman constantly ever since last night. Does she know I'm here for her?

"You must have really liked that Rachel sandwich." She's dressed in similar clothes to yesterday, except today she wears a long black coat that mirrors the color of her hair. She smiles, but I see something behind that smile. Something I wouldn't have seen if I hadn't been looking for it. Something that might have been there yesterday, too.

"Yeah, it was so good I had to come back." What am I supposed to say? I've spent all afternoon waiting for you, hoping you'd show up so I can interrogate you about what happened between you and my future husband? And expect you to answer honestly?

Reflexively, I glance down at Laura's hand, noting she's not wearing a wedding or engagement ring. So either Laura isn't in a relationship right now, or she doesn't believe in those things. Or maybe my fiancé drove her from believing in the institution of marriage.

"Are you coming or going?" Laura asks.

"I'm... Um..." This is the perfect opportunity and I'm blowing it. I can't let it slip through my fingers. The partners will just have to wait. Now's my chance to learn everything I possibly can about Laura Blackwell.

"Coming," I finally say, getting ahold of myself. "And don't forget. Today it's my treat."

FIFTEEN

WINTER

We make our way to the counter, but I hold back. "Why don't you tell me what you want and go grab a seat?" I say, eyeing the cashier who couldn't have missed the fact I've been sitting in his café for two hours already.

"Thank you, but I can order," Laura replies, walking right up. "Give me the pastrami deluxe, no cheese and a pickle on the side. And make sure you toast the bread this time. Last time the bread was soggy."

The cashier looks slightly annoyed. "Anything to drink?"

"That tepid water you call green tea will suffice."

I'm slightly puzzled. Is this the same woman who couldn't decide what she wanted yesterday? And today she rattles off an order without a second thought?

Laura stands to the side as I realize I'm up. I smile at the cashier, praying he won't say anything about me being in here so long already. He narrows his eyes, then glances at the table Cams and I occupied. "Back so soon? What will it be this time?"

Maybe Laura will think he meant from yesterday. "I'll just have the green tea as well."

"Twenty-one eighty-five."

I hand over my debit card without looking at Laura. She

doesn't say anything about the cashier's remark and neither do I; instead, I take my drink from him along with my receipt. This isn't how I wanted to make a second impression. Now she's going to think something's up and there will be no way for me to pretend like *something* wasn't going on. I shuffle awkwardly back to the same table I'd shared with Cammie. Laura takes her time unbuttoning her long coat, then hangs it on the seat and sits down.

I can't think of anything to say. Of all the questions I have for this woman, for all the ways I hoped this would go, I find myself dumbstruck with no way out. I can't just come out and blurt out what I know. And every second that passes only increases the tension.

"You ate already?" Laura finally asks, breaking the silence. She says it like I killed someone. Immediately I know I'm busted. What else does she know? And can I throw her off the trail?

No. Fenton got us into this mess by lying. I'm not going to do the same thing. "I'm sorry," I say. "I didn't mean to deceive you. I came here around one, with a friend of mine. I was... hoping to run into you again."

"A friend?" she asks, turning to look at the few remaining patrons.

"She left about half an hour ago," I admit.

She takes a long sip of her tea. "I guess that means you figured out who I am."

My gaze and heart rate shoot up in tandem, and I lock eyes with the woman. I can just barely make out my own reflection in Laura's cat-eye glasses. I didn't expect to break this wall so quickly. Is she going to accuse me of stealing her husband? Or something worse? Did she lure me here to... I dunno... attack me?

Nothing makes sense and she just continues to stare at me like she's a predator, deciding how slowly she wants to devour her prey.

Finally, she breaks into a grin, then a laugh. "You should see your face." She takes a sip of the tea, then reaches over and pats my hand with perfectly manicured nails. "Let me save you some consternation. Yes, I am your fiancé's first wife."

I let out a breath. It's all true. But that still doesn't explain what she wants with me.

"So yesterday wasn't a coincidence."

"I'm sorry, no." Laura's grin fades. "I didn't want to scare you off. Let me guess. Before yesterday you didn't know he was married before, did you?"

"It's... it's been a trying couple of days," I say. I don't like being in the dark, especially with strangers. I could try to play it off, like Fenton told me a long time ago, but what good would that do? I'm trying to *gather* information; maybe the best way to do that is be upfront with everything I know. I'm more likely to get the truth out of her rather than Fenton. In my lap, I clench and unclench my hands.

"I'm sure it came as a shock. He doesn't like telling people about me."

"Did you send it?" I ask, my voice cold.

Laura's mouth turns into a frown. "Send what?"

"Your book. Did you send him your book?" I don't mean to be so brash about it, but this woman owes me some answers.

"My book? I don't have... Do you mean one of my manuscripts?"

I huff and manage not to grit my teeth. "Yes, whatever it's called. Did you send it to him?"

"Sweetie," Laura says with sympathy that makes it sound like I'm a lost child, "I haven't been in contact with him for years."

I narrow my gaze. This is too much of a coincidence to accept that she just *happens* to show up in my life the day after her book arrives on my doorstep. But I can't force it out of her. Better to just play along. "Then why track me down?"

Laura pulls a deep breath in through her nose and takes a long exhale. She reaches into her purse, removing a small mirror case. When she pops it open, a row of perfectly aligned cigarettes stare back at her. She withdraws the first one, sticking it in her mouth.

"Hey!" the cashier yells across the small room. Everyone in the restaurant stops and turns to look at him. He's pointing at Laura.

"No smoking in here." Now everyone is looking at us. I must admit it's more than a little creepy. There's no sound in the place other than something grilling in the back.

Laura already has her lighter in hand and sits frozen in place, prepared to ignite. She turns back to me. "Care to go outside? I need a smoke."

I'm *not* letting her out of my sight. "Sure."

Laura leaves her coat but grabs her purse and I do the same, following the woman out to the front. The sun is shining, but it's still on the chilly side with the wind gusts coming across the face of the building, rattling the small pennant flags on the line strung between the light post and the building.

"Aren't you cold?" I ask, holding myself.

"I've got all the warmth I need," Laura replies and lights the cigarette, the lighter disappearing back into her purse. The lenses in her glasses had darkened in response to the sunny weather and now look like sunglasses. "The reason I sought you out was because I saw your engagement announcement in the paper a few weeks back. It just took me a while to find you."

Where was this going? "To congratulate me?"

Laura chuckles and pushes the smoke out through her nose. "No. To warn you." She glares at me over the top of her sunglasses. "How much do you really know about Fenton Byrnes?"

I stiffen. I do my best not to let it show, but from the sad smile Laura gives me, I know I've failed. She takes a long drag from the cigarette and blows it out away from us, studying me, like I'm some kind of specimen. "What do you mean?" I ask, trying to sound stronger than I am.

Laura drops her gaze, kicking around some of the gravel beneath her feet. "He never told you about me. I figured that much already. But I thought it was my duty to warn you. No one else could."

"Warn me about what?" I ask, unsure of anything now. Had someone come up to me and told me I needed a warning about my fiancé before I ever found that book, I would have laughed in their face. But now I'm not so sure. What else could he be hiding?

"You guys have been together a couple of years now, right? I think I read that."

"Three."

"I was with him for less than that, only two. But I knew him longer... before we officially got together. And I saw things in those years I never want to experience again. He tried to convince me, tried to tell me he was going to counseling and getting himself straight, but I could never put myself in that situation again. I loved him, but once was enough for me."

Fenton's been in counseling? Wait a second. "Are you saying... he hit you?"

Laura takes another long drag. "Maybe I let it go on for a little too long. I should have seen the early signs, the bruises when he'd grab me too hard, or push me away. But when it finally came to blows, I was done."

I'm speechless. Fenton has never gotten physical, ever. Not even a hint of hurting me. He's one of the gentlest people I know. For Christ's sake, he doesn't even like killing spiders! There is no way they are talking about the same person. "I... I just... can't believe that," I eventually manage.

"Good," Laura replies, finally looking at me. "Then it sounds like all that work he did really helped. If he's never been that way with you, then that's great." She drops the cigarette and puts it out underneath the toe of her black pump. "But you see where I'm coming from, right? I couldn't in good conscience let anyone else get themselves into that situation without knowing all the risks. Have you guys talked about it, then?"

"Well... no," I admit. This makes no sense. Fenton wasn't like that, and I'm not about to stand here and agree with this stranger I don't know about my fiancé's behavior. "Did you file a police report?"

"I tried, but I'll give you one guess who put a stop to that."

My heart picks up, realizing that any report filed against a Byrnes could be easily squashed. "Lazarus."

"He smoothed the whole thing over. Convinced me to take a payoff if he could guarantee Fenton would never touch me again. I actually made it all the way to the police station, but he was there, waiting, in that ridiculous black Escalade or whatever it is." She laughs, but there's no humor in it. "I don't even know if it would have made a difference. You know he has connections all over town."

"So does Brian," I say, thinking back to Fenton's text conversation with him. He'd been the first person Fenton had called after this all began.

"Oh, don't even get me started," Laura says, pulling out another cigarette. She offers me the case. Under any other circumstances I would absolutely and unequivocally refuse, but I find myself reaching for the case and taking it. Her hand is shaking as I remove a cigarette and perch it between my lips. Laura holds up the lighter and ignites the end for me. It's time to see if these things really do take the edge off. I inhale, not too deep, as I don't want to scorch my lungs the first time, and a little jolt of electricity surges through me. I don't cough, but it burns all the same and I hold the smoke for a moment before blowing it out.

"How do I know you're telling the truth?"

Laura looks taken aback. "I guess you don't. You believe what you want to believe, but I don't really have anything to gain by telling you all this."

"You do if I leave him. Revenge."

Laura blew her smoke away and I copy the gesture. "I worked too hard in my own therapy sessions to fall back into the revenge spiral. Make no mistake, I was mad for a long time. But I got over it. If you guys are happy, then that's great. But if something ever happened to you and I hadn't said anything... well..."

I take another drag, and this one comes a little smoother. "I appreciate what you're trying to do. But look at it my from my perspective."

Laura exhales. "I get it. If some random lady came up to me and told me things about my husband, I'd probably tell her to fuck off."

"You're married?"

She nods. "Five years now."

"But you don't have a ring."

Laura stares at her ring finger. "We don't believe in them." Then, after a beat, "Yeah, we're those people. No rings, no hyphenated last names or anything like that. Just two people who love and live together. And get all the tax benefits."

I take another drag on the cigarette. It warms me from the inside out; I can see why people do this. Despite my anger, I'm also slightly euphoric. Like I just discovered some long-lost secret. If only Daisy could see me now. I smile at the prospect and relish a few more pulls on the cigarette without saying anything. Can I trust this woman? Her accusations about Fenton were terrible, but what if he really has done those things? It isn't out of the realm of possibility that his family could cover them up. From what I've seen, they could cover almost anything up. Lazarus's influence extends far and wide beyond our little corner of Connecticut.

"Anyway," she says, blowing out another puff of smoke. "Did you say someone sent you a book? *My* book?"

I nod.

"That's... kind of concerning. Which one?"

"*The Last Man I'd Marry*," I say, and suddenly the title doesn't seem so nebulous. "Wait, did you write that about Fenton?"

Laura removes her glasses and pinches the bridge of her nose before replacing them. "That was so long ago. I haven't thought about the books in years. I never got serious about it, you know? I mean I tried, but they just never went anywhere. I'd actually forgotten about them until you said something."

"*Someone* remembered it. It looks like a professional book. Like one you'd pick off the bookshelf."

"Do you have it?" she asks, an inkling of hope in her voice. "I wouldn't mind seeing it."

"Fenton took it," I say. "I... I'm not sure what he did with it."

"Oh," she replies, and my heart breaks a little for her.

"If it makes any difference, I really enjoyed what I read. *Before* I learned who you were."

She smiles. "Thanks. I spent a long time on that manuscript. I just wish an agent would have taken a chance on it."

"Do you have any idea who might have published it—or, I guess, made it pretty for you?" I ask. "And sent it to me?"

She shakes her head. "No clue. But let me check with some of my friends. I sent it to a few people back in the day, you know, to get their opinions. I can't imagine any of them doing something with it without telling me, but I guess you never really know what someone will do, do you?"

My thoughts go back to Fenton. "No. You don't." I pause, letting the air hang between us. "The dedication…"

Her eyes go wide and she looks mortified. "Oh no. Is that still in there?"

I nod, thinking back to it. Though now that I do, I realize I've been focusing on the wrong part of the dedication. The "I love you" part. But there was a much more ominous aspect to that dedication.

And I have the perfect opportunity to find out what it means right now. "What made you write 'you'll never get rid of me.'"

She lets out a long breath. "It was never supposed to go to print. I guess whoever got their hands on it didn't make any changes." She pauses. "I wrote that when I was angry with him. He'd just told me I wasn't getting anything in the settlement. We were already three months into the divorce proceedings. It was meant as a kind of 'fuck you.'" She gives me a nervous laugh.

"I can understand that," I say. "He can be a frustrating man sometimes."

She laughs, the tension around her evaporating. "I guess if anyone understands, you would. Listen, can I get your number? Then I can text you if I find out anything about it?"

"Yeah. Of course." I drop my cigarette and put it out under my own shoe. So that's what that feels like. I dig into my purse and pull out my phone. Laura rattles off her phone number, and as soon as I add it, I hit send. A little chime goes off inside Laura's purse.

"Perfect," Laura says. "Now that the ugly business is out of the way, care to have a second lunch?"

"Absolutely," I reply, following my new friend back inside.

SEVENTEEN
WINTER

I don't bother going back to the office. By the time Laura and I finish at the café, it's nearly five o'clock, so it's better to just go home and make up the work tomorrow. I've got three missed calls from Sidhara, none of which could be as interesting or important as getting to know more about Laura and her life. She's a web developer working for a major company based in Hartford. She met her husband only a few months after leaving Fenton, though it took them a little longer to get together. And she is understandably shy. But the more I listened to the woman, the more I found I could relate to her. We both came from broken families, both have an older sibling working out of the country somewhere and are both highly determined and motivated. Between the two of us, we boiled down Fenton's type to a very narrow band. And while that was funny in one sense, it's also a little concerning. What had he done—screwed up with Laura then gone out to look for an exact replacement with me? Like Laura was his practice run? I can't be sure until I confront him.

Which is exactly what I'm prepared to do as I pull up to our home... until I see the other car in the driveway.

I don't even bother opening the garage. Instead, I ease in behind Fenton's car, keeping the noise to a minimum, then cut the engine and take a deep breath. The burn of the cigarette is still back there. Some part of me can't come to terms with the fact I actually did that. I'd refused to smoke every day of my life until today, another symptom of being the "good child." But in that moment, I'd needed something, something decidedly non-Winter. If I could do that, I can get through this.

It seems spring has gone back into hibernation after all, because when I get out of the car, I can see my breath in front of me. I sneak up the walk as quietly as possible, hesitating when I reach the front door. Behind it, muffled voices shout back and forth, neither of them clear enough for me to make out what they're saying. There are at least two people in there, maybe more, and from what I can tell, the conversation isn't a good one. As soon as I open the door, I'll give myself away because of that damn security system. Why it doesn't chime on the back door or garage I don't know. But if I go through the garage, the rolling door will alert them just as easily. I toy with the idea of sneaking in through the back, but when they catch me standing there, and they eventually will, I'll have no excuse. I don't want it to look like I'm the one hiding anything. I want to keep Fenton thinking he's controlling the only avenue of information about his former life. He can't be the only one holding all the cards.

I hold my breath and open the front door, the chimes singing overhead as I toss my keys to the side table.

"Winter? Is that you?" Fenton's voice comes from the living room.

"Yeah," I reply as casually as I can. He hasn't texted all day. Or called. Or anything else. Either he saw me at the office and is waiting to confront me, or he's actually trying to keep his distance for once.

"Hey, Win." Brian's voice echoes from the living room. I suspected he was here from spotting the Range Rover outside, but is there anyone else?

Please, God, not Lazarus, please not Lazarus.

When I turn the corner, it's just the two men, sitting across from each other. Fenton sits on the same couch where I chucked his phone at him last night. He doesn't give me an accusatory glare or any indication he knows where I was this morning. I breathe an internal sigh of relief.

Brian stands and gives me a brief hug like he always does. During which all I can think of is how he's lied to me for years about Laura. "I understand this guy is being a royal shit to you lately."

I smirk, playing along. "Something like that."

"Brian... don't," Fenton says.

His brother waves him off. "*I* wanted to tell you about Laura from the beginning. But *some people*"—he stares at Fenton as he says it—"thought it would be a bad idea."

"I appreciate that," I reply, surprised by his candor. Could that be true? Could Fenton have been the one who kept the rest of his family quiet about his ex? Or was it the other way around? Was it a family mandate not to talk about the *failed marriage?*

"And now that you know, I want you to know I'm working on finding out who sent this book to you. Or him. I've got some of my best people looking into it."

"Your best people?"

"Private detectives, a few beat cops on their off time. You know, nothing serious but enough to make some inquiries."

I frown. Should I tell them I've met Laura? With Brian involved, what's the point in hiding? Other than the fact it might upset Fenton. Not that I care very much about that at the moment. But I also like having Laura all to myself, like my own personal secret. And now that Brian has informed me of his investigation, it has lit something deep within. I need to beat Brian at his own game. Not because I don't like Brian, but because it's not his job, or his life. The book had been sent to *my* house, to *my* fiancé, and it wasn't his responsibility to figure this out. Somewhere, maybe while talking to Laura, I realized the book was a message, either to me or Fenton. And I'll be damned if someone else figures it out before I do.

"Do you think Laura might have sent it?" I ask, probing him. It's time to see just how much he knows.

Brian glances at Fenton, then back at me. "I guess it's a possibility?"

"Brian," Fenton warns.

"I'll make sure to check into it. If it is her, I would be very surprised."

"You don't think it is."

"Not at present."

Good. That confirms Laura's story as well. But it also means that Brian might be talking to some of the same people who know Laura. Should I call and warn her to hurry up, or at least mention that my soon-to-be brother-in-law is on the case? So she won't be surprised if he or one of his underlings shows up at her house one day?

"So that's it, then?"

"That's it," Brian says. "I just wanted you to know, so you wouldn't worry that someone out there might be stalking you. We've got this thing covered."

"I thought I heard you guys arguing before I came in."

"Oh, that was just my stupid brother telling me he didn't think we should tell you yet. I explained to him that you can't keep things from the woman you love, because that gets you into deep, deep trouble." He stares at Fenton again.

"Sounds like sage advice," I reply. Fenton's doing the smart thing and staying mostly quiet. That tells me he knows how serious this is.

"I like to think so," Brian says.

The room falls into an uncomfortable silence.

"Okay, I'm outta here." Brian grabs his jacket and heads for the door. "Hey, Win, if he keeps giving you trouble, just send him back over to the house. Watching him ask Dad for a place to sleep last night was one of the best moments of my life."

"Would you just leave already," Fenton says, his head still down.

Brian smirks. "Night, you two. Try not to kill each other while I'm gone." A moment later the door chimes, signaling his exit.

"So," I say, slumping down into the chair Brian just vacated. "How *is* your dad?"

"Winter, I am so, so sorry," Fenton says, looking up. "The last thing I wanted to do was hurt you."

"Then you should have told me the truth from the beginning. All of it."

"I know. It won't happen again."

"You're right, it won't." I'm still not quite sure how I'm going to manage this, but for the moment I have the upper hand I'm not about to let it go.

"Tell me what you need me to do."

I ponder a moment. It's in these moments I find being mad at him difficult. And yet on some level I suspect it's an act to get back in my good graces. He always goes into this supplicant mode whenever he's royally messed up, and he's never done anything this bad before. Which means he'll be compliant for a while.

"Is there something you were looking for in the office?" he asks. "Something I can help you find?"

"No. I was just going through some stuff," I reply. "I'll clean it up later."

His lips form a line and he nods like he knew that was coming. "Don't worry, I already took care of it," he replies, pushing himself up from the couch. "Guest bedroom tonight?"

I nod absently, my thoughts drifting to Laura.

"Why isn't there anything left of her?"

"What?" he asks, midway though standing up.

"You're not stupid. You must know I was looking for her in those files. But there's not even so much as a picture. Why?"

"Win," he says in that maddening way he does when he's irritated with me. *He's* upset? "Can we just drop this, please?"

I want to tell him I'm not dropping anything. But what am I really fighting for at this point? He's admitted to their relationship, they had a failed marriage and they divorced. What else is there? What do I really want from him?

"Fine," I say. "Sleep well."

"You too." He heads off to the guest bedroom at the other end of the house. It's like I can feel our bond crumbling between us. His deception and subterfuge are the driving forces behind all of it.

If all this falls apart, it will be because of his actions, not mine. But someone out there knows something. Otherwise why send the book at all? Laura claims it wasn't her, but that could have been another lie. Hell, maybe Fenton himself sent it. Maybe he wanted an easy way out of this marriage. Though I can think of a thousand better ways to go about it.

All I know is someone wanted either me or him to see it. Beyond that, I don't know its purpose. But if neither Laura nor Fenton sent it, then who? And for what purpose? Is it a warning? Or something more?

As I watch Fenton saunter down the hall, I can't help but look at him differently. Could he have really hurt Laura like she said? I never would have believed it before today. But then again, he's shown me over and over he's capable of far more than I ever knew. And he's managed to hide it so well for so long. I've heard of relationships that change once the wedding ceremony is over. Where one spouse will turn into a completely different person. Is that what's going to happen with Fenton? Will he turn physical and abusive after we're married?

I don't want to stick around to find out.

But at the same time, I just met Laura. And I'm still not sure I completely trust her. Despite what she says, she might be trying to drive a wedge between us.

Maybe the book was meant to open up the possibility in my mind that my husband isn't who he says he is. And if that's the case, then I need to find out everything I can about him, starting with his relationship with Laura. I can work backwards from there. Because right now, all I really know are the past three years. Before that... anything is possible.

I listen to him rustling around in the bedroom for a few minutes, shuffling and getting ready for bed. Who is he... really? Is he the kind and charming man he's shown to me since I've met him? Or is someone darker lurking beneath the surface? And considering who his father is, it isn't out of the realm of possibility.

If there's nothing here and nothing in his office, then I'll just have to get more creative. The county records office should have records of marriages and divorces. It would be the next most logical place to look. I'll also be able to see if he was ever married at any other point in his past. I'll head over there tomorrow after work, see what I can't dig up.

Dead tired, I head for the bedroom, only to have my phone beep from my purse. It's a text from Cammie.

Shit. I completely forgot.

> Hey, what's going on? I've sent you like three texts. Are you coming over or not?

I type back a quick reply to her. With everything that had happened with Laura and then coming home to both Brian and Fenton, it slipped my mind.

> I'm sorry, I got hung up and there have been some... developments. Rain check?

She sends back a text a minute later.

> Yeah. Sure. Just let me know.

I can tell by the clipped words I've pissed her off. And rightly so. I promised to come look at the van and I didn't do it. I am a shitty friend.

> Not ignoring you. Call you tomorrow with details. Big developments.

I wait a moment for another response, but none comes. I'll have to smooth things over with Cammie tomorrow. While I'm scrolling,

I realize I've missed three voicemails as well, all from Sidhara. The first two she just waits long enough to hang up. But she actually left a message for the third.

"Winter. Where are you? We have to get this second proposal done or we are going to lose these bridge contracts. Call me as soon as you get this."

I grimace and toss the phone on the bed. Great. I've pissed off my best friend and neglected my work, and I still don't have anything to show for it. How could both have slipped my mind so easily? That never happens. I'll go in early in the morning to do some damage control there too.

I guess all it took was one tiny push for all the dominoes of my life to begin to fall.

EIGHTEEN
FENTON

Fenton listened carefully as Winter rustled around the living room for a bit and then all went quiet. For once in his life, he was glad he had listened to his brother and his father. They had gotten rid of anything and everything related to Laura years ago. As much as it had pained him to do it, it had all been destroyed. A necessity at the time, they'd said.

He'd been understandably upset. He'd wanted to keep a few things to remember her by. A few gifts, things that were special to the both of them. The pictures from their trip to the Grand Canyon. The painting she'd given him on their first anniversary. She'd done it herself in sort of a Jackson Pollock style and it had hung above the mantel in their old house for most of the time they were together. But Brian had insisted it be destroyed, along with everything else. There could be no trace, he said. Nothing that could ever lead back to Fenton.

He supposed he couldn't blame Brian too much—he was as much a victim of circumstance as a willing participant—but that didn't absolve him of everything he'd done since. All the cover-ups, all the lies and deceits. Fenton had hoped to avoid it all, but somehow it had still come back to haunt him no matter what he did.

And what was all that crap he'd told Winter tonight? Fenton almost laughed despite himself. And why had Brian told her he was investigating it? Didn't he know Winter at all? Now she would only be more interested. When he'd seen the state of the office this morning, he'd known immediately she wouldn't give this up. She wasn't one to let things go, not until they had reached her satisfaction.

He wasn't going to bring it up. She could search his office all she wanted. There was nothing there to find. What concerned him more was the book and the ominous dedication written in the front. It meant someone knew. And whoever that person was, they were intent on tormenting him.

He didn't want Winter involved. Not in something like this. It was his mess and he had to clean it up. But despite his protestations, Brian thought it was best they tell her at least some of the truth. And Fenton wasn't even sure that decision hadn't come from Dad somewhere along the line. Brian said she needed an ally at the moment, someone she could trust more than Fenton—a person who could control the narrative—rather than someone out of their control, like Cammie, putting ideas in Winter's head.

Fenton sighed, pulling his shirt over his head and heading into the guest bathroom. He'd had the wherewithal to grab his toiletries before Winter came home, figuring he'd be relegated to the guest room for the time being. After Fenton revealed he'd been married, there was no pretending anymore. The fact was they still had no clue who sent the book, but whoever did had some very damaging information on the Byrnes family, Fenton in particular. And Dad, for all his faults, would never stand for that. Fenton was sure they would get to the bottom of it eventually.

Whether or not his relationship would survive was the real question.

NINETEEN
WINTER

I awake early, invigorated. There's a small irritation in the back of my throat, probably from the smoke. What had I been thinking? A lifetime of healthy lungs and I go and cut four or five months off of my life for no good reason. But I guess when I'm ninety, another four months won't make a difference. Plus, it isn't like I'm going to do it again. That's all in the past. The first order of business is to get work squared away and then head down to the county courthouse. Then patch things up with Cams.

I pass the guest room, listening to Fenton's soft snoring permeating the closed door. How late had he been up? For the first time a bit of guilt gnaws at me over how I'm treating him. This is the man I love, after all. But that doesn't excuse his behavior. And as much as I want to believe he isn't capable of those things Laura said, as much as I want to go into the guest room and embrace him, I just can't do it. There have to be consequences, otherwise he'll just do it again. I'm not going to be pushed around by anyone, especially not the person I plan to spend the rest of my life with.

I fix myself a quick cup of coffee and head back into the bedroom for a shower. As soon as I'm ready, I'm out the door before Fenton even shows himself, which is how I prefer it. I have too much on my plate to deal with that awkwardness this morning.

As I pull out of the long driveway, I wave to Janet, who is out getting her morning paper. The older woman blows me an overly compassionate kiss and smiles. I pull onto the main road and grab my phone, quick dialing the second number on my list.

"Hello?" Cammie says.

"Hey, Cams. I'm sorry about yesterday. A lot happened."

"Oh, hey, Win. Can I give you a call back? We're elbow deep in engine parts and I—"

"Laura showed up yesterday after you left," I say hurriedly. "She knows I know who she is. She said Fenton was abusive towards her and that's why she left."

"Holy shit." Cammie pauses. "Do you believe her?"

"I don't know." I speed up and pass a slow truck on the two-lane highway. I need to get into work as soon as possible.

"What are you going to do?"

"I figured out how to prove he was married before. I'm going to go pull the county records on my lunch break. Get the marriage and the divorce records."

"That's... not a bad idea."

"But I wanted to give you an update since I didn't get a chance to call you back yesterday. When I got home, Brian was here. He said he's personally investigating the book."

"That's good. Right?"

"I guess. It just makes me itchy. You know Lazarus has his hand in this somehow and I want to find out everything I can before he suspects something. I've never had a good feeling about that man and I certainly don't want to be indebted to him. That doesn't ever seem to go over very well."

"You think he'd actually believe you owed him?"

I grimace. "If he puts a bunch of resources into finding out who sent the book, including his other son, and then comes back and tells me his efforts were all for me, so I could have a happy, stress-free marriage, then yeah, I think he would think I owed him a favor. And from everything Fenton has told me, I do not want to owe that man anything."

"You make it sound like he's part of the mafia."

"Yeah, well. You know rich people. They've always got their hands in something."

"C'mon, Win, that's kind of ridiculous." A metal clang rattles through the phone. "Shit. I gotta go. I'll call you back later. Don't do anything rash."

I hang up and shove the phone back into my purse. *Don't do anything rash...* like what? I'm not putting myself in danger. All I'm going to do is head down to the Clerk's Office. But I can't help but think that perhaps I'm picking at a scab that should not be disturbed. Someone had gone to a lot of trouble to conceal Fenton's first marriage and people don't do that without a reason.

"What the hell is going on here? I thought we had this thing locked down! That's what you said, wasn't it? 'Locked down'? Of course that was two days ago, the last time either of us saw you, and now I'm getting calls from the city asking if we're still putting in a proposal!"

Henry paces his office while Sidhara and I sit in the other two chairs, facing his desk. We usually meet in here because he's got the biggest office, despite the fact it gets hot as hell in here in the afternoon. It was a compromise he said he was willing to make. I take a deep breath, trying to figure out a way to explain myself out of all this.

"What the hell could have been so important that you completely forgot to tell us about the site visits?" he screams before I can even answer his last question.

"Henry, calm down. Let her talk," Sidhara says. She's a much more reserved person than our colleague, but even I can see storms brewing behind her dark eyes.

"Well, I can't wait to hear it!" Henry adds, falling with a *thump* in his own seat behind his desk.

I lean forward. "I had planned on calling you. But I've had a bit of a family emergency the past couple of days and it slipped my mind." It's the best I can do without getting into the minutiae of the book and everything else. The truth is I *did* forget. If I tried to explain it all now, they'll think I was losing my mind.

"Everyone is all right?" Sidhara asked.

I nod. "More or less. It's just been... a stressful few days. Which is why I came in early this morning to get some of the new drafts done for the proposal. I'll have them all finished before I leave today."

"That's just great, as we were supposed to submit them this morning."

I turn to Henry, doing my best to keep my temper under control. I'm not the only one who can finish proposals, even though I was the lead on these jobs. "I know, and I said I was—"

"Do you not want to do this anymore? Is this how you go off on your own? This was your idea, if I might remind you. Bring the three of us together, become the most respected engineering firm in the state. Because right now it looks like you have more important things on your plate."

"I told you I was sorry," I say through gritted teeth.

"No." Henry shakes his head. "No, I don't think you did. You gave us a half-assed excuse about a sick family member and then justified it. What was so important you couldn't even call Sid back? At least let us know you hadn't done any of the proposal work? At least let us know we were still in the running for the jobs!" His face has gone all red.

I don't respond well to men screaming in my face. So I'm not about to give him the satisfaction of a response.

"That's enough," Sidhara says. "It doesn't matter anymore. She's here now and she said she'll finish today. Do we still have the time to submit our final proposal or not?"

I glance at the clock. Henry isn't wrong; it was due at the city this morning, something else I've forgotten. I completely neglected everything yesterday. It was as if the day had existed outside of time and I somehow thought I could come and go as I pleased, without any consequences. Why had I thought that? Was it because this mystery had become so compelling? Or was it just the surprise of seeing Laura again, of learning about this bombshell that had turned my life upside down? It's a puzzle to be deciphered, one in which the stakes are higher than anything I've ever faced at work. Perhaps that's why everything else had seemed—and still did to some extent—less important.

"If I work through lunch, I can get it done in time. I'll call Carter down at the city. He'll give us an extension, I'm sure of it." I won't have time to get to the Clerk's Office, but I don't have much of a choice. We can't afford to lose these contracts. And if I can get it done quickly enough, I might be able to swing by before the courthouse closes for the weekend. I glance at Sid. "Can you double-check my work? I need a second pair of eyes to make sure I don't miss anything."

"Of course."

The two of us stand, leaving Henry still slumped in his chair.

"Great. What am I supposed to do?" Henry asks.

"What you always do," I say. "Call the inspectors. Make something up about why everything is late, but let them know it will all be filed today." I leave the room with Sid on my heels.

"What am I supposed to make up?" Henry calls after us.

"Whatever your tiny brain can come up with," I say under my breath.

TWENTY

WINTER

The drafting takes longer than I expect, and by the time we're done and have actually sent it off to the city, it's already 4:15.

"I gotta go," I tell Sid. "I have people to attend to."

"You sure everyone is all right?" she asks again, that calm demeanor never betraying her.

"Everyone will be fine. I just worry. You know how I am," I reply, shrugging my jacket on.

"Listen," Sid says, pulling me aside. "Whatever is going on with you, it's affecting all of us now. I need to know you have a handle on it. We can't afford to sacrifice jobs, not right now."

I glance down and retrieve my arm from Sid's grip. "I know. You're right. After that Williamson debacle we can't afford to lose any more contracts. But I can practically guarantee we're getting these jobs. The site manager practically told me the other day we're the only real consideration in the running."

"You know how much can change in two days."

Tell me about it.

I want to say it out loud, to try and explain what's going on, but Sid and Henry don't care about any of that. And it isn't their problem. "It will be fine, I promise. If they don't like the proposals, I'll go down to the office itself and make the case in person." I glance at the clock. 4:20. "I really gotta go."

Sid doesn't say anything else, only presses her lips in a line as I walk away. This is all a matter of resource allocation, and I just need to make sure I don't forget anything else. I pull out my phone and type in a reminder to check on the contracts first thing Monday with the site manager. A little follow-up might push things in our direction, even if we are slightly more expensive than the competition. GWH is all about quality and reputation, and the site manager knows it.

I brush out the doors, my stride quick and purposeful. The Clerk's Office is only about ten minutes away, but will they still process my request before they close? If only I hadn't been so frazzled yesterday, I could have planned all this out. Not that waiting until tomorrow for the certificates will hurt anything, but I need to get out in front of this and find out what is really going on before Brian comes back and feeds me some bullshit line Lazarus crafted. Brian is a nice enough guy, but he's too loyal to the family. Which is something I admire about Fenton; he was willing to leave that all behind. It can't be easy to say no to a comfortable, all-your-needs-taken-care-of life. At least I assume it can't. I wouldn't know.

The Southerland clan didn't exactly struggle, but things hadn't been easy either. Especially after Dad left with his new girlfriend in tow, something I still haven't forgiven him for. We see each other at Christmas and sometimes Thanksgiving, but that's about it. And maybe Lucille really is a nice person, but I don't care to find out. I'm just grateful she and Dad don't have any kids. I can't imagine a stepbrother or -sister more than ten years younger than me and, what, twelve years younger than Daisy? And Mom would have a fit. No, it's best to leave Dad and Lucille in their nice little fantasy world where they don't have to worry about raising anyone and can go off on their vacations.

I slip behind the wheel and crank the heat as soon as the car is on. I wish this cold snap would move on already. It's supposed to be spring, for heaven's sake.

Pulling out of the parking lot, I push the speedometer above normal on Highway 6. I'm not normally a speeder, but this is an emergency. And if I get pulled over, then so be it.

I push the accelerator harder. The speedometer inches up to forty-eight. Forty-nine. Fifty. Fifty-two.

Adrenaline pumps through my veins. It isn't the speed, but the fact the cops are vigilant on this stretch of road and speeders get caught all the time. I've never needed to get anywhere fast enough to justify a ticket. But now I get it. Maybe it isn't about getting somewhere fast but challenging and beating the system. I push the accelerator a little harder. Sixty-six and blowing past other cars on the four-lane highway. I almost want to whoop with exhilaration but stop myself.

The Clerk's Office comes up quickly on my right, a two-story nondescript building which, from the look of it, was built sometime in the 1960s with its thin windows and mix of brick-and-masonry construction. Most of the parking spots in front are already empty, so I yank the car to a stop in the closest one to the door and hop out, trotting up to the doors.

"Hi," I say to the woman manning the front desk. "I'm looking for some public records."

The woman makes a point to check her watch and then returns her gaze to me. "Type?"

"Marriage and divorce."

The woman sighs and pulls out a form from one of the filing cabinets beside her. "Fill this out and we'll mail them to you in four to six weeks."

"Four to six weeks? I can't wait that long."

The woman sits, unmoving. Just staring at me with her small black eyes and silver hair done up in a tight bun.

I compose myself. I have to remember I need this woman's help. All she wants is to go home away from this job. "Is there any way to speed that up?"

The woman stares at me for longer than necessary and I can't help but feel like she's intentionally stalling. Like the records office is this one woman's domain, and no one's getting past her if she doesn't approve it. Finally, she opens her mouth. "We process in-person requests Monday through Friday, nine a.m. until four p.m."

Is that a smirk on the woman's face? They don't have Saturday hours? With it being Friday, I won't get back here until next week, which means an excruciating weekend in the house with Fenton, both of us tiptoeing around each other. I can't live like that.

The other option is to accept everything I've learned and drop it. To just forget about the book, about Laura's warnings and about Fenton's lies. To somehow turn back the clock and pretend like none of this ever happened.

But that just isn't something I can do.

And what if there were other records? What if he'd been married more than once? Maybe I needed to prove he wasn't lying about anything else; that there hadn't been anyone else before Laura. Because right now, I'm not sure.

I need access to those records. Today.

"Is there anything you can do?" I ask, already knowing the answer.

"Winter?"

I look up, past the silver-haired lady to a figure emerging from a small office off to the side.

"Janet?" The sight of my neighbor anywhere but her own house catches me off guard. In fact, didn't I see her just this morning, getting the paper? "Do you... work here?"

The woman at the desk harrumphs.

"I do. Part-time. Do you need help with something?" Janet asks.

I glance back and forth between the woman and Janet. "I'm trying to get some marriage and divorce records."

"We process in-person requests Monday through—"

"Oh, can it, Mary," Janet interrupts. "I'll take care of her; you go back to your solitaire."

Mary purses her lips again, then turns so her back is to us.

"Come on, dear, you just follow me."

"Are you sure?" I ask, falling in step behind her. "I don't want to be an inconvenience."

"It isn't. This is the most excitement I've had all week. With the exception of your prowler, that is. Still never saw anyone, but I wouldn't put it past some hobo to go out there, stumbling around in the dark." She lets out a brief laugh.

But this person wasn't stumbling. They weren't even moving. They were just staring right at me. As if they were looking into my soul.

"Don't keel over from a coronary," Mary calls out from the desk, now a good eight or ten feet behind us.

"Go home and drink your medicine, Mary!" Janet calls back. Then, whispering to me, "She always gets pissy around five o'clock. If you come in the mornings, she's bright as a bluebird."

I'm in awe of Janet a little bit. She has more bite in her than I'd expected. I've only known her as the kind lady next door.

She leads us into a different office. It only has one small desk with a computer, but three of its walls are covered with stacks of filing cabinets.

"Are these the records?" I ask.

"Only the last ten years. Everything else is in the basement." Janet sits down behind the computer. "Who do you want to see?"

I hesitate. I thought I'd be looking through the files myself, or at least telling someone I don't know personally. But Janet knows Fenton. She's been his neighbor ever since he bought that house and started refurbishing it. This is all so embarrassing. But if I want answers, I don't have a choice.

"Umm. Byrnes and Blackwell."

Janet glances up briefly, then returns to the screen. "Marriage or divorce?"

"Both."

"Do you have the dates?" she asks, her voice completely even. I hope she knows how much I appreciate her not giving me any accusatory stares or lip service.

Shit. The dates. I didn't think to ask. "Do you need them?"

"Nope," Janet replies. "It will just take me a little longer. Give me a few minutes, if you don't mind. Within the last ten years, right?"

"Right." I take a moment to glance around the room, not that there's anything to look at except for filing cabinets, but I don't want to stare or appear like I'm inviting further discussion. The best thing I can do is examine the typography on the labels affixed to the cabinets themselves until she's finished.

"Okay, I think I got it," Janet says after a few minutes.

"Really?" I turn, trying to keep my voice even. This is it. Until this moment I wasn't completely convinced the marriage had actually happened.

"Looks like the wedding date was... oh, just under the cutoff. August 29, 2008. And both parties divorced on October 21, 2010. Reason listed is irreconcilable differences." She glances back at me. "They *always* put that."

A breath of air escapes my mouth. So it's all true. He really had been married. It doesn't bother me as much as I thought it would. After all, had he told me, maybe it would have been something we could have bonded over. Sometimes I think he ignores all the progress I've made on purpose.

Now comes the hard part. The question that has been on my mind since I came up with this idea. "Janet, can you see if there are any other marriage records for Fenton Byrnes? Other than this one?"

"Sure." Janet typed a few keys and studied the screen some more. For a second I'm sure my arm is going numb and I shake it out. Just nerves.

"Looks like this is the only one. I don't see any other records attached to his"—she corrects herself "—*that* name." Janet stands and opens the bottom drawer of one cabinet. After a moment she pulls out a plain-looking document. "Here it is. Do you want copies?"

I nod, taking the paper in my hands, trying to keep them from shaking. "Please."

"Let me pull the divorce record first and then I'll copy them both for you."

"Thank you," I say quietly, struggling to get the words out. My eyes scan the page. It's real. Everything matches, and that is definitely Fenton's signature at the bottom. August 29, 2008. Almost ten years ago. At least now I know he was telling the truth. And it wasn't as if he'd been married only a few months before we met. Laura had said they'd only been married two years, which meant there was at least a five-year gap between when they got divorced and when he and I met. Five years is a long time. Maybe he really did change. Especially without any other relationships. Of course, just because there are no marriage records didn't mean he hadn't dated, though that wasn't a big deal. It isn't like I expected him to abstain for five years.

"December, December," Janet mutters as she heads over to another cabinet. She withdraws another, thicker set of documents. "Let me get these copied for you," she says, her eyes all business as she takes the marriage certificate from me.

I have the proof. I should be furious, but instead, I feel a little better. Knowing that he actually came clean and there aren't any other secret marriages goes a long way to helping me regain some small amount of trust in him. Maybe we can work this out after all. It isn't hard to believe he'd hidden the truth from me; I know I can be harsh about that kind of thing. Haven't I been in similar situations? Wanting to tell someone something important and waiting too long? And then it becomes too late and you just look like an ass for never saying anything. So you keep quiet. And that's exactly what Fenton had done. It just happened to involve the one thing he knew would trigger me. Things might just be okay.

Janet comes back into the room, one set of papers in each hand.

"Winter, I don't mean to alarm you, but I think we might have an issue here."

I look up. I hadn't even realized I'd been staring at my own shoes. "An issue?"

"Look at this," Janet says, placing the marriage certificate and the divorce filing beside each other in front of me.

It takes me a moment to see what she's talking about. On both pieces of paper, Fenton's signature is nearly identical. But Laura's is not. On the marriage certificate it has clean, swooping lines in a very script-y style. But on the divorce filing, it doesn't quite look right. There is a messiness that isn't present in the other document. Like someone tried to copy her signature and hadn't done a very good job.

"What does it mean?" I ask, all sense of relief now gone, replaced by fear and trepidation.

"It means a different person signed each of these documents."

TWENTY-ONE
WINTER

I take a deep breath and examine the documents again. Giving them both a close look might change things. Maybe if I squint hard enough, I can make the signatures match.

"I don't mean to intrude," Janet says softly, "but how important is this?"

I draw a second breath, trying to work out the implications. Maybe Laura had been drunk, or high? Or incapacitated in some way so she couldn't sign properly? Maybe she'd just been nervous? I mean, how many times have I tried to sign the stupid little pad at the grocery store only for it to come out an unintelligible mess?

I lay the documents on the desk and rub my hands down my face. Am I making too big a deal out of this?

"I... don't know," I finally reply.

"Listen," Janet says, still whispering. "I have a friend who used to work for the FBI doing handwriting analysis. I could get him to take a look for you. This might not be anything."

"And it might be something." I scan the rest of the divorce signature page. There's only one lawyer listed, the Byrnes family counsel himself, Jackson Willoughby. Wasn't it customary to have two lawyers present in these types of proceedings? There had definitely been two lawyers when Thomas and I went through our divorce. Had Fenton forced Laura into something she hadn't wanted to do?

FBI agent. Janet said FBI agent. One who could decipher handwriting styles. That sparks an idea in my brain. "Do you think he could look at something else for me?" I ask.

"I don't see why not."

"Does he live here in town? Is he close?"

Janet nods. "He's retired. Doesn't live too far from us, actually. Jack's got himself a small farm out there, keeps a few chickens. I think he's got a goat now."

I'm out of my chair and hugging Janet, almost knocking the older woman off-balance. "Thank you. You have no idea how much this helps."

"I don't want to see you hurt," Janet replies. "I know we haven't known each other long. But every time I see you, I feel like you're carrying this… weight. Like you've been through more than your fair share."

The sudden empathy makes my eyes prickle. "You can tell that?"

Janet pats my hand, not unlike my mother used to do. "We'll get you straightened out. I'll make some more copies of these and drop them by Jack's on the way home. What else do you want him to look at?"

No one else knows about the book, but this is a safe bet, right? I am *sure* Janet didn't deliver it and this guy is FBI. "I received an anonymous package in the mail, but it was hand-addressed. I wonder if he can compare it to these two signatures."

"He's thorough. I had a landlord once who'd forged my signature on a rental agreement. He'd written up something that said he was no longer required to pay for the water utilities and signed my name to it. So when they shut off my water due to lack of payment, I took it over to Jack—he was still working back then, field office— and he ended up writing me a four-page report on why my signature didn't match the one on the landlord's document. One look from the judge and the jerk had to not only pay three months of utilities, but a reconnection fee, and punitive damages to me for putting me through it. All to save twenty bucks a month." She grins, her straight teeth a brilliant white. "He'll do a good job for you."

"Will he..." I begin, not quite sure how to phrase the question.

"He doesn't have to know it's you if you don't want him to," she replies, reading my mind. "Nobody else has to know. As far as I'm concerned, it's your business and no one else's."

"Thank you," I say again. This woman is a lifesaver.

"Do you have the package with you? I can drop it off at the same time."

"I..." Damn. Brian took it. Which means there's no way I can get hold of it. Odds are he's stashed it away or given it to one of his father's cronies by now. Why didn't I just take a picture of it when it was still at the house?

"No, and I'm not sure I can get it back."

Janet gives me a look that's full of sympathy. "Well, if you happen to find it, let me know. I'm sure Jack will be happy to take a look."

"Thanks," I say, though I can't help but feel defeated and out of options.

We leave the Clerk's Office together, Janet locking everything up. Mary must have slipped out unannounced sometime while Janet was pulling the files, for which I'm grateful. I don't need anyone else sticking their nose into my business. After agreeing to get back in touch as soon as I get the package, we say our brief goodbyes and head off in opposite directions. Presumably, Janet is off to drop the documents with Jack while I'm left to wait for... what? Someone to tell me the signatures are or are not from the same person?

Wait a minute. I can find out myself. I don't have to wait on Jack. Without the package I can't even prove someone sent the book to our house anymore. But I do have access to a resource who can tell me what happened when the divorce was finalized: Laura.

Since I already know who she is and that she was married to Fenton, there's no reason I can't ask her about the divorce records. The only problem is I have very little reason to trust her. But maybe I can catch her off guard. I could tell her I'm worried about what Fenton might do, and that I've been looking into his past to try and find out. That's what we have in common, and it might make her more amenable to answering questions about the divorce. I fumble for my phone and dial Laura's number. The other end rings longer than I expect and I'm about to hang up when she answers.

"Winter?"

"Hi, good afternoon." I glance at the clock on the dash. "Or I guess it's evening. I can't wait for daylight savings time to end; I hate these long nights." God, I'm rambling because I'm nervous.

"What can I do for you?" she asks, her voice guarded.

"I was hoping we could meet again. I have some more questions. About Fenton."

There's silence on the other end. "What else can I tell you that you don't already know?"

She seems... off. The friendliness of the past few days no longer there. Maybe she had a tough day at work? And maybe we're more alike than I realize. I'd be upset too if someone just called me up out of the blue asking to go to dinner. But if I'm not going to be able to ply her, I might as well get it out in the open. "I found your divorce records in the courthouse. I wanted to ask you about them."

"You did?" She sounds surprised.

"I have a friend who works over there. She pulled them all for me." There's a long pause on the other end.

"Oh," she says. "Let me look at my schedule and call you back." She ends the call without another word and I'm left there holding my phone, surprised at her sudden abruptness.

I sigh. I've upset her... somehow. Though I don't really know why. But I can't dwell on it. I grab my copies of the marriage and divorce records and stuff them into my purse. That way, I'll have them when we meet and she can tell me immediately if that's her signature or not. With any luck she'll be able to tell me what happened at that last meeting that had her so distraught that the County Clerk thinks they aren't the same signature.

I start up my engine, the car rumbling against the cold and try not to make any assumptions about what any of this means. But I can't help my mind from drifting. From building worst-case scenarios. I haven't done that in a long time, but like an old friend that just won't leave you alone, the thoughts come roaring back. First my mind goes to my bank accounts. If things don't work out with Fenton, I'll be back on my own, which means renting again for a while until I can find a place. I've saved some money not needing to pay rent or a mortgage, but it might be difficult finding my own place for cheap. When we'd first moved in together, I was more than happy to pay half the mortgage, until I learned Lazarus had already bought the house outright. Apparently, it had been a gift of some kind to his son. But Fenton told me that his name was on the property, not his father's. I hadn't been able to relax until Fenton had shown me the title which confirmed it. Just the possibility of Lazarus owning the house we live in is enough to put my nerves on end. There is just something wrong about that man.

But if we do split up, it means I'll never have to deal with them again. *If* they let me go. The Byrnes family had been reluctant to let me in when Fenton and I first started dating. But over time, I'd been begrudgingly accepted, if not outright welcomed. But I recall Brian saying that once you're in with the Byrneses, you never really leave. I couldn't tell whether he was being serious or not, but I recall him looking me dead in the eyes as he said it.

I just hope I don't have to test that theory.

TWENTY-TWO
WINTER

As I pull up to the driveway, Fenton's car is already there. But instead of being parked in the garage like usual, he's left it out.

Why is he home already? I almost always beat him home on a weekday, especially on Fridays. I'd hoped to have some time to decompress and figure out how to handle him for the weekend before he got home. Do I confront him? Or do I keep silent and until I find the truth behind it all? Maybe some people wouldn't think that's a big deal, but it's often the little details which reveal the most about the secrets we keep. It means something, and I'm not letting go until I know what that something is.

When I get inside, Fenton is in the office, working at his drafting table. That explains why he's here; of all days, he's decided to work from home today.

"Hey," he says. "How was work?" Like everything is normal.

"What?" I ask, having forgotten all about the proposals to the city until he said something. "Oh... fine. We got everything submitted on time." He's awfully calm for all that's happened the past few days. I head into the kitchen. I need something to take the edge off.

I don't like this. Why is he acting so confident? Does he really think this might all blow over and we'll go back to normal? But then again, how do I expect him to act? I don't want him on eggshells around me all weekend. We both still have to live in this house together and I'd rather not be miserable.

I pull a bottle of wine down from on top of the fridge. It's a white, but I don't feel like waiting for it to chill. I grab a tumbler and fill it with ice, then pop the cork and pour it over the ice.

The ice sours the taste, and I pour the glass in the sink and shove the bottle in the freezer. Fifteen minutes ought to do it.

He appears in the large opening to the kitchen, leaning against the frame. "How are you?"

"I'm a little frustrated, to be honest." I busy myself with putting away the dishes that are still in the dishwasher.

He's silent for a moment. "I'm frustrated too."

I stifle a laugh. I bet he is. "What do you have to be frustrated about?"

"I just feel like you're pushing me away. Like you don't want to talk about any of this."

I can't help it; the words come fast and hard. "You *lied*, Fenton. All because you didn't want to face the consequences. We're supposed to be partners. To share everything. And yet you kept it from me." I throw a pan into the sink, which makes an awful, harsh clang. "How would you like it if you found out I'd been lying to you for three years? For our entire relationship? How do you think you'd cope with that?"

"I don't—" He pauses.

"Don't what?"

"Nothing. Never mind."

"No. Please," I offer. "Let's hear the excuses."

He shakes his head.

"Okay, you don't want to talk? Then I will. You knew I was married once before. You knew I found out Thomas was cheating on me and was keeping his relationship with that woman secret for *years*. You knew the day I found out was the day I called a divorce lawyer. And yet instead of being honest and open about it, you kept this from me. And whether you meant to do it or not, it still hurts just as bad. And I can't keep from thinking, *What would have happened if that book had never shown up?* Would I have ever known about her? Or was that just a secret you were going to take to your grave?"

His eyes meet mine, but he doesn't respond.

"You never were going to tell me, were you?"

He finally breaks eye contact. "No." And there it is. The truth.

Despite being mad as hell, I need to know more. He's finally opening up and I'm not going to let this opportunity pass. "Why not?"

He furrows his brow and opens his mouth to say something before closing it again. "I just couldn't," he finally says.

"That's not a reason." Tears form in my eyes. I turn and finish putting away the dishes. "And it's not enough."

"I can't tell you how sorry I am."

I close my eyes and let out a long breath. Despite the rage of emotions flooding through me, he's given me a glimmer of the truth. Part of me wants to try and work this out with him, the other part just wants to leave and be done with him. "It's obvious you're not going to be honest with me about this. Which means I don't think we have anything else to discuss." My hands are trembling.

"Win... I *can't*."

I feel my world crumbling around me. Here is the person I'm supposed to trust with my everything, to build a partnership with, to build a life with. And he's hiding things from me. Even now. "Just... leave me alone."

"For how long?"

"Jesus, Fenton," I say, out of both frustration and anger. "The rest of the evening." I reach into the freezer and grab the wine again, even though I can feel it's still warm. "Just stay in the office, okay? I don't want to see you again tonight." I push past him and head down to the main bedroom.

"Fine," he says, hurt in his voice. He turns and disappears back into the office.

His absolute refusal to tell me his reason is not only infuriating, but incredibly hurtful. Does he just think I can't handle it? Does he really think that after what I've been through I'd just shut down? I hoped I've at least proved him wrong on that point. But I can't deny that part of the reason I'm still going strong is my own pride. I have to figure out what I've missed.

An hour later half the bottle is gone and I'm stuck playing a stupid game on my phone. I don't even perceive time anymore; the only reason I know the time is because it keeps staring back at me from the top of my phone. Maybe I should go stay at a hotel until I get some answers. I also realize that I might not be entirely lucid at this point. Between a harrowing day at work, everything at the courthouse and the fight we just had, I'm exhausted. But every time I try going to sleep I can't seem to get images of him with Laura out of my head. I grab the bottle and take another gulp, only to be met with air.

My phone rings at exactly the same time, and I notice on the caller ID it's Laura. I replace the bottle on my nightstand and tap my phone. "Hello?"

"Hi. Is this a bad time?"

"No," I reply, my heart rate picking up. "Did you look at your schedule?"

"Yes. Unfortunately, I'm booked through the weekend. I've got some family visiting and I don't think I can get away."

"Oh," I say, sitting back on the wet part of the bed. "I understand."

"But I have some free time now. What was it you wanted to ask me?" she says.

I really wanted to do this in person. To gauge her reactions. To see if I could tell if she was lying to me or not. But this will have to do. "You're going to think I'm crazy," I say, laying back on the bed.

"Try me."

I take a deep breath, feeling the fuzziness from the wine. "Okay. I told you I went to the county courthouse today and pulled the records for your marriage to Fenton. But your signatures on the marriage certificate and the divorce agreement don't match."

Silence on the other end. Shit. I've gone too far. She must think I'm a full-on psycho.

"Huh," she finally says. Not anger. Not accusation. More like... curiosity.

"Laura, I'm sorry. I shouldn't have been so nosy. It's just, I can't get Fenton to tell me anything and I don't have any idea what's going on. I kind of feel like I'm going a little crazy."

"What do you mean?" she asks.

"I can't find anything about you," I say. "There's nothing. No pictures, no documents, records, bills, mementos, nothing. It's like he's wiped you from his life."

"You think I'm lying," she says.

I sit up, alarmed. "No, no. Not at all. I saw the papers; I know it was official. It's just... weird. There's nothing of you here. It's like you never existed."

"I see," she says, and I'm sure she's about to hang up on me and never talk to me again. "Have you looked in the crawlspace?"

"The what?" I ask.

"The crawlspace. There's a trap door in what used to be the house's kitchen, back when it was built. In the middle of the floor. If he's got something to hide, my bet is it's down there."

"I've never seen any trap door," I say, adrenaline clearing my head.

"Have you ever looked under the rug?" she says, and part of me wonders how she knows we have a rug.

"No..." I say.

"It's probably still there. At least it was the last time I saw that house, back before he began renovations. He used to keep stuff down there for storage, since the house doesn't have an attic."

"You... saw this house?" I ask.

"Like I said, it was before he finished all the renovations. Everything... kind of fell apart at the beginning. But it was a good place to store stuff. It was cool and dark down there."

I can't help but be curious now. Is she right? Now that I think about it, I don't believe I ever *have* seen under the rug in our living room. The house has always been furnished, ever since I moved in. "I'll take a look."

"Well," she says. "Good luck. I hope you find what you're looking for."

"Wait," I say before she can hang up. "What about the divorce? What happened? Why is your signature all messy?"

"Oh," she says. "I was probably a little tipsy. It was a difficult time for me. I just wanted out. After all, it's not every day you leave the man who assaulted you. I remember being nervous because I thought they might try to stop me from going through with it. You know how that family is. I was terrified Lazarus would find a way to keep me in the marriage. So I might have had too much."

At least I know my fears are justified. It doesn't surprise me Lazarus pushed her to the edge just because she wanted to leave. I won't give them a chance to do that to me. "I'm so sorry," I say.

"Thank you. Good night, Winter."

"Night," I say, hanging up. I stand, the room rolling for a brief second as I steady myself against the door to the en suite. It takes me a second to stabilize myself before tiptoeing to the bedroom door and cracking it open. It doesn't sound like Fenton is still in the office. He must have gone to bed.

What if it's true? What if there's a hidden compartment under the floor? Do I dare look with him still in the house?

The more dominant part of me, probably propelled by slight inebriation, says yes. That no matter what I find, it's my right to search. This is my house too, after all. Another, smaller part of me, says this might not be the best idea.

I shut that part down and make my way down the hallway toward the living room.

TWENTY-THREE
WINTER

I creep through the house as quietly as I possibly can, though the room is tilting slightly and I have to catch myself a few times from toppling over. Had I known Laura was going to drop this bombshell on me maybe I wouldn't have downed half a bottle of warm pinot grigio.

Fenton is in the bedroom, a bit of light spilling out from under the doorframe. Good. I'd half expected to come out here to find him sprawled on the couch again. But I still need to be quiet; the last thing I want is for him to come out here and try to make up more excuses about what he can and can't tell me. I also really want to see if this so-called *hiding place* is actually there or Laura's just having fun at my expense. I really don't know if I can trust her or not.

But I want to. After all, we're very similar.

I stop at the couch, looking around the edge. Thankfully, it's not one of those monsters that takes an entire moving crew. It's much more understated and mid-century modern. Though now that I think about it, I'm not even sure who chose this couch. It was already here when I moved in. In fact, I never made any of the decisions about what goes into this house. It's supposed to be a merging of our lives, and yet all I see when I look around is Fenton.

My eyes land on the little vent under the window again, but I turn away quickly. I move over to the edge of the carpet, wondering what's the best way to do this. I have no idea where the door could be, so I'm not sure which side of the carpet I need to roll up. I lift up one edge, trying to peer along the floor into the darkness, but I can't see anything. I want to sigh in frustration, but I stop myself before I can make a sound.

Okay. So no matter what I do, I'm going to have to move the couch. There's really no way it can stay where it is. I get up under one side and walk it over until its legs are no longer on the carpet and set it down as carefully as I can. I wait a second to see if there's any movement from the other room. But no shadows pass the light spilling out, and so I creep over to the other side.

Once the couch is off the rug, I get in the middle and begin rolling, revealing the polished wood floor beneath me. I never really noticed before, but it looks like the floor has been refinished, like it could be original to the home, just with a new sand, stain and lacquer.

I only get the rug about halfway before it runs into one of the side chairs. What if she was just screwing with me? It isn't like she's seen this house since it was finished; he might have had the trap door removed from the revised plans. I mean, this place has had some major work on it. You can't even tell this room used to be the kitchen. The only reason I know is because it has the fireplace and Fenton once told me that was where they used to cook all the food back when the house was built.

Once the chair and a small side table are out of the way, I continue rolling, until I uncover a small metal hook embedded in the floor itself.

I stop rolling, my heart pounding as I look down at what could very well be a door. I look back over my shoulder, still no indication he's heard me. It only takes a few more rolls to completely uncover the door embedded in the floor, the antique hinges on the other side mark where the door ends.

"Son of a bitch," I whisper, then clasp my hand over my mouth.

Did he hear that? A long, slow breath escapes my lungs. I know I should wait until he's not here to open this door, but my curiosity gets the best of me. I've come this far; I'm almost there.

I hook my finger under the clasp nearest to me, giving it a slow pull. There's no catch, it's just held down by gravity and the door lifts open without resistance. The smell of dankness fills my nose as I open it all the way, peering into the pitch-black hole.

I can't believe this has been here the entire time and I've never known about it.

Pulling out my phone, I turn on the flashlight and shine it down into the hole, anticipating finding a treasure trove of hidden memories. But instead I'm greeted by only a single white banker's box. I reach in and pull the box out, setting it on the floor in front of me. Screwing up my face, I lean back into the hole, shining the light all around the crawlspace, but I don't see anything else. Just the one box? What the hell?

Still, my heart threatens to break through my rib cage. This is it. This is exactly what I've been looking for. He wouldn't keep any of his sensitive documents at his office, where he couldn't get to them at a moment's notice. He'd keep them here, right under his feet. Where they're safe. Whatever is in here, he never wanted anyone to find. Probably most of all not me.

I glance back toward the bedroom again. Does he know? Does some part of him sense that I've found his secret hiding spot, that I'm about to uncover all of his secrets?

Steeling myself, I remove the lid and almost cry out.

At the very top, bound together by a piece of metal spiral, is a stack of papers with a neatly typed title, *The Last Man I'd Marry* by Miranda Meriwether.

It's her book. But this is a much earlier, less refined copy. It isn't double-printed, or professionally bound, and doesn't even have a cover. This looks like what someone would have printed out from their home computer and bound themselves.

I'm not sure what to do. I just sit there, holding the manuscript in my hand, reading and rereading the title over again.

He has her manuscripts. This entire time he's had them. Underneath the top one sits another one, and another under that one. Had he made copies? And why keep them, of all things? Could he have taken this and made it look as if it were the kind of book you'd find in a bookstore? He would have needed special software, which wouldn't have been hard for him. But he would have also had to create the cover, set up the binding...all of it. That's a lot of work for one book. But, I suppose there are places out there that do that kind of thing.

But why go to the trouble? Maybe as a test? To see if I would open it? Is this all some kind of sick game to him?

The very fact he keeps them buried beneath the home we share unnerves me. Why keep your ex-wife's unpublished works? Unless there's some deeper meaning to them, something I could only learn by reading them. Could it be the text itself?

I set *The Last Man I'd Marry* down and pick up the one under it. *Undesirable*. My heart pangs. If Laura's first book was a warning, this one is a cry for help. Assuming, that is, she was still writing about her relationship with Fenton. I turn to the dedication page.

Remember what you did. What happens is your fault.

I shiver.

What could she mean by this? Did it refer to how he'd hurt her? And if so, why would he keep them? A traumatic reminder of his actions? She said he'd seen a therapist, maybe it was their idea. Though I can't imagine Dr. Hobart ever suggesting I keep my ex's manuscripts if I was written to be the bad guy in them.

But, to be fair, I haven't read them all the way through. Maybe that's not the case here.

I peer down into the opening again, shining my flashlight around, despite my shaking hand and find nothing but the blackness of the crawlspace staring back. This box is the only thing he's hidden. I thought there would be more, pictures of their life together, mementos, anything that might remind him of her. But all he'd kept was her box of "books." I check the stack, and five different manuscripts are present. In a way they almost remind me of movie scripts in the haphazard way they're presented here. They almost reek of desperation.

Some dust from the crawlspace finds its way to my nose, and even though I try to hold it in, I can't help myself and sneeze into my sleeve. It makes an echoing sound through the room and down into the crawlspace.

Footsteps approach from the other side of the door. "Win? Are you out there?" He opens the door, and as soon as he sees me, he stops cold.

It takes him a moment to register the scene. But as he does, I see something I've never seen in Fenton before. Not like this.

It's anger. Pure, and white-hot.

And for the first time since I've known him, I'm afraid.

TWENTY-FOUR

WINTER

I have the brief sensation of floating, as if gravity has turned off somehow. My whole body has gone numb and I have to look down at my hand to make sure I'm still holding the manuscript. My eyes travel slowly across everything. The couch pulled out of the way, the rug rolled up haphazardly, the trap door open to the darkness beyond, and the white box full of manuscripts from my fiancé's ex-wife.

His hoard of secrets, exposed and out in the open. The one person he's tried to keep everything from finally learning the truth. He doesn't move, but his glare could cut through glass. Then, as if someone has turned a switch, he softens, and the man I know is back, though there is still a look of consternation on his face.

I slam back into my body, my own fury bubbling up. It isn't enough that he never told me about his previous marriage, something that I would have forgiven. But to discover he's hidden her writings right under our feet this entire time? Those times when we'd made love on the couch, had he been thinking about these *things* only a few feet away? I drop the manuscript in disgust. He winces slightly as it hits the floor. Something about the movement incenses me. I bend down, grab it, and slam it down again. He doesn't jump a second time, only stands, as if in disbelief.

All I have to do is get him to admit he sent the book to torture me and this will all be over. I can leave and move on, just like before.

"What... are those?" he finally asks.

My eyes widen at his brazenness. "You know exactly what they are." I consider picking it up again and throwing it at him.

"Winter, I don't. Was... was that in the *floor?*" He takes a cautious step forward.

"No, sir. You're not going to play dumb with me." I say it with such conviction; I have found all the evidence I need. He's not going to weasel out of this.

"Those aren't..." He steps closer. "Oh my God. Her books?" His breath hitches. "Were they in the *crawlspace?*" He's almost yelling, as if *he* can't believe they're real.

"Right where you hid them," I say triumphantly.

"Shit. *Shit!*" Fenton's hand goes to his pocket and he withdraws his phone. "You didn't touch any of—dammit, how many did you touch? Don't move!" he yells, frantically dialing.

"Of course I touched them. I wanted to read—"

He holds up a hand to cut me off while he speaks into the phone, which only infuriates me further. What is he playing at? "Hey. It's me. Get over here now. Winter found something. Yeah. I think it's all her books." He pauses. "Under the house! What? I don't know, just do it. Yeah... yeah, I know. Okay." Fenton hangs up and turns back to me. "Don't touch anything else."

He *has* to be joking. "What are—"

"Winter, I didn't put those there," he says, staring directly into my eyes. "I don't know who did, but whoever did has access to this house." He pauses. "How did you find them? How did you even know about—"

"About your secret passage?" I ask. "I already told you—I was looking for evidence..." I trail off, some of my anger flowing out of me.

"Evidence of what?"

"That you were still seeing her," I finally admit. "That you never stopped seeing her."

"Winter, honey," he says, approaching me, but I take a few careful steps back. I don't want to fall into the hole.

"No, stay back," I say. Laura's words about him bruising her come rushing back to me. It's not safe to be around him.

"Winter. I'm not seeing Laura anymore, okay? I can't. She's— she moved far away."

He doesn't know. Or he's pretending not to. I don't know what to do anymore. "Who was that on the phone?"

"Brian. He's coming over here to bag all this stuff up."

Bag it up? Just like the first book? I grab the first manuscript, holding it close to my chest. He's already made the book disappear. I can't let him take these too. They're all I have. They're all *she* has. Laura will want these back.

"Sweetie, please. It might have fingerprints, you're contaminating—"

"Don't 'sweetie' me," I growl. "You've been hiding this behind my back the entire time, don't you dare deny it."

"Winter, I swear to you—to everything I have—I did not put that there. I haven't seen that box in eight years. I destroyed it. Along with everything else that belonged to her."

Why does he have to do this? Why make this so difficult? I've caught him red-handed. Why can't he just admit it and move on? Wouldn't it be easier for everyone, instead of going through this entire charade? "Stop. Lying. To. Me."

"What do you want me to say? It's the truth." He turns away for a moment, then faces me again. "I made a mistake, okay? I should have told you about Laura from the beginning. But I couldn't. She's gone, out of my life now. I want nothing else to do with her. If a machine existed that could erase memories, I would wipe her in a millisecond. I *don't want* to remember her. Do you understand? I don't want anything to do with her, so why would I keep something like this? Do you think I'm so shallow I can't let go of some stupid books from ten years ago just because she wrote them about me? That wasn't a great time in my life. Why would I want that reminder around all the time?"

"Then you knew they were about you," I say. "About how you hurt her."

His chest rises and falls with each tortured breath. I've never heard him so intense before; something about all this has struck a nerve, but not necessarily the one I thought.

He nods. "I know. I broke her heart."

"And the bruises?"

He furrows his brow. "Is that what she wrote?"

He doesn't know I didn't read the whole book. Right now I'm going off Laura's word. But honestly, that's good enough for me. "Yes."

He sighs. "It was an accident. I didn't mean to hurt her."

"That's no excuse," I snap.

"You're right, it's not. And I spent a lot of time working through those issues in therapy. I... I didn't want you to know about that side of me. It's a side I've tried very hard to forget."

I relax my grip on the manuscript slightly. I can understand Fenton wanting to put his past behind him. Didn't I do the same thing? When was the last time I reached out to Daisy, or Mom? The truth is I don't, because I don't want to open those wounds again.

Maybe Fenton is doing the same thing.

"If you didn't put these down there, who did?"

"That's what we need to find out," he replies. "Someone else must have a key. I'll need to get the locks changed, immediately. And... I'm not so sure we should stay here."

My mind goes back to my ghost at the end of the driveway and goose pimples appear on my arms. If he's telling the truth... if he really didn't put these here, then someone else has gotten in our home. Maybe even while we're in it.

But that doesn't make sense. People don't break into homes to *leave* things, they do it to take them. Unless they have an ulterior motive. And right now, there are only two people who I can think of who might want to disrupt things. Laura... for obvious reasons. But also Fenton's father, Lazarus. Maybe I thought I had been accepted too soon.

He was never very happy about Fenton going off on his own, leaving the family... according to Fenton anyway. Is this some kind of sick punishment for *him*? A reminder that he already had one failed marriage? Maybe Lazarus sent the book to torture his own son. I don't know for sure.

"You can't let Brian come over here," I say, resetting my gaze.

"Why?" Fenton asks, still intense.

"Because if your father planted this to frame you, Brian will destroy any evidence."

"My father?"

"If what you say is true and you didn't put that down there, which I'm not saying I believe, then someone is framing you. Can you think of anyone better than your dad?" I'm still not ready to tell him about Laura. If it *was* her, I'll handle it on my own. But Lazarus is the big boss. I'll need Fenton's help to figure out if it was him.

"He wouldn't do that to me. He wouldn't go that far."

"Then who would? Who else wants to see you suffer? And like you said, who else even knows they exist?"

Just say her name, just do it and admit to it.

Fenton shakes his head. "I don't know."

This is how I know he's lying about some part of this. Any reasonable person would suspect their ex first. But Fenton seems incapable of the idea. But it still doesn't make sense. I need to keep the evidence. If Brian decides to take everything, I'll be right back to square one.

"If I'm right, and your father is behind this, what are the odds Brian knows about it?" I ask, rethinking my options.

"High." He turns away from me and curses. "And he would have known the first thing I would do is call Brian. That man and his *fucking* games." There's that anger again, but it isn't directed at me this time. Instead, it's reserved for his father. He shakes his head in disbelief, then turns back to the hole in the floor. "I'd almost forgotten about this. When I bought the house, it had been used as a storage unit for canned goods. It's a lot cooler closer to the earth and the dirt acted as..." he trails off.

"Acted as what?" I ask.

Fenton bends down, staring at the side of the box. "Look at this." I lean over; his hand points along the bottom of the box. "Little to no dirt. If it had been in that hole any amount of time, it would have gathered dust and the bottom would be filthy. Plus, you remember when we had that storm a few months ago and it was raining like crazy?"

I nod.

"That rain seeped up under the house. This is close enough to the outer wall that it should have soaked through at least a little. The bottom of the box should have some water damage, but I don't see anything. Which means it hasn't been in that hole long."

He's right. There are no telltale signs of the water damage normally found on cardboard after it gets wet, and the box is relatively clean. Had he kept it under the house for years, it should be a lot dirtier. Which means it was placed here recently. Probably within weeks. Maybe even days.

"What do we do about Brian?" I ask, now very unsure of the facts. "He's coming."

"If this was Dad, he'll cover all this up. Hang on." Fenton runs into the kitchen and returns with a box of gallon-sized ziplocks.

"Here, put the one you've got on the floor, and grab one of the ones you haven't touched yet, but grab it by the edge if you can. We'll put it in here."

"You think you can pull fingerprints off it?"

"Maybe. Right now we just need to preserve it and keep it out of Brian's hands. At least until we know his agenda."

I can't argue with the plan. I just have to make sure to keep those manuscripts in my sight and not let Fenton take them. I shouldn't have touched any of them, but I'd been so shocked I couldn't help it. I lay down the already-crumpled manuscript and reach into the box with both hands, removing two more manuscripts at once by their edges. "I want them both. Just in case."

Fenton nods and holds out a gallon bag. The first one doesn't quite fit all the way, but it is in enough that we can handle it without risking contamination. He holds out a second bag and I deposit the second manuscript into it.

"Okay, leave the rest. We'll tell him this is all you found," Fenton says, gathering the two together and wrapping them in a plastic grocery bag.

"Wait, what are you doing with those?" I ask.

"Hiding them. Just until he leaves."

I hold out my hand. "Give them to me, I'll hide them."

Fenton stops. The tension is palpable. What is he really going to do with them? Get rid of them? Destroy them like everything else?

"Fenton," I repeat. "Give them to me." I urge my hand forward.

"I was just going to hide them in the kitchen," he says.

"Now." My outstretched arm trembles.

He hands the bag over, staring at me. "Just hurry up. He'll be here any minute."

I retreat to the bedroom and slip the bag in the back of my closet, behind a large pile of clothes I never bothered to pick up off the floor.

When I look up, shadows move across the back wall, announcing the arrival of a car in our driveway.

TWENTY-FIVE
WINTER

"Well, well, you found the jackpot," Brian announces, entering the house.

I barely have just enough time to get back in the living room before the door bursts open. He didn't even knock. Fenton barely looks at his brother. His gaze is still stuck on the box. Brian glances at me, a smile on his face.

"If you want to call it that," I reply, trying to keep the conversation light.

"How in the ever-loving hell did you uncover this?" Brian asks, approaching the disheveled room and hole in the floor. "I didn't even know this was here."

"Accident," I stammer. "The vacuum always catches on this one part of the carpet and I guess I just finally got fed up with it." I point to the top of the trap door. "Turns out it was that little ring." While it was obvious the ring sat flush in the wood, it was plausible the vacuum could have caught it.

Brian eyes me for a minute, and I can feel the scrutiny of his gaze. I remain steadfast until he turns his attention back to the box. "Did you know about it?" he asks his brother, his attention finally off me.

"I honestly forgot about it was there," he replies. "After the renovation..."

"Right." Brian turns to me again. "What did you touch?"

"I pulled the box out, so the outside of it, and the lid. And the top manuscript. That's it."

"Okay," Brian replies, pulling out a pair of blue latex gloves from his back pocket.

"It hasn't been here long," Fenton says.

"I see that. I'm going to ask this because I need to. Did either of you put it there?"

"Of course not," Fenton replies, anger in his voice. If he's not genuine, it's a good act.

"And have either of you let anyone in this house recently? Anyone you might have taken your eyes off for a minute?"

"I think we would have seen someone hauling a big box into our house," Fenton shoots back.

"That's not what he means," I say. "He thinks someone might have copied our house key."

"You are too sharp, sis. Have I ever told you that?" Brian winks at me, then bends over to inspect the box.

I don't feel like being winked at. I feel like someone who is unfamiliar with her own home. A stranger in the place where I'm supposed to feel the safest. I run through the list of people who have a key in my head. Me, Fenton, Brian... that's it. As far as I know. And Brian is only to use it in an emergency. No one else should have access to this house.

"What about the security system?" Fenton asks.

"Whoever has your key also has the code," Brian says. "I suggest you change it immediately."

Fenton nods. "Right."

"You haven't given anyone access to the house that you know about?" Brian repeats.

"I haven't," Fenton says, turning to me. "Have you?"

I shake my head. I can't even meet the neighbors properly. How am I supposed to invite someone over to my home?

"And there's no other maintenance access under the house? No outside door or anything for the crawlspace?"

"Not unless someone made their own door," Fenton says. "I specifically didn't install an outside door because of security reasons. Access can be from inside the home if necessary. I don't like the idea of someone crawling around under my house."

Brian nods. "Then we need to inspect your locks and windows. Someone got in here recently to do this. We need to determine the point of entry."

Not if it was you, I think. "Should we call the cops, then? If we're dealing with a breaking and entering?" Not that I necessarily want to involve the police, but this has grown beyond the scope of just family matters. The police wouldn't know what to do with an errant book delivered to their house, but a burglar was another matter. But again, who ever heard of a burglar bringing something *into* the house?

"Don't worry," Brian says. "I can handle it. I'll let a few of my friends down at the station know and they can help me do a full inspection tomorrow. For tonight I can at least check your locks."

Fenton and I exchange a quick glance. He looks worried. Neither of us likes it when Brian circumvents the police. It doesn't help that Lazarus has so much influence with the local boys in blue, but Fenton used to tell me about how Brian could sometimes get problems to go away with the family connections down at the station. It's one of the reasons he never wanted to work for his father. I can't help but wonder just how deep Lazarus's power goes.

"Trust me," Brian says. "It will save you guys a lot of headaches." He pulls out some large black bags from his coat pocket and begins the process of placing the manuscripts inside them. I find it odd he just happens to carry gloves and black bags with him wherever he goes.

"What are you going to do with those?" I ask.

"Find what I can. Maybe I can grab a match on one of these."

My heart jumps. "A match? Do you mean you found something on the book? Do you still have it?" Of course Brian has it. Why would Fenton do anything else with it? And if Brian has it, maybe I can still snap a picture of that cover for Janet.

Brian smiles that stupid placating smile. "Don't worry. When I have something substantive, I'll let you know. You just take care of each other."

I can never tell if Brian is genuinely concerned for us or if is all some elaborate ruse to cover up his true purposes. The other night he seemed different. It's almost like whenever there's a crisis, a different Brian emerges. One who answers to one person only.

"Are you both planning on staying here tonight?" Brian asks.

"We're not sure yet," Fenton says. "Even if we do, I'm not sure I can sleep knowing someone has access to the house."

"For your own safety, I'd suggest you move somewhere secure."

Fenton gives him a hollow laugh. "Dad's house, I suppose?"

Brian shrugs. "Or a hotel."

"I may have something that could help." If someone got in this house and planted that box, it means they've been watching us for a while. Maybe a long while.

"What?" Fenton asks. He's grown indignant and grumpy. The mere mention of his father's house has put him in a sour mood.

"I saw someone. The day we got the book. They were standing at the end of the driveway. At first I thought they might just be looking at the house. But now I'm not so sure."

"What did the person look like?" Brian asks. "Man or woman?"

"I couldn't tell. Too far away. Maybe a man. I called Janet, but she didn't see anything. I'd completely forgotten about them until now." A white lie, but a lie nonetheless. Now Fenton has me doing it. But I don't feel like explaining I could have imagined them. I don't owe anyone an explanation.

Fenton shakes his head and turns away from me. "That does it," he says after a pause. "We're not staying here. Something is going on, and I'm not about to be one of those people who gets killed in their sleep because they didn't pay attention to the signs."

"Normally, I'd say you're overreacting, but I think you're right on this one," Brian says, bagging up the box. "Sounds like someone is deliberately stalking you. They're obviously looking to mess with you, if this box is any indication. The sooner we find out who it is, the better."

His familiarity with the box reminds me he knows all about Laura. And yet he hasn't questioned a bit of this. Is that because he really knows what Laura is like? Maybe Brian knows she's back in town. Given his resources, I wouldn't put it past him. Fenton may not suspect his ex, but Brian isn't as emotional.

"How long... I mean, when can we come back?" I ask.

"I'll check the home tonight and you should change your locks. I also suggest you get some security cameras. We can never be too careful."

"But they'll—" Fenton begins.

"Do you want to know if someone is coming into your house or not?" he asks. "Get those cameras that connect to your phones. You'll be notified immediately."

I can see the consternation on my fiancé's face, but he doesn't argue. Though part of me agrees with him. I don't want to be under constant surveillance either.

I exchange glances with Fenton again. It feels less like we're on opposite sides now. With the possibility that Lazarus could be behind this out in the open, it's like we have a common enemy. I still don't know what to think about all this—about his relationship with Laura, the manuscripts, all of it. But one thing is for sure, Laura was telling the truth about him. He *had* hurt her. Intentional or not, I'm not sure it's something I can forgive. Will that happen to me one day too?

"I'm going to get a hotel," he says, sneaking glances at me. "Do you..."

"Yeah," I say. "Until we can be sure." At least I won't have to worry about someone breaking into a hotel room. And it will give us a break from each other. We can stay in the same building, but I think separate rooms for now, just like here. Until we can figure out where all this is going.

Ten minutes later I've packed an overnight bag. We meet back in the living room where Brian has already removed the box and the bags, presumably storing them in the back of his car.

"I'll stick around and do a quick check, then come back in the morning with a few off-duty uniforms. You know, get them to look around, make sure nothing looks out of place."

"Thanks, Brian," I say as I toss my bag in the back of my car.

"No problem," he says. "See you both tomorrow." He heads back into the house, presumably to begin his sweep.

"Hey," Fenton says over the top of his Mercedes. "Do you want to take one car?"

Bruises.

"No, that's okay," I say. "Where should we meet?"

"There's that motor lodge a couple of miles away."

Ugh. The motor lodge. I guess it will do, though it doesn't strike me as the safest place. I give him *the face.*

"Or there's a DoubleTree out past Bristol," Fenton adds, checking his phone.

"The whole idea is to go somewhere safer than here, right?" I ask. We stayed at the motor lodge once when the power went out after a particularly nasty storm. And personally, I'd never like to visit the *Connecticut Chainsaw Massacre Inn* again.

He nods.

"DoubleTree," we both say simultaneously. I have to suppress a grin. This is the old Fenton I know. The one I fell in love with.

"See you there."

"Yeah," I say. "See you there."

TWENTY-SIX
WINTER

We ended up in two adjoining rooms for the night. While I agreed to connecting rooms, the first thing I did once in mine was to make sure the door between us was locked on my side. I didn't feel like arguing about it in front of the front desk and it doesn't matter anyway—not for one night.

But at the same time, I can't help but lament what we've become. I can't believe it's come to this. Here we are, sleeping in two different rooms like strangers, when we're engaged to get married.

I toss and turn all night, a million different thoughts running through my head. Some of them even involving me opening that door and crawling into bed with him. I miss his arms around me. I miss the closeness. And I feel like we're on the verge of losing what we have. And all because of a stupid little book showing up out of the middle of nowhere.

There's an easy solution to this: which is, I let it go. I accept what happened has happened and I allow myself to trust him again. The appearance of that box—and the fact Laura was the one who led me to it makes me think she's toying with me... with us. I don't believe Fenton was responsible for sending the book. He's responsible for a number of other things, but not that.

Maybe... in time, I might be able to trust him again. But it's a big if. I need to speak with Dr. Hobart about everything that's happened over the past few days. And despite what Brian says, I think we need to get the police involved. Someone—and I think I know who—is stalking us.

As I turn over and watch the first rays of sun begin to break over the horizon, I consider telling Fenton about Laura. He deserves to know that *she's* the one out there, torturing us. That she was the one who told me about the box under the house.

But then again... she *had* been right about Fenton's temper. A temper that left her bruised and ended in their divorce. What if I tell him all this and he turns on me too? At the same time, what if I try to leave and that's what sets him off?

I think I need to confront Laura one more time before admitting anything else to Fenton. She says she didn't send the book, but how can I believe that? The fact that she knew about that cubby under the house *and* there was something down there for us to find has me on edge. What is her endgame?

"Heard anything from Brian?" I ask as Fenton and I sit across from each other in the hotel's small breakfast bar, each of us barely touching our overcooked eggs.

"He cleaned up last night, said he didn't find any points of entry," Fenton says, moving his eggs around on his plate. "Nowhere they could have gotten in without breaking something."

"Which means they had the key."

He nods.

"And the security code."

"Yeah."

And just like that my confidence in Laura being behind all this evaporates. How would she have access to our home? And why would she even want it? She said she's happily remarried. Why put us through this?

"When are you getting the locks changed?"

"Today," he replies. "I'll get new ones from the hardware store on the way back home." He's in a sour mood, but I guess I can't blame him. We've both been through the ringer.

"Do you trust Brian?"

He looks up. "What?"

"It's just... he has a key. And he can probably figure out how to disable the security code to the house. And he's the first person you always call when you get in trouble."

"So?" He's on the defensive. "He's my brother."

"Doing your father's bidding."

"Don't start that again." He pushes his plate away. "We should get back home."

"Are you serious right now? Fenton, someone has been in our *house*. And we just left the most likely culprit back there to get rid of any evidence."

"It's not Brian," he says without even missing a beat.

"Are you sure about that?"

He stares at me. "He doesn't have a motive."

"You were the one who told me your father wasn't the kind of man who let things go easily. What if he's... I dunno, trying to scare me off or something. We just made the announcement a few weeks ago. What if all this is nothing more than an elaborate ruse to get me to leave you?"

"Why would he do that?" Fenton asks.

"Because if I'm not around, maybe he can bring you back into the family business. He's a proud man. Maybe he doesn't like you going off and making it on your own."

He pauses for a moment before shaking his head. "No, he wouldn't do that. He likes you, you're my fiancée."

I shoot him another look.

"Listen, you have to understand... my father—"

"Is the kind of man who gets what he wants," I say. "If he wants me gone, he'll find a way."

"He *wouldn't* do that."

"Yeah? Is that what you told Laura too?"

Fenton glares at me before getting up and grabbing his

overnight bag. "I'll see you back at home. Or... whenever." He heads out to his car, leaving me alone.

I feel bad, but it was a fair question. Could Lazarus have been behind Laura's departure? She didn't give me many details on what happened with Fenton regarding the bruises. Maybe there's more to the story.

I pull out my phone and dial her number, but it goes straight to voicemail.

Shoot.

As I dump what remains on our plates into the nearby trashcan, I wonder if Janet's friend has made any progress on the signatures from those records. She said she'd call... but I should check in with her anyway. That, and I really don't want to go home right now.

I should check in with Cams too. I feel bad about the other night. She's always been there for me and what have I done? Only called when I needed something. Maybe I should go over and surprise her with some coffee.

I nod to myself, my mind made up. I'm not sure if I should tell her about everything that's happened because I don't want it to feel like I'm dumping on her again. And some time away from all this nonsense will be good for me. I've been running at a hundred miles per hour for days now. I need to stop and take a few breaths. Figure out just where the hell I am.

As I get in the car, resolve blooms in my chest. I'm going to make this right.

TWENTY-SEVEN
FENTON

Fenton fumed as he pulled into the hardware parking lot. This was all spiraling out of control and he wasn't sure what to do about it. First the book and now an *entire box* of them? And buried underneath the house no less.

He hadn't gotten a wink of sleep. He'd hoped Winter might reconsider them staying together, but that had been nothing but a pipe dream. If she didn't want to sleep in the same room in their own house, why would she want to in a hotel? Not to mention he felt bad for shooing them to a hotel in the first place.

But someone had been in the house... *recently.*

And Winter thought it was his dad. *Or Brian.*

He leaned his head back against the headrest. Maybe he should just come out with it and tell her the truth. This was driving a wedge between them and it would destroy everything unless he was honest.

But then his father really would bring the hammer down. The police would get involved. There would be an investigation. Everything they had worked so hard and so carefully for would fall apart and Fenton would probably end up in jail.

Were those his only options? Come clean and go to prison or try to keep the secret and maybe lose her anyway?

He got out of the car, heading into the hardware store. His head hurt and he didn't want to think about this anymore. Five days ago everything had been *fine*. And now...now everything was a mess there was nothing he could do about it.

He had to stop and ask three different clerks before he found one who could tell him where the home locks were located. And by the time he found what he was looking for, Fenton realized he knew nothing about buying or installing locks on a house. Were they all the same size? Could they be swapped out for a different lock? What about the brand?

He had to laugh at himself. Here he was, an award-winning architect who could design the most impressive home Connecticut had ever seen, and yet he couldn't even figure out basic home maintenance.

Well, there was nothing like trial and error. He grabbed three of the same item off the shelf and headed to the self-checkout.

The more he thought about it, the more coming clean to Winter started to become appealing to him. When they'd first gotten together, he hadn't given Laura a second thought. He'd trained himself to never think of her again and only occasionally would thoughts of her invade his mind. But he was always quick to push them away. He thought this business with her was done and over with, that he'd closed that chapter of his life long ago.

But apparently some things just didn't stay buried, no matter how deep a hole you dug. It had taken Fenton a lot of time and work to get over losing her. A lot of self-reflection and hard work on himself. Hard work his father hadn't deemed necessary. He'd said Fenton was weak, that he needed to steel himself against these kinds of things because they would just keep coming. Life was a gauntlet, and if you didn't build your defenses, it would kick your ass every day until you died.

But Fenton didn't want to live that way. He wanted to thrive, not be afraid of the next thing around the corner. Which was why he had broken off from the family, gone off on his own, built something for himself. Though, he had to admit, the best parts of his life hadn't begun until Winter had shown up.

He'd been enamored the first moment he saw her at that gala in Boston for all the young professionals in the field. She'd been wearing that floor-length dark-maroon dress that had made everyone else in the room disappear. At first he didn't think he could work up the nerve to approach her, until he remembered that sometimes life was about taking chances. And he knew in that moment, if he didn't say something, he would regret it for the rest of his life.

She had been charming and funny, warm and compassionate, and—as it turned out—lived only about twenty miles from Brighton. They'd spent the entire night talking and laughing and Fenton had found himself falling in love for only the second time in his life. He knew that night, Winter Southerland would be the woman he'd marry.

Brian had been strangely happy for him, pouring on the congratulations when they made their relationship official and Fenton proposed.

His mother and father, however, had been more reserved. He sensed his father's quiet judgement at taking a second wife after what happened with Laura. But Fenton wasn't about to let that stop him. And he enthusiastically introduced her to the entire family.

Things had been good. The past had stayed there... buried, right where it should be.

Right up until that book showed up.

And now... it was all on the verge of falling apart. He needed to find out who was behind all this. Because right now, they threatened everything. His father had nearly torn him a new one the other night when he tried to explain. Lazarus knew better than anyone what was on the line here. Someone knew about Laura... but to what end? Extortion? Money? There hadn't been so much as a demand.

Just a cryptic book, and now a box of manuscripts. *That* was what really worried him. Fenton had burned all her old stuff himself. Tears had fallen down his eyes as he watched their life together turn into nothing but ash.

But someone else had copies. And they were *taunting* him.

As he pulled into the driveway, Fenton's heart dropped a little when he saw Winter's car wasn't there. He supposed he couldn't blame her. And yet, he'd hoped she'd start coming around soon. Surely she could see he wasn't the bad guy here? They needed to be a team about this. Because it affected them both.

He grabbed the bag of locks and stepped out of his car into the garage. He entered the house through the connecting door, paying close attention to the lock itself, trying to figure out how he would get the old bolt off and the new one on. He'd have to borrow some of Brian's tools; there weren't any in the house anywhere.

But as he stepped into the living room that had been put back in order, rug over the hole in the floor, couch over the rug, side seats and tables all back in place, Fenton stopped cold, dropping the bag of locks on the floor with a *thump*.

There, in the middle of the coffee table, was another brown paper package with his name carefully written across the front.

Winter

I sigh as I pull up to the house. Two coffees that have probably gone cold by now sit in the cupholders of my car. Cammie hadn't been home when I dropped by; the new mobile grooming van missing from their driveway. They probably took it out on a test drive. I called, but it went straight to voicemail.

I can't blame her. After how I blew her off the other night, I'm probably not the first on Cammie's list of people to talk to. I'll try again later, maybe this afternoon if I get the chance.

But what really gets me is the fact that Fenton's car is already in the garage, though the door remains open. Then again, where else would he be on a Saturday morning? Still, I just wish I could go in, take a nice, long, hot shower and let all this melt away for a hot minute. I didn't see any reason to take a shower at the hotel knowing we'd be coming right back home.

As I get out of the car, leaving last night now seems silly. It's hard to believe, in the cool morning light, that someone could have been lurking about out here, waiting for us like some kind of serial killer. Did we overreact? Or did we just let Brian push us out, so he could conveniently clean up any evidence he left behind?

I'll never know for sure. But one thing I *do* know is I need to get that book from him. That way I can get it to Janet who can get it to her FBI friend. And it's the only way I'll know that Laura was telling the truth about the divorce records. Which will go a long way to me trusting her on everything else.

The door chimes the familiar song as I open it, finding Fenton in the living room, staring at the table. Everything is back as it was. Either he or Brian must have rearranged the room.

"Hey," I say, pushing down what I *really* want to say. "When did you get back?"

"Win..." Something in the tone of his voice makes me stop cold. "Don't freak out."

My eyes travel to the table and that's when I see it. Another brown-wrapped package, identical to the first one that showed up a few days ago. And on the cover, Fenton's name written across in a scripty font.

"No." My heart is about to burst out of my chest. "...Where? How?"

He shakes his head. "I don't know. I just got home. It was here—"

"It was Brian," I say. "He must have left it."

Fenton turns to me. "Win, seriously?"

I stare at him like he's crazy. "*Yeah*. Seriously. He was here last night, Fen. He had the chance when he was 'cleaning up.' Why can't you see that?"

"Because it isn't possible," he yells back.

"Why not?" He looks like he's about to say something, then clams up again. "Why can't you just be honest with me?"

He just shakes his head and pulls out his phone.

"What are you doing?"

"Calling Brian," he replies, his voice devoid of any emotion.

I step forward and snatch the package off the table. It feels just like the last one. I have no doubt another one of Miranda Meriwether's books is inside.

"What are you doing?" he says mid-dial.

While I'm not happy about the appearance of another book, especially one *inside* our home, at least I no longer need to track down the first one. I can give this book to Janet for the handwriting analysis. "You're not getting rid of this one."

"Win," he says, "put it down."

"You can't just erase someone from your life!" I yell. "She exists. She's real, no matter how much you want to pretend she isn't." Everything that's been simmering under the surface comes to a boil. "How could you do that to her, Fen? To someone you claimed to love? Things between Thomas and me may not have been perfect, but I didn't start pretending like he stopped existing as soon as we got divorced. Is that what awaits me? You'll just conveniently forget about me one day and move on?"

"Win, you don't understand," he says.

"Then explain it to me."

A war of emotions erupts across his face, each battling for supremacy. He wants to tell me, I know he does. But something is keeping him silent.

"Is it Brian? Your dad? Why won't you talk about her?"

His breaths are rapid and short, and sweat has broken out across his brow. "Just... give me the book. I'll take care of everything."

I take a few steps back. "No. You'll give it back to Brian."

"Win, why would I want to give it to Brian if he was the one who put it here? Don't you see? It doesn't make sense."

He's right. But I still can't help but feel there is more going on here. And now that I have it in my hands, I'm not letting go of it again. Letting the first book out of my sight was a mistake, one I won't make again.

"I'm going to find out what's going on," I say, almost in a whisper. "Whether you want to tell me or not. I'm going to find out."

"Win, don't. *Please.*"

He approaches me slowly, like a predator preparing to pounce on his prey. Laura's description of the bruises comes back to my mind again. I need to get out of here... away from him. "You're never going to be honest with me. Which means I need to find out on my own."

"You don't know what you're saying."

Now he's trying to gaslight me? I feel myself growing closer to the door. Can I get out without him catching me? What will I do if he does? He's stronger than I am... He could easily hurt me.

My bag is still on the floor at my feet. Without thinking, I kick it as hard as I can and it hits his legs, tripping him up for half a second.

But that's all I need.

I'm out the door and dashing to the car as he calls after me. I can feel him right on my tail, but I manage to get in my car and lock the doors just as he comes up to the side, jerking on the handle.

"Win. Let me in."

I start the car. Thank *God* I never took my keys out of my pocket. I put it in reverse.

"Win, please, don't *do* this." As he yells "do" he slams his hand on my side window, producing a large spider crack through the glass. He steps back, almost surprised at the force of the hit.

But I'm not stupid. I know what he's capable of.

I hit the gas, and the tires spin in the gravel of the driveway and the car rumbles back until I hit the small cul-de-sac. Fenton remains standing in the driveway as I put the car in drive and peel away, my breathing ragged and my heart practically in my throat.

I can't afford to stop at Janet's now; he'd just catch me there. I need to meet her in a neutral place. Somewhere Fenton won't think to look.

I glance in the rearview, watching as he grows smaller in the mirror and I realize there's no going back.

There is only forward.

TWENTY-EIGHT
FENTON

Fenton slumped down on the living room couch. He couldn't believe this. She'd actually been *afraid* of him. He drew his hand through his hair. He tried calling her cell, but it went straight to voicemail. There was no point leaving a message. And for a second he'd considered going after her, but that would only put her in more danger. If she got in a wreck trying to get away from him...

What a mess. What a royal, fucking mess. And now there was another package to boot. Apparently, Brian's investigation wasn't going very well. How many more packages would show up at his doorstep? And what was the endgame?

He glanced at his cell. Twelve minutes since she left. He couldn't put it off any longer.

He dialed.

"Enjoy your night out?" Brian said on the other end. "Listen, I'm headed over in a few minutes with a couple of officers I rounded up. Are you decent?"

"I'm not in the mood," Fenton replied before explaining about the second package and what had just transpired with Winter.

"You *let* her take it?"

"I didn't *let* her do anything," he argued. "You should have seen her. She was *terrified* of me. She looked at me like I was going to kill her."

His brother was silent on the other end.

"It was on the living room table. Did you move anything back last night?"

"No. I wanted to leave everything as it was for when I came back with a few uniforms. When I left the house looked exactly as you left it. I even left the trap door open."

"Then whoever it was decided to clean up too. The living room is back in order again."

Again, his brother said nothing.

"Well?"

"Well, what?" he asked.

"You're the expert, what am I supposed to do here?"

"First, calm down," Brian said. "We're not going to get anywhere if you're hysterical."

Fenton wanted to tell him to fuck off, but that would only make things worse.

"Next, you need to find your fiancée."

"How am I supposed to do that?"

"Track her phone. Remember when I told you to install that tracking program on there?" Fenton didn't reply; he only shook his head. "You did install it, didn't you?"

"*No.* Because I don't believe in spying on my future wife," he replied.

"Then that's just great," Brian said. "Good job, Fen." He huffed. "She is going to get herself killed."

Fenton sat up straight. "Killed? What do you mean? Did you find something?"

"Everything I've found points to the person behind this as being unstable in some way."

"Winter thought it might be Dad."

Brian replied with a mirthless laugh. "If it were, I'd know it."

"Would you, though? You know how cagey he can be. How many secrets he keeps. He doesn't tell you everything. He doesn't tell anyone everything; that's the whole deal, remember? Compartmentalize so no one person can screw over everyone else."

"I remember those breakfast-table discussions just as well as you do. But I have access to most of his stuff. If something were going on, I'd know. I'd see changes in personnel. He'd never do it himself; he'd get someone else."

"Yeah, good point," Fenton said, sitting back. Their father never got his hands dirty. That was always work for someone else. "Do you really think Winter is in danger?"

"I think if she digs too deep, she will be. So far this person seems fixated on you, but she might accidentally make herself a target."

"Brian, I have to tell her. I can't keep lying to her."

There was a muffled noise on the other end of the line. When he came back, he was much closer to the receiver. "Are you crazy? What do you think she'll do? And I can guarantee you, if you do tell her, Dad *will* get involved. And I'm not sure how he'll react. You might not be safe."

"He doesn't have to know."

"You think she won't go to the police? Or worse? Look at what she's done already."

Fenton rubbed his forehead. There had to be a way out of this. Why couldn't anything in his life just be normal? That's all he'd ever wanted. Nice, quiet and normal. "You have to find this person before she gets hurt."

"What do you think I've been doing?" Brian yelled. Clearly, his anger was getting the better of him.

"You haven't done anything! You come over and tell us not to stay—"

"Which might have just saved your lives, by the way," he interrupted.

"—but you're still no closer to finding out who this person is, or why they're doing this to me."

"I'll find them. I'm close. But if you think I'm doing such a shitty job, why don't you come with me? Put some skin in the game for once."

He pinched his brows together. "Come with you where?"

"I might have something. One of your neighbor's surveillance cameras picked up a car that might have been watching your house over the past few days. It might belong to the person who broke in."

"How did you get access to our neighbor's surveillance cameras?" Fenton asked.

"You don't need to worry about that. I've been keeping a running tally of all the cars coming and going from your neighborhood and matching them to their respective houses. Some are visitors; I can't find any connection for this one. And it was parked far enough away so as to not look suspicious."

"Then how did you find it?"

"Like I said, I haven't just been sitting on my ass over here. I have resources, you know. And I matched an address to the car this morning. Do you want to come or not?"

Going with Brian might help this go faster. And it would allow Fenton to keep a closer eye on his brother. Even though he didn't suspect him, he couldn't help but feel something was going on, given how easy it would have been for Brian to set all this up. If for no other reason than to prove his brother's innocence, he'd go. Whoever was sending these packages obviously knew about Laura, and no one knew more about Laura than Fenton. Maybe he'd see something Brian might miss. As much as it hurt to remember everything they'd been through, if doing this would put all of this to rest, it would be worth it.

"Fine," he said. "I'll be right there."

TWENTY-NINE

WINTER

I'm parked in the lot of a fast-food restaurant and I can't keep my hands from shaking.

I can't believe Fenton did that. He's *never* been that volatile before. But I honestly felt like my life was in danger for a few seconds. Part of me can't seriously believe he'd hurt me, but another part wonders if I've ever really known him at all. If he could do that to my window... what could he do to me?

Thomas was never like that. For all his faults, he never got violent. We had our fights and raised our voices. But it never came to slamming doors... or breaking windows.

I can't stay another night in that house with him. Not now. Laura was right about that much. After calling Janet I tried reaching Laura again but couldn't reach her. I left a quick message, but I really would like to see her again today. I need to explain what's happened.

Who knows? She made it out of this relationship. Maybe so can I.

It takes Janet another fifteen minutes to arrive in her silver Crown Victoria and by then I've managed to calm down a little.

"Winter?" she asks as she gets out of the car. "Are you okay?

You sounded—" Her eyes go wide as soon as she sees me. "Oh my God. What happened?"

I must look as bad as I feel.

"Oh, I'm fine," I lie, putting on my best fake-it-till-you-make-it smile. "I didn't sleep well last night and uh..." I look at my cracked window. "I had a little accident on the road."

Janet reaches out and puts her hand on my forehead. The action startles me and I step back instinctively.

"Hon, you are warm. Are you sick?"

"No, just a headache," I say. "But I've got the other hand-writing sample." I hand over the brown paper wrapping that was around the book itself. I took the liberty of opening it up while waiting for her, and found the professional version of Laura's second book, *Undesirable*, inside. Of course, there was no other note or letter explaining the package.

"I spoke with him after I got off the phone with you. He'll be happy to take a look at all three right now if you're free." She looks around me like she isn't sure if I'm alone or not.

"Oh," I say. "Um, sure. That would be great." The sooner I have an answer to this mystery, the better off I'll be. Plus, it's not like I have anything else to do. Cammie isn't home and I can't get Laura to call me back. And I'm definitely not going back home. Not while Fenton is still there.

"Care to follow me?" she asks.

I nod and climb back in my car.

I follow her through town, my leg bouncing the whole way. To know I'll have an answer to all of this soon is a relief, but also very stressful. I know one thing; I'm ready to be done with all of it. I just want to put all this behind me and begin the process of starting over. *Again.*

I sigh. I'll have to call Mom. I'd get in contact with Daisy, but it isn't like we're close. And being with her would be stressful anyway. But I'll need a place to stay until I can find a new apartment. I had a great apartment when I met Fenton. It was low-cost, tons of amenities and had a view. And it's unlikely I'll find any place like that again anytime soon. Maybe I should look for a place that allows pets. If Cammie is still speaking with me, she can help me find a dog that needs a good home.

Ten minutes later we pull into the driveway of a modest home on the east side of Brighton. The house has been painted a very pleasing blue color and a row of flowers have been planted along the front beds. Fenton never wanted flowers planted around the house; he said they contrasted with the "lines" or whatever bullshit reason he came up with.

"You'll want to get that fixed as soon as you can," Janet says as I join her on the sidewalk. She's referring to my window. "That's a driving hazard."

I nod. "I'll take care of it soon."

"Okay. Here, come along. Now, his name is Jack Keever and he's been retired about five years now. But he's very smart and knows exactly what he's doing."

I pause. There's something about the way Janet keeps going on about him. "Is he… your boyfriend?"

She laughs. "Heavens, no." Then she gives me a little elbow in the side. "But I wouldn't mind, if you know what I mean." She rings the doorbell.

The door opens to reveal a tall man with a full head of graying hair and a nicely trimmed beard. He's wearing a pair of dark jeans, complemented by a comfortable button-down shirt that's been rolled up at the sleeves. I'm slightly taken aback.

"Janet," he says before turning to me. "And you must be Winter."

I shake his hand; he has a strong grip. "Yes, uh, *thank you*, for helping me with this. I know it must be a pain in the ass."

He chuckles. "Nonsense. Plus, I owed Janet a favor."

The woman beside me practically *titters* and I work to hide my smile.

"Here, come on in. I have the samples set up already. Just waiting on the last one." We follow him into the house, which is sparse, but clean and organized. What else should I expect from a retired FBI agent?

"How long were you in the job?" I ask.

"As long as they'd let me, twenty-seven years total," he says. "I would have stayed longer if I could. It's hard to leave a job like that."

I can't even imagine *doing* a job like that.

One of the spare bedrooms in his house is set up like an office, with a large desk taking up most of the room. The desk has all manner of mementos on it, presumably from his time with the Bureau. But in the center sit Fenton's prior marriage and divorce certificates. Two large lights sit on the edge of the table and Keever switches both of them on. "Do you have the third sample?"

I hand over the brown paper wrapping. I was careful not to tear it anywhere, just in case.

"Perfect." He takes a seat and removes a pair of special glasses from one of the drawers. They're outfitted with small magnifying glasses on each lens, and when he puts them on, his dark brown eyes fill up the oculus.

"Will this take very long, Jack?" Janet asks.

"Shouldn't," he says. "Now, Winter, this isn't an exact science. I can give you an indication, but no certainties, okay?"

I nod.

"Having a third sample will help tremendously, that way we can look for any consistencies over the three different items." He sits in his chair and leans down closely to the marriage certificate. "You're asking if the person who signed Laura Byrnes is consistent across all three samples, correct?"

"Yes, that's right," I say. This will tell me once and for all if Laura was the one who left these books or not. And whether she's behind all this. My hope is it will also clear up the confusion about the marriage and divorce certificates.

"Well, I've already taken a look at these two documents, so let's look at what you've brought today first." He pulls the wrapping into the light and leans over closely, examining every curve with his glasses millimeters from the surface. In his free hand he holds a pen and makes notes on a notepad next to him without even looking up.

After a few minutes he sets the sample down, moving to the marriage certificate. He repeats the process before moving on to the divorce records. When he's done he sits back, removing his glasses.

"Well?" I ask.

He purses his lips. "I'm not sure what you're hoping to hear, so I don't know how this news will come to you. But none of these are a match to each other."

"Wait, what?"

"The one here, signed for the divorce, was made by someone attempting a poor copy of this one, here." He holds up the marriage certificate. "I had hoped the third sample would explain the inconsistencies, but it only adds to the problem. It was written by a different person as well."

"Then Janet was right. The person who signed the marriage certificate did not sign the divorce papers," I say, making sure I'm understanding him correctly.

"I'm afraid not."

"How sure are you about this, Jack?" Janet asks. "I was only guessing."

"About as sure as I can be," he replies. "Sometimes there are anomalies, people have off days. But there are always at least a *few* markers that are always consistent across writing. That's not to say they *couldn't* have all come from the same person, but in my professional opinion, that's highly unlikely."

I frown, staring at the three samples before us. "What does that mean?"

"It means most likely someone attempted to forge Laura Byrnes's name on the divorce records," he says. "And this." He holds up the wrapping the book came in. "This is a total mystery."

Then Laura couldn't have left the book. But it also means she didn't sign her divorce records with Fenton. At least, she didn't sign them herself. "Is it possible she could have hired someone to sign for her?"

"If that were the case, it would be indicated in the record," Keever replies. "As in, *Jack Keever signing on behalf of... etc., etc.* But I wouldn't be signing *her* name. This is a forgery, in my opinion."

Does that mean Laura and Fenton are still technically married? Is *that* what this is all about? But if so, I still don't understand how. How would sending these books either strengthen or weaken that relationship? But the bigger question is, does Fenton know? If the end of their marriage was never finalized, then he cannot legally marry me.

"Okay," I say, gathering up the documents. "Thank you anyway."

"I'm sorry that wasn't what you were looking for," he says, standing. "But I hope it helps in some way."

I nod. "It'll help. I'm just not sure how, yet."

"Is there anything else I can do?" Janet asks.

I give her a quick smile and a shake of my head. "No. But thank you. You've already done plenty. Both of you."

"If I can be of any further service, please let me know," Keever says.

I pause. "Have you ever heard of someone breaking into a house to *leave* something? Not steal it?"

He chuckles. "You mean like a television?"

"Or to plant evidence."

His face darkens. "Yes, I have come across that a few times in my career."

"Any advice on how to handle it?"

"Document everything. And get the police involved if they're not already," he says. "If someone is trying to frame you or someone you know, having the facts is the best thing for you right now."

"Oh, Winter, I had no idea," Janet says.

I feel tears prickle my eyes but quickly wipe them away. "No, it's probably nothing. Just some prank, I'm sure."

"I don't mean to be an asshole, but if someone planted evidence in your house, it's no prank," Keever says. "Trust me."

"Do you have any idea who it could be?" Janet asks. "Does Fenton?"

I want to tell them that they just exonerated Laura, which only leaves one other suspect, which happens to be Fenton's family. Namely his father. "I think I might."

"Go to the police," Keever says. "Get your story on the record right now."

I nod. "Thank you both, again."

"Good luck, honey," Janet says, patting my arm. "And if there's anything else I can do, please let me know."

"I will." I head back out to my car and toss my "evidence" in the passenger seat, emotionally wiped. I'm not sure where to go from here. The signatures don't match.

Oh my God. If she never officially divorced Fenton, that means her marriage isn't legal. I try calling her, but it goes to voicemail again.

"Laura, it's Winter. I need you to call me immediately. I have some information you need to hear. Please."

I don't care that I sound desperate. She needs to know so she can begin taking steps to fix it.

And in the meantime, I need to take Keever's advice and get this all on the record.

I don't see how I have any other choice.

THIRTY

WINTER

"I'm sorry, ma'am, I just don't know what you want us to do."

I've been standing in the lobby of the Brighton police department for the past three hours waiting to talk to someone and now that I'm finally sitting down with a detective, *this* is what they're telling me?

"I don't know how to be much clearer," I say. "Someone broke into my house"

"And yet, you've said nothing is missing," Detective Marsh replies. "No jewelry. No money or other goods."

I take a deep breath. I've already explained the entire situation *twice*. What is it that she's not understanding? "That's right. But they left something."

"The box."

I nod.

"Full of your ex-husband's manuscripts."

I shake my head. "No, Fenton is my *fiancé*. And they were *his* ex-wife's manuscripts."

"Right. Sorry." She makes a little note on her pad, but I suspect that was on purpose. To see if I could keep my story straight. "And these manuscripts... they belong to a Laura Byrnes."

"Her maiden name was Blackwell." I've already handed over

the marriage and divorce records. "And I'm not sure they're actually divorced."

"Because of the signatures."

"*Yes*." God, it's like talking to a brick wall.

Marsh leans back, sighing. "What exactly is it you want us to do, Ms. Southerland?"

"I don't know... put out an APB or something. Assign someone to watch our house. *Something*."

She purses her lips. "Frankly, this isn't much to go on. There's no evidence of forced entry. Nothing missing. No indication anyone wants to harm you or your fiancé."

"What about the person at the end of my driveway?"

She gives me a pitying look. "That could have just been someone out for a nighttime walk. The fact you haven't seen them again reinforces that possibility."

"But... you have to be able to do *something*."

Marsh scans back over her notes. "You said your fiancé got upset when you left earlier today. Did he get violent with you?"

I think back to the window on my car. Do I tell her? It could have been an accident, Fenton might have just hit it the wrong way. Then again, he did still hit it. "Not... exactly."

"Has he hurt you? Put his hands on you?"

"I think you're missing the point here," I say. "There's no way Fenton could be behind this. It's someone else."

She sees the resolve in my eyes and decides to drop the matter. "I'll be frank with you, Ms. Southerland. Accusing Lazarus Byrnes of anything in this county is a dangerous proposition. Accusing him without actual evidence? I don't care if you're about to be his daughter-in-law or not, that's just playing with fire."

"Is that a threat?"

"It's a fact. I've watched Byrnes take down very powerful people for far less. If you want my advice, I'd drop this entire matter. I don't even have to enter it into the record."

Keever's advice comes back to me. "No. I want it on the record. Because when something worse happens—when someone gets in my home and tries to attack me—then I'm going to come back to this conversation right here. Assuming I'm alive."

She blows out a puff of air like I'm being overly dramatic. "Have you replaced your locks?"

I shake my head. "I don't know. Fenton was supposed to earlier today."

"That would be step one. Step two would be to get some cameras for the house. You said you don't have any right now?"

"No," I admit.

"Do those two things. I'll see if maybe I can't have some of our patrols ride by a few times tonight, okay? Just to keep a lookout."

"Thank you," I say. At least that's something. But I don't even know if I'm staying at that house tonight. I'm not sure even with two doors between us that staying with Fenton is a good idea.

"You look like you want to say something else," Marsh replies. She's watching me carefully. I know she's waiting for me to give her a sign that Fenton has stepped over the line, but I don't do it. I still love the man and I don't want to see him in jail, despite how much of a dick he's been lately. Whatever he is, it's not a criminal.

Finally, she gives up. "I'll tell you what. I'll hang on to this for a day to give you some time to decide. If after sleeping on it, you want it entered into the public record, I'll be happy to do it for you."

I scoff, getting up. "The gaze of Lazarus Byrnes reaches farther than I thought."

"Be careful who you make an enemy of in this town, Ms. Southerland," Marsh says. "There aren't that many places to hide."

I walk out of the station more frustrated than when I went in.

Brian was right. Lazarus's influence goes far. How long until he hears about this from his police buddies? And what happens when he finds out all this is coming from me?

Lazarus has always been suspicious to me. Closed off, cold and not particularly happy about our relationship. Every time I've met the man, he's lorded his power over people like he's some kind of king. Fenton has told me on more than one occasion he has dirt on everyone, because he never knew when "it might become useful." On the outside he runs a successful logging company. He'd been one of the first innovators to start importing wood from Russia, Brazil and—most profitably—Canada, selling them at premium prices here in the States. But it's his business *behind* the business that really brings in the money. The enforcement jobs, keeping the competition out of their small corner of Connecticut and keeping the cops fat and happy. Not to mention all the "imports and exports" coming and going with the logs. But I'm not supposed to know about that.

Maybe that was the problem; Lazarus was afraid Fenton might reveal too much to me, and with his independent streak, he can't keep tabs on his son like he does Brian. Fenton could probably bring his father's entire operation down if he wanted to, but as far as I've seen he wants nothing to do with it, good or bad. He just wants to make his own way in the world and leave his father to his own machinations.

Fenton has spent so much time trying to get away from his father's reputation and everything that went along with it that it's become like a second identity for him. And maybe the logging magnate wouldn't be so good at his job if Lazarus's own father and grandfather hadn't built all those longstanding relationships back when the town was new and small. But today, just like the town, Lazarus's reach has grown further and deeper than ever. And Fenton sits at the end of a long line of power.

All of which contrasts deeply with my own past. A moderate life, regular parents, regular sister, right up until the day Mom found out Dad was cheating with Lucille Touffey and kicked him out of the house. They separated for a few months at first, while they "worked things out." Then he moved back in with promises it was all over, and everything was okay again.

Unfortunately, it didn't last.

Dad came back *with Lucille in tow* to pick up his stuff before I finally overheard what really happened. After his first round of affairs, Mom had convinced Dad to come back despite him not wanting to. She said it was the best thing for us girls and we needed our father around, like she didn't want him there to help take care of things for her too. I hated how she always tried to pin that on us. But, of course, he just kept on cheating behind her back. He hadn't even been back in the house a year before it started up again.

After that, I decided I was no longer going to be the reason anyone split up. And I made damn sure anyone I dated had none of my father's hallmarks. And yet, despite all my work, it happened to me too. Like when I found those text messages between Thomas and his coworker. There hadn't been any reason to question Thomas about it; it was all there in black and white. I was on the phone with the divorce lawyer that day. He'd made his choice clear and I wasn't about to stick around for it.

Maybe there's just something about the Southerland clan that attracts us to cheaters. Mom was innocent, but Daisy—Daisy swung the exact opposite direction. Said if anyone was ever going to cheat in the relationship, it was going to be her. That sounded toxic to me, but you can't tell my sister anything without her arguing with you, so I just let it go.

I thought maybe if I was careful and kept my eye out, I could find someone who wouldn't fall into that category. I thought I'd found that with Fenton. For three years we were happy.

And maybe what he's done isn't cheating, but it's still lying. It's still hiding himself and his past from me. I needed him to be open and honest and he's proved he's neither of those things. But now that I think about it, he was practically groomed by a master manipulator, so should I be surprised he's good at it as well?

I grit my teeth. I'm tired of this song and dance; it's time I got some answers. If Lazarus is the one who sent the books, then he'll know Brian never recovered the one we found this morning. And if Brian doesn't have it, he'll assume either Fenton or I do. But he won't know about Janet or Jack. He doesn't know I know about the divorce papers, which I might be able to use to my advantage. Someone as smart as Lazarus must know what happened with his son's first marriage all those years ago. And maybe I can leverage what I know to get him to reveal enough to give himself away. I don't expect him to come right out and say it, but I have to at least try.

If he wants to get rid of me, he's going to have to tell me that to my face. And then again, maybe all this is nothing more than a trial, to confirm I can't handle the pressures of being in this family, with its secrets and power struggles and shady dealings. It's meant to scare me off because I've aligned myself with his ostracized son, and no one says no to Lazarus Byrnes.

I smile as I pull out of the parking lot. I can't wait to see his face when I march up to the house and announce I won't be scared away by a little book. It's going to take something much, much worse. And perhaps that challenge will finally earn me enough respect to be left alone.

THIRTY-ONE
FENTON

"You need a shower," Brian said as Fenton walked in through the side door.

Fenton sighed. He didn't want to get into it with Brian right now. "What am I doing here?"

"You... get to be my sidekick," Brian said, shooting him a grin. Fenton knew that grin. It had caused him considerable trouble when they were kids.

"Sidekick?"

"We're going stalker hunting," Brian replied. "We're going to find out whoever knows about Laura and we're going to shut them up. For good."

Fenton shook his head. "God, I hate this. I hate what you two do. This whole business."

"This whole business kept you out of jail eight years ago, don't forget that," Brian said, suddenly intense. "Would you rather Dad hadn't been there?"

"I sometimes wonder if things would have been simpler."

Brian scoffed. "Really? Okay, then. I guess I'll just go let him know..."

Fenton grabbed his arm. "No. I didn't mean it. I'm just under a lot of stress right now."

The lone kitchen light above them flickered once. Brian frowned at the light for a brief second before returning to Fenton. "I know you are. And I'm just trying to help. But it means Dad has to be kept in the loop."

"Yeah." Fenton sighed. "Yeah, I know. Let's get this over with."

Brian nodded and disappeared into one of the back rooms for a minute, returning holding his 9mm before stuffing it in his belt.

"Jesus. Really?"

"You can't be too prepared. The one time I don't have it on me will be the one time I really need it. So I carry it everywhere."

Fenton couldn't argue with that logic. He gave Brian a resigned look and they both left through the side door, Brian locking it behind them and letting the screen clap shut. They piled into his car and Brian put in the address in the GPS. "Have any favorite tunes? Because we're going to be here for a while."

Almost thirty minutes later Brian pulled his Range Rover up to a small crest, just off the side of the main road.

"Is that it?" Fenton asked.

Brian consulted the GPS. "Says it's that development right down there."

"I'd say 'development' is being a bit generous."

"You're a stuck-up little snot sometimes." Brian gave him a toothy grin. "Everyone's got to live somewhere."

They stared down into the community of mobile homes, each one identical to the next. It was one of the nicer mobile home neighborhoods, with each plot clearly marked and most tended and kept well. Some even had miniature white picket fences.

"Which one is it?"

"Address just says 1805 Salem Drive. It could be any one of them. We'll just look for the one with the car."

"And then what?"

"Wait until they leave and take a look around."

"You mean, break in."

"I mean, do whatever we have to do to find out who is threatening you. If that means breaking into a mobile home, then yes."

"What if they have a family, other people living there?"

Brian shook his head. "No way. My psychological eval tells me this person is a loner. Most likely very isolated from everyone else. He's probably a hermit, only leaves when he absolutely has to."

"Which means?"

"Which means we may not be able to wait. His next venture out could be to leave another book at your house. And that might take days. We may have to go in while he's inside."

"Fuck," whispered Fenton.

"See? Now aren't you glad I brought this?" Brian smiled and patted the gun in the wood-paneled console between them.

Fenton just rolled his eyes.

They took a few minutes to drive around the neighborhood. It was a series of two concentric circles, a smaller one inside of the larger one, connected on both ends by long lanes providing two entrances and exits out of the development. They found the car on the outer circle, sitting next to a light-blue mobile home. It had no personal decorations outside and the grass had grown far longer than at its neighbors'.

"Yep, that's him all right," Brian said as they passed. "Might as well have a big bullseye on that thing."

"What do we do?"

"We'll wait him out for a few hours. If he doesn't come out by the time it gets dark, we'll make our way inside."

They left the park and took some of the smaller roads off to the north. Brian used the GPS to swing them back around so they were parked in an adjacent neighborhood (one with slightly nicer houses) with a perfect view of the mobile home.

Two hours later, nothing had changed and Fenton was growing anxious.

"Let's just forget this. Let's go back home, and—"

"And do what? Forget all about it? What happens when the third book arrives? Then the fourth and the fifth? What then? You think he's just going to stop? He's building up to something. He's building *himself* up to something. The first one was on your stoop. The second in your house. Do you want to wait around and find out where he puts the third one?"

"We could leave. Winter and me. We could just leave for a few months. Until things calm down."

"And how do you think she's going to feel about that?" Brian asked. "Leaving her job, her friends? She won't even stay in the same hotel room with you, much less leave on a cross-country adventure. How do you see that panning out?"

Fenton didn't reply. Brian was right; there was no way around this now. He didn't want to tell his brother the details of how Winter took the book. He'd only get accused of losing his temper again—something Fenton hadn't done in *years*. But lately... lately things had been more difficult. More... uneven. If he ever wanted a chance at a normal life again, he had to see this all the way through.

Brian elbowed him. "Look."

Fenton squinted to see through the twilight. A dark figure emerged from the mobile home and promptly got in the car and drove away.

"Finally."

"Should we follow him? What if he's going back to my house?"

"I think we'll learn more by checking the place out while he's gone. It's better this way. We don't have to get our hands dirty."

"It always makes me nervous when you say that because it never ends up working out."

"You worry too much, little bro."

And you don't worry enough.

Brian exited the vehicle and closed his door without a sound. Fenton tried to do the same but ended up pushing it too hard. Brian gave him a sidelong glance as he stuffed the gun in the back of his belt.

They made their way across the small field separating the two developments. There weren't many trees out there, only a few at the edge of each property. Most of it was overgrown grass and muddy earth. When they reached the mobile home, Fenton noted that lights were on in both neighboring units.

"It's fine. If anyone asks, tell them we work for the property owner and are checking for gas issues," Brian said.

"How many times have you done this?" Fenton asked.

"I thought you didn't want to know about the business." Brian made his way up the three stairs to the door and pulled a small black piece of plastic out of his pocket. From this he pulled an even smaller piece of metal, shaped in different ways. It was in the lock less than a minute before he had the door unlocked.

Brian put his ear to the door, listening before nodding to Fenton and turning the doorknob.

The door opened into a dark space, and Fenton couldn't see anything other than the dark outline of shapes against what little light filtered in. The windows were covered by standard blinds, mutating the light into long parallel beams. Brian closed the door behind them and flicked on the light.

The room was surprisingly bare. To their right was the modest kitchen, missing an oven, and with a refrigerator that had to be at least thirty years old. Beside that, almost in front of them, sat the couch, a ratty, plaid specimen from another era. Off to the left was a hallway and doors to what Fenton assumed were the bathroom and bedroom. The place was completely devoid of any personal touches.

"Kind of looks like your house," Fenton said. "Just smaller."

"I'll decorate when I get a day off," Brian replied, taking a close look at what little was in the room. "Look for anything that you might recognize. Any papers, manuscripts, anything of Laura's." He tossed Fenton a pair of latex gloves.

Fenton took a deep breath and began his search. Not that there was much to search through. The house looked like it had been cleaned out. Or hadn't been lived in for a while. He made his way into the kitchen. The countertops were all Formica with old, wooden cabinets underneath that were not much thicker than MDF. The lack of stove was odd, leaving the disconnected gas line hookup and scuff marks on the floor where the old one had been removed. Whoever was taunting him apparently didn't need an oven for meals.

Fenton opened the fridge to find very little: a carton of old milk, a half-used bottle of ketchup and a Styrofoam container with some soggy fries. The freezer contained a couple of microwave dinners.

"Anything?" Brian asked, returning from the bedroom.

"Not much."

"It's been more or less vacated as far as I can tell. No clothes. No personal effects. Not even a toothbrush."

Great, so whoever lived here had completely vacated? That didn't make much sense.

As Fenton searched, the phone in his pocket vibrated. He pulled it out, but it came through as a blocked number. Still, there was a message attached.

GET. OUT.

His eyes went wide. He looked around for a camera or something that could have caught them coming into the mobile home, but there was nothing of the sort. His phone vibrated again.

NOW.

"Brian, we need to go," Fenton said.

"What? We're not done yet," his brother called from the back.

"C'mon," he said, urgency in his voice. "Let's go!" Fenton ran outside, looking to his left and right and seeing no one. The whole area was dark.

"Hey," Brian said from behind him. "What—"

Fenton grabbed him by the shirt collar, pulling him out of the doorframe. Brian pushed back, forcing Fenton off him. "Don't you ever grab me."

"We have to *go!*"

"We go when I say we go."

Fenton didn't have time to argue. He didn't know what it was, but the message had a strange urgency to it. And he wasn't going to ignore it. He began running for the car.

"Hey!" Brian called from behind him. Fenton could tell he was trotting after him. Good. Whatever it took.

It happened in slow motion.

There was a small pop in the air, like someone bursting a balloon a few feet away, and then sound disappeared for a moment. A gust of air hit Fenton, knocking him forward as an eruption exploded in his ears. He looked back to see the roof of the mobile home launch itself up into the air while every window in the home exploded. A giant fire followed the shattering glass, pouring out of every opening, including the door they'd just run through. The roof reached its maximum height and fell back to earth, smashing into the mobile home and enraging the fire.

"Brian!" Fenton called. "Brian!" There was no answer. Though he could barely even hear his own voice.

On the edge of his vision, he thought he saw the dark form of someone running from the scene, but the figure was too far away to be Brian. He glanced down and saw smoke rising from a body on the ground. He crawled over, the heat from the flames making him shield his eyes as he inched closer. He was vaguely aware of people running and yelling all around him, yelling at him. But he had to reach Brian. The gun was still in his hand.

He grabbed his brother by the shoulders, pulling him away from the flames while another smaller explosion came from somewhere inside the structure. The entire area was awash in flame light.

Once he'd dragged him a suitable distance—just beyond the

trees and into the tall grass where they'd come from—he flipped Brian over.

He was breathing, but unconscious. Second-degree burns had scorched his face and had melted the gloves to his hands. He'd been too close to the explosion. Fenton tapped his burned cheeks as lightly as he could.

Brian jerked his eyes open, trying to scramble away from Fenton, waving the gun at him.

"Whoa! Easy, it's me. Easy!"

Brian stared at him a moment but didn't move, keeping the gun outstretched.

"Here," Fenton said, his own hand shaking. He put one hand on the barrel of the gun. As soon as he did, Brian's grip relaxed and he let go. Imitating his brother, Fenton shoved it behind him in his belt. The last thing he wanted to do was get shot tonight.

"Brian. It's me. There was an explosion."

"Explosion." His voice was rough, like he'd been smoking his entire life.

"Yeah, you got burned. Can you walk? We have to get out of here." Already the sound of sirens filled the air.

That seemed to rouse him. Brian blinked a few times, took a look at the burning husk that was the trailer, then looked back to where they'd parked the car. "We have to go." He looked down. "My hands." It was as if he could comprehend it but couldn't feel the pain.

"We'll get you fixed up."

Fenton helped him to his feet. Brian stumbled twice but made it to the car on the other end of the field.

"Keys?" Fenton asked.

"R…right pocket." Brian closed his eyes and leaned on the car, moaning slightly. He was going into shock. Across the way, the first fire trucks arrived.

"Here." Fenton unlocked the doors and helped him into the passenger seat. "Don't touch anything until we can get those off you." The gloves were one thing, but the burns on his face were another. And there was no telling what other injuries he might have suffered. If he went to the hospital, it wouldn't take long before they put two and two together. It wasn't like there were a lot of exploding mobile homes around here. Fenton only knew one place he could take Brian and get him the help he needed without a bunch of questions.

But it was the last place he wanted to go.

THIRTY-TWO

WINTER

I glance at the clock on my dashboard. It isn't much past six and the sun has already disappeared behind the tree line as I pull up to the giant wrought-iron gates. Will I be interrupting their dinner? Do I even care? Hell, I'm mad enough to knock the bowl of gruel right out of his cold hands if I have to.

The black orb on the small metal pad beside the gate stares at me as I press the button. "Winter Southerland," I say clearly.

"Welcome, Miss," a formal voice answers. Was that Jakoby or Warren? I will never get used to the idea of butlers. "I don't see you on the schedule for this evening."

"I want to talk to him. It's important."

"I'm sorry, Miss Southerland, but you know the rules. You'll have to—hold, please."

I sit back against my headrest. Lazarus isn't a coward; if I'm right and he knows why I'm here, he'll let me in. His pride won't let him hide or be intimidated by a woman half his age.

"Please park near the west wing of the house," the voice says before promptly cutting off. I'm about to ask which side is west when the iron gates screech open in front of me. They're at least ten feet high, attached to stone walls on either side. It's as if I'm entering the gates of hell.

Not too far off, I think, steeling myself.

The driveway is all gravel, and I have to drive slowly to avoid kicking anything up that might damage my car's paint. This is a deliberate choice on Lazarus's part, I'm sure of it. To intimidate people by making them literally crawl up to meet with him, with his imposing house looming in the distance. Or else risk damage to their expensive vehicles.

The last vestiges of light fade from the sky as the property lighting clicks on. I pass giant Italian cypress trees on my right, a lamp on every other tree to highlight the height of them all. The view on the left is reserved for a wide expanse of well-groomed grass, with a huge three-tier fountain, complete with its own lighting. Lazarus is nothing if not ostentatious. Of course, Abagail was sure to have her input as well. It's their way of showing off their tremendous wealth.

I've only been here twice before, but it isn't the type of house you forget. When I first saw it, I would have described it as a modern-day castle. A giant monstrosity done in the French Revival style, though updated sometime in the past twenty years so it has all the modern amenities—Fenton's words.

I can't understand how people live in places like this. They always seem so cold, so impersonal and so cut off from reality. It's as if the Byrneses have walled themselves off from everyone and everything, hiding in a cell of their own design.

As I pull up, I try to discern which side of the house is west. It's not like my car has a compass built in. I make good money, but not *that* good. Giving up, I drive up to the front entrance and park underneath the giant portico, the kind I assumed only existed at fancy hotels. The ten-foot oak doors accentuated with iron details are all that stand between me and the answers I need. I saunter up to them, but before I can knock, the latch clicks and the door opens to reveal Warren, looking slightly annoyed.

"This isn't the west wing, Miss."

"Sorry, Warren. Tell him he needs to put signposts out there. There are too many driveways."

Warren doesn't respond, only closes the door behind us.

"Winter. How nice." Abagail Byrnes approaches me, her light gray hair tied up in a bun and her long white robe dragging on the floor. She reaches in and gives me a half hug and phantom kisses each cheek. "What brings you to visit? How is my son?"

I manage a smile. My fight isn't with her. "He's... good. Busy, you know. I came to see your husband. I hope I'm not interrupting anything."

Abagail scoffs, rubbing my shoulder lightly. "If he didn't want you here, you wouldn't be here," she says in that cold way I've never encountered with anyone else. It's as if she tries to be friendly but doesn't really know how.

"He'll be in his study. We were just in the middle of dinner."

"Oh, I'm sorry, I should have called—"

Abagail smiles. "Yes, you should have. But you're here now. Go see him." The smile doesn't quite reach her eyes. She turns and disappears into some corner of this maze of a house. Great. I've already pissed off one of the two occupants of this house, might as well make it two for two.

Which way is the study? Considering the last time I was here was six months ago and this house has more doors and hallways than a city block, I can't exactly be chastised for not remembering. I look at Warren, hoping for some help.

"This way," he says, somewhat exasperated. Warren isn't what anyone would call a typical butler—I don't even know if he *is* the butler—but he wears a smart suit and has the most penetrating blue eyes. Fenton told me he's been working for his family since before he was born and still he doesn't know much about the man's personal life. Was it possible he did jobs for Lazarus? I start wondering if *he* could be the one who left the book in our house. Or is Warren nothing more than a glorified house sitter, taking care of the home and nothing else? I admit, I have no clue how many people Lazarus keeps on his personal payroll.

Warren directs me to a large wooden door on the same floor, full of ornamentation and molding. Something much too opulent for a normal house, but it fits here. Still, it's cold and foreboding. No wonder Fenton doesn't like coming here. This whole place is impressive, but it's also obnoxious. Give me a warm throw and a soft couch over this any day.

"He'll be waiting for you in here, Miss." Warren opens the door but does not step inside. My heart picks up an extra beat. I've never been in this room before, only passed it once. The floor is a dark cherry hardwood, covered in opulent carpeting that doesn't reach the walls. Floor-to-ceiling antique bookshelves line every wall that doesn't have a window, and those are flanked by dark-red curtains. Lazarus isn't a hunter, but if he was, I'm sure a couple of animal heads would look right at home in here. In the middle of everything sits a ginormous desk, complete with green-shaded work lamp and a high-backed chair containing the man himself.

Except that it doesn't really accomplish its goal.

The chair fails miserably to contain him; the presence of Lazarus Byrnes could not be constrained within one piece of furniture alone. He's not heavyset, but he is a large man. Large and imposing. As I survey the room, I doubt ten rooms of this size could contain him.

"Good evening," he says, staring me down, his dark-grey eyes matching his wavy hair. As a younger man he'd probably been impossible to resist, at least until people got to know him.

"Good evening," I reply, doing my best not to let my voice waver. Everything about this room screams intimidation, but I'm not going to cave. Not when I'm this close.

Lazarus continues to watch me, picking up a glass half full of brown liquid in his massive hand and taking a long sip before putting it back down, his eyes never leaving mine. He could wrap that hand around my neck and strangle me easily. "Can I offer you something?"

I shake my head. "Just a moment of your time."

Lazarus sits back in his chair, his hand still on his glass. He gestures with his other hand to a chair in front of his desk. "The rest of my evening is yours," he says, his voice dripping with sarcasm.

Internally, I wince, but I take the seat anyway. Now that I'm here, I'm not feeling as confident as I had been driving up here. I'd been so sure about my plan all the way up until this moment when I'm in front of this man who has power I can't even comprehend.

"It must be awfully important to come at a time like this." He takes a sip. "Outside of business hours." His voice is low, measured, every word carries his gravitas.

"Are you..." I falter. I'm about to accuse the most powerful man within fifty miles of harassing his own son and future daughter-in-law. Maybe not the best idea.

"Am I what?" he asks. "Annoyed? Inconvenienced? Upset?" With each word his voice grows deeper. "Spit. It. Out." Any trace of a smile has disappeared from his face.

"Are you the one sending the books to Fenton?" I somehow manage to ask.

Lazarus narrows his eyes. "No."

I bite the inside of my cheek. He's so damn direct. I need to ask in a better way. "Do you have anything to do with the books? With what happened between Fenton and Laura?"

Lazarus sits very still, considering me. He's not going to answer. He'll just sit here and deny everything. Why did I think this could work? This was a bad idea. A very, *very* bad idea.

"Those... are two very different questions," Lazarus finally says.

"I want an answer to both," I reply.

Lazarus's face turns into a sneer. "What makes you think you deserve one? Just because you are marrying my son? You think you can come into this family and dictate terms to me?"

"I deserve them because they affect me. And they are tearing your son and myself apart."

Lazarus leans back again. "I can't say I'm surprised. He never was good under pressure." He takes another sip.

"Is this all some kind of ruse? A test? To see if I'll break too?"

He doesn't reply. Only watches me. His gaze unnerves me.

"I have the divorce papers," I blurt out, having lost all my composure.

He arches an eyebrow. "Divorce papers?"

"From the county courthouse. The ones that were filed when Fenton and Laura got divorced."

"And?"

"And I want to know what happened. Why is her signature different? Fenton's is the same, but Laura's is different."

"I wouldn't know," he replies, taking another sip.

"You bastard," I whisper. "I know you're doing all of this. The books, all of it. To get back at him for not being part of your little mafia up here. Whether you admit it or not. And you're not going to get away with it." I stand to leave.

"Stupid little girl," Lazarus says, his voice deep and resonating. "If I wanted to torture my son, I wouldn't send him some flimsy books. I'm much more creative than that. And if I didn't want you to be part of his life, trust me, you wouldn't be."

A chill runs through me, but I stand my ground. "Is that a threat?"

"You'll know when I'm making a threat." The smile returns to Lazarus's face. "Unless you're dumber than I gave you credit for." He takes one last sip, draining the glass, but his eyes are still on me.

"I'm smart enough to know that rich people like you make sure you have insurance on everything, including your family," I say, having found my voice. "And whatever this has been—whatever you're hoping to accomplish—you're only going to tear your family further apart. If you're too much of a coward to admit it to me, at least admit it to yourself."

Lazarus shoots up out of his chair faster than I think possible. Before I realize what's happening, he's leaning over the desk, his nostrils flaring. "How dare you," he says through clenched teeth. "Your generation's reputation for lack of respect is well earned."

"I don't respect liars."

He stands up to his full height. Was his side of the desk higher? He looks about six inches taller than the last time I saw him.

"Is this what you did to Laura? Intimidated her into leaving? Forced her to sign the divorce papers under duress? Is that why they're different?"

"You should have taken my son's advice and stayed out of this. You don't know what you've gotten yourself into," he rumbles.

"What do you mean?"

"Because, you stupid girl. Laura is dead."

Obviously, he's lying. He's just trying to rattle me. He doesn't know I've been talking to Laura this entire time; the woman has been my primary source of information. And she sought me out, not the other way around. I hadn't even known Laura existed until after I met her.

"You're lying," I finally find the strength to say, my focus on Lazarus. *Don't break eye contact. Whatever you do, don't let him see you as weak.*

Lazarus scoffs. "I don't care if you believe me or not. The fact of the matter is she's dead. Believe whatever you want or need to. It changes nothing." He sits back down in his chair. I take it as an invitation to do the same.

"You're telling me the woman I've been talking to for the past four days is dead? Or didn't you know she was back in town."

Lazarus's eyes widen, but it's very subtle. Like a fly landing on a lampshade, the movement is so small it's barely perceptible. But I can tell I've surprised him. He hasn't anticipated me talking to her. Maybe I should have kept it in my back pocket, but it's out now. Nothing I can do about it. *"Never give the man any advantage, never let him get one over you, because you'll never get out from under his boot."* Fenton's words.

"Interesting," Lazarus says. He picks up his cell phone, which acts as a paperweight for a small stack of papers on the giant desk. He types something out, but I can't see the screen. Who is he contacting? And what is he telling them?

Maybe the best tactic would be for me to indulge him. "Okay. Let's say Laura is dead, as you say. What happened to her? How did she die?"

Lazarus finishes typing and sets his phone down again. A smile creeps across his face. "I'll leave my son to tell you that story."

"Fenton knows?"

"Of course Fenton knows. He was there."

The room feels smaller, even though I know this is nothing more than Lazarus playing his games. I keep pushing. "Did he do something to her? Did something happen?" Laura's words echo in my head. His grip, the bruising. How he'd lost control.

Lazarus sits silently on his side of the desk, his smile never wavering. "My son has a nasty temper when he doesn't get his way."

"Why did you even tell me if you're not going to give me any details?" I demand.

"Who says you deserve them?"

I draw back, disgusted. Was this how it was going to be?

Lazarus stands, taking his glass over to the small bar area on the left side of the room. It's filled with an array of bottles, all with names I don't recognize. But knowing Lazarus, they all probably cost at least five hundred dollars apiece. He picks up one with a gilded label, but all I can read is, *Aged 35 years*. He returns to the desk with the glass half full.

"Oh. I'm sorry," he says in mocking tone as he notices me looking at his glass. "Did you want one?"

I don't dignify the comment with a response.

He takes his seat across from me again, relaxing back into the chair. "The thing you have to understand about fathers and sons is their relationship is complicated. You wouldn't know, as you don't have any brothers and of course your father was a womanizer and a cheat."

I bite the inside of my cheek to keep from saying something I'll regret. How did he find out about Dad? How much does he know about me? He probably used all his contacts to learn as much as he could the day Fenton and I went on our first date. Still, I don't like him knowing my personal business. This man is not family to me, he's a stranger. And it's unnerving to hear such personal information come from someone like him.

"See, sometimes, little boys have trouble listening. And they won't do what's best for them. And those little boys grow up into little men, and they grow stubborn. So you have to institute what I like to call 'creative punishment.' For their own good, of course." The smile never leaves his face. He's enjoying this way too much. Too much to be healthy, too much to be sane. Not that anyone will ever call him on it. Fenton had been the only one to break ranks, and look what Lazarus is doing to him.

"My boy, as you know, likes to think of himself as... independent. See, he doesn't appreciate all the *advantages* that I've afforded him over his short life. And he's happy to propose to someone with a questionable heritage, someone who is no doubt looking for a big payday after a few years."

My cheeks are burning, the blood rushing to my head. This man has the uncanny ability to get under anyone's skin. "I don't care about Fenton's money. Or yours."

"Believe it or not, but I actually think you're telling the truth." He holds his glass out to me in a mock salute and then takes a sip. "I actually quite like you, Winter. I wasn't sure before tonight, but it takes some balls to come in here and face me. Stronger and richer people have tried and failed, so I'll give you points for that."

"I'd hate to see what you do to the people you really *don't* like."

He considers that a moment. "No, you wouldn't. My actions are as much for your benefit as my son's. If you're going to be part of this family, you're not going to be skirting the edges, flitting to and fro as you see fit. Unity keeps a family strong. And strong families endure. Don't think I'm picking on you; I would test anyone my sons bring into my orbit."

"Is that what Laura did?" I swallow, unable to believe I'm about to ask this. "Is that why she... died?" The way he said it, I don't believe it was any kind of accident. But the question remains, who killed her? And if she is dead... who have I been talking to?

"I think that is enough for one night," he replies. "Not every secret needs telling."

"What if... what if I decide to go to the police?"

He laughs, almost choking on his drink. "I received a very interesting call from Detective Marsh today," he says, running his finger along his glass. "She told me you stopped by to see her."

I swallow again, *hard*.

"We both agreed it was best if she just destroyed your report. Better for everyone, don't you think?"

That's it. I've played my last card. He has the police in his pocket and the means to cover up any crime. He may have had Laura killed, and then found a way to make it all disappear. That would explain why Fenton destroyed everything of hers; why he keeps nothing around. It isn't because he doesn't want to. It's because it would be evidence in her murder.

Suddenly, I'm not so sure I'm going to be able to walk out of this house as easily as I walked in.

As I take a deep breath, ready to ask him if he's going to kill me, the door flies open to reveal Warren, his face flushed, and his breath ragged.

"Sir!"

Lazarus looks up, and within seconds he's on his feet and out the door behind Warren without giving me a second glance. I'm momentarily startled, not sure what's happening. I stand to follow, only to realize I've been left alone in this man's study. I need to make my escape now. I'll never get a better chance.

I leave the office and retrace my steps back out to the main atrium, following not only my original path, but a cacophony of voices coming from the front entrance. I turn the corner to find

Lazarus yelling at two men I don't know, while Abagail stands, her hand over her mouth.

When I peer around the corner, I'm surprised to see Fenton standing beside Warren, both of them tending to a man seated, with his back to me.

And from the looks on their faces, I can tell something is very wrong.

THIRTY-FOUR

WINTER

"Fenton?" I ask, my escape momentarily forgotten. "What are you doing here?"

Abagail looks up, tears in her eyes as Fenton turns away from the man slumped in the chair. "What are you waiting for?" Lazarus roars. "Get him downstairs immediately!" The two men hoist the figure in the chair up between them and help him down the corridor. As they turn, I gasp, realizing it's Brian. His face is covered in burns and his eyes are closed. I can't tell if he's breathing or not.

"Oh my God," I say. "What happened? He needs to go to a hospital!"

"There's a medical area downstairs," Fenton says, approaching me and leading me away from the crowd. "Dad has a surgeon on retainer; they're already on the way."

"On retainer? For what?" I'm practically screaming. "What do you need a surgical center for? In a house!"

"Trust me, you don't want to know." Fenton wraps his arms around me, dragging me away from his parents and Warren who are following Brian and the others down the corridor. "Let's go. You don't want to be here for this."

"What happened to him?" I sniff the air. It smells of sulfur and ash, and it's coming from Fenton. "What happened to *you*?" I note his grip on my arm and pull free from it. He doesn't fight me.

"Brian thought he'd found the person sending the books. It was a trap. It almost killed both of us."

I pivot, grabbing him, struck with the possibility that he might be hurt, which pulls at something primal in me. "Are *you* okay?"

He waves me off. "I'm fine. I was far enough away. Brian was a lot closer. He lost consciousness in the car on the way over."

"Good," I say, surveying him. "You're sure you're not hurt?"

He nods again. This is the closest we've been physically since the book arrived. But at the moment I don't care. I can't believe he was almost killed. Everyone else has already gone with Brian, leaving just the two of us. But I can hear the opening and closing of large doors in the distance. "Can they help him here? Wouldn't he be better off—"

"We can't risk it. I seriously thought about it, but then they'd start asking questions and anyone who saw the house explode would figure out we were there. That's information we don't want going around."

I take a step back. "It's your brother's life. Who cares if anyone knows if you were there or not?"

"In cases like this, we don't get emergency services involved. There's paperwork, and we can't chase down this person and deal with an inquiry as to why we were in someone's house when it exploded."

"You really are your father's son after all," I say.

He furrows his brow and looks at me. "What?"

"Nothing. Did you say *house explosion*?" Everything is coming so fast it's taking my brain a second to catch up.

"Mobile home. If someone hadn't texted and warned me, we would have both been inside when it went off. We were lucky."

Warren returns to the hallway, his face somewhat flushed. He doesn't say anything, only stands by the hallway where they took Brian, his hands clasped in front of him.

I return my attention to Fenton. "Who warned you?"

"No idea. It came from a blocked number. I'm just glad they did."

So now my fiancé has a guardian angel?

"I need to sit down," I say. I find an ornate chair in the massive foyer. I reach it just in time to feel all the strength leave my legs. This is getting serious; could this explosion be connected to the books? "Okay," I say. "Why did the house explode? And what were you doing?"

"I assume it was a trap in case someone that wasn't supposed to came snooping," he says. "Brian had a lead on the person living there. Said the address matched to a car he'd seen in our neighborhood that might have been surveilling the house. So we went over there."

Is he telling me that there really *is* someone out there watching us? Keeping tabs on us? "Do you know who it is?"

He shakes his head. "The house is registered to 'Cary Grant,' and unless a movie star from the last century has risen from the grave, we have no idea who it could be. I saw a dark figure running away after the explosion. But that's it."

"And Brian...?"

"Caught the edge of the blast. He's got some pretty bad burns. But don't worry. Dad knows some of the best doctors around."

I scoff. "I bet he does." What sort of business doesn't have surgeons on retainer for when employees or family members almost get blown up?

Silence fills the air between us as I try to process everything. Part of me wants to go back into Lazarus's study and search it now, knowing he definitely won't be coming back for a while. The other part just wants to give all this up, to leave Fenton and this insane family behind. I don't need this.

"Wait, what are you doing here?" Fenton asks, bringing me back out of it. "I didn't think you wanted my family to have the book."

"They don't," I shoot back. "I came here to confront your father. To force him to tell me what's going on."

His eyes go wide. "Did he... uh..."

"Don't worry, apparently I'm not good enough to know, given that I'm just marrying you for your money."

"No, you're not. Is that what he said?"

I push myself out of the chair. "I don't want to get into it." I shoot a look at Warren. He stands impassive and as still as a Roman centurion. The last thing I want to do is give Lazarus's spy more information he can report back to his boss about me.

"Where are you going?" he asks.

"A hotel," I reply. "Unless you don't plan on going home tonight. Then I'll stay there."

"You can't," Fenton says. "We don't know if it's safe. Whoever broke in is still out there. Why don't you stay here? There are plenty of bedrooms."

"I don't think so." Wasn't this the same man who just a few days ago wanted nothing to do with his father? And now he's willing to stick around and let Daddy take care of everything? "What happened to not wanting to be part of this madness? Of this life?"

"Winter, I *am* part of it. Whether I like it or not. I was almost killed tonight. I can't just pretend like it didn't happen."

"I'm not asking you to," I half shout. "But that doesn't mean you have to be a lapdog to that monster you call a father."

It doesn't escape my notice that Warren visibly tenses.

"I'm not a lapdog. I don't even want to be here. But I *have* to. At least right now. At least until this is sorted out."

"So you'll reject your father, but only when it's convenient. Is that it?" I make my way towards the door.

"Hey!" he yells after me. "That's not fair."

I spin on him, the full fury of everything I've felt the past four days coming to a head. "Fair? You want to know what's not fair? How about the man you promised to love for eternity keeping enough secrets to fill a vault with? About learning that he was previously married from the *other* woman? Is that fair?"

He looks away, his eyes downcast.

"All I want is a straight and clear answer. That's all I've ever wanted."

He hesitates. Here it is, the crux of everything. He's still keeping secrets from me, despite his promises to be honest. For whatever reason, he can't make the right decision. Why can't he just stop lying and tell me? What's he so afraid of?

I don't think he's going to say anything, but he drops his head. "Then ask. Ask whatever you want and I will tell you the truth."

My eyes are already wet, but I don't bother wiping them away. I want to leave him standing here, looking foolish, but he's laid down the gauntlet, which means I need to pick it up. There's only one way to tell if he's ready to be honest with me or not. After this, I'll know for sure if this relationship has any chance of a future or not.

I steel myself. "Then tell me. Is Laura dead?"

Fenton lifts his head, stares directly into my eyes, and nods.

It can't be true. I expected Lazarus to lie, and at this point I shouldn't be surprised by Fenton doing the same. Then again, Fenton has successfully lied to me for years and I never saw it. Maybe I'm not seeing it right now.

I take a breath, centering myself. "Then can you explain to me who I've been talking to the past four days?"

His brow creases and he shoots a cursory glance to Warren. "What?"

"I met a woman. She claimed to be Laura Blackwell. She was the one who told me you were married before. And that you had been physically violent with her."

"That's... not possible," he says.

"She also told me about the hatch in the floor of the house."

"No," he says, more to himself than me.

I glare at him under hooded eyes. "It's what happened."

He takes me by the shoulders. "Winter, I swear to you. Laura is dead. She died eight years ago."

I pull out of his grasp for the second time. I don't want his hands on me. "I don't even know why I asked. You're just going to lie no matter what."

"It's not a lie," he insists. For a moment I pause from the intensity of his voice. He shoots a glance at Warren who looks like he wants to step forward and say something, but he remains rooted to the spot.

"Then prove it. Take me to her grave," I say.

Fenton stands there, his mouth open for a moment. He turns back to Warren, who looks similarly alarmed before looking me in the eye again. Fenton sputters. "I... I can't do that."

"Why not?"

"She was cremated."

I scoff. "That's convenient. I suppose you scattered her ashes in the ocean?" I say, all of it with an air of skepticism. If Laura is dead, then who did I meet at the Stone Inn Deli? And why would she pretend to be someone she's not?

"It's true, Miss," Warren says, finally stepping forward. "Laura died eight years ago. I was there. We all were."

While I don't doubt Warren would lie for the family he works for, there's something about the conviction in his voice. And he is now the third person who has told me she's dead.

I swallow, hard. Suddenly, my throat is very dry. I don't know what it is, but the both of them insisting it's true makes me consider the possibility. "How did she die?"

Fenton and Warren exchange glances. "Maybe you should come and sit down," Fenton says, regaining his composure. "Come into the kitchen. I'll get you some water. You look like you're about to topple over." He holds his hands out to me, about to take me again, but I step away.

"Fenton, *how*?"

"She was... murdered," he says.

I look at him, then at Warren, then at this entire house. And finally it all makes sense. The veiled threats from Lazarus, the cover-up, all the work this family has done to bury their secrets. Laura tried to come into this family but, just like me, hadn't quite fit. And eventually they had just gotten sick of her. So they disposed of her, just like Lazarus had told me I would be. Was this what happened when you didn't measure up to the Byrnes name?

Is anyone who doesn't fit the mold branded a problem and removed?

Not only that, but I think about what Lazarus said about his son. That Fenton had a temper. He already admitted to hurting her. Did he kill her as well?

"Was it you?"

"Win... please," he says. "Let's just talk about this. You're talking nonsense."

I back away from Fenton and Warren; I have to get out of this house, away from these people. If I stay here I'll end up just like her. I pull the engagement ring off my finger and toss it at Fenton. It hits him in the chest and falls to the floor, clinking on the marble. "Stay away from me," I say.

"Winter, you don't understand," he says, reaching out for me. Warren approaches as well. This is how it's going to happen. I know their secret now; they can't let me leave, I'm too much of a security risk. "Come on, let's just..."

I shake my head. If he thinks he's keeping me in this house, he's sorely mistaken. I reach behind me and feel the large wooden door, my only escape route. I manage to press the handle, the door opening at my touch. I half expected it to be locked, but they might not have had a chance after what happened with Brian.

"Miss—" Warren says as I get the door open. "Please."

I turn and bolt for my car, fumbling for the keys in my pocket, thinking any second I'm going to trip and fall face first on the gravel. But I manage to reach my car as Fenton and Warren come rushing out of the house after me. But instead of chasing me to the car, Fenton stays on the porch, watching me. I don't question my good luck; I just get in the car as fast as possible.

Without looking back I throw the car into reverse and peel out, then kick the car into drive and floor it, sending up dirt and gravel all over the place. Half of it hits my car, but right now I don't care. I barrel down the driveway, not even bothering to slow. I'll slam through those gates if I have to, but I find they're already open when I get back to the entrance. I don't question it. I just need to get as far away from this place as I possibly can.

What now?

Fenton will tell his dad I know their secret. And Lazarus may sic the cops on me. He already has full control over Marsh. I can't go back home—Fenton has access to the house and would probably have people waiting there for me.

I fumble for my phone, dialing my mother's number. It would be a good two-hour drive, but at least I'd be safe. But it goes straight to voicemail. It's very possible she's not even home right now, maybe even off on one of her mission trips. And I have almost nothing with me to my name. My overnight bag is still in the foyer of the house from where I used it to get away from Fenton the first time.

I gun it when I reach the blacktop, skidding onto the double yellow. All that matters is getting away. If it's really true and Laura is dead, then who have I been talking to? Someone impersonating her? There's no doubt in my mind now that she's the one who's been sending the books, but to what end?

It doesn't matter. I can't be involved in this anymore. It's going to end up getting me killed. I've stumbled into some mafia-level shit here and I'm not about to stick around to be silenced when I voice a differing opinion. But what does that mean? Do I leave my job? Leave town permanently? I can't exactly stay here; Lazarus has people everywhere. I need to get as far away as possible, maybe California. Maybe Canada. Just somewhere they won't look for me.

"Goddammit!" I yell, rolling down all the windows, feeling the cold wind whip through the car. I need to feel the cold up against my skin, to remember that I *can* feel. That I haven't been sucked into this so far that I'm not still me. This is so much worse than Thomas. If I'd just walked away the minute I realized Fenton was keeping things from me, none of this would be happening. I might not even be on Lazarus's radar. But it's too late for that now.

Whoever "Laura" is, she's done me a massive favor. I never

would have known about any of this if not for those books showing up. They were the key; they cracked this world open for me to see. Maybe she wasn't completely honest with me either, but she dropped the breadcrumbs for me to find, and they've led me here. And they may have just saved my life. I owe her a debt I can't repay.

And then there's the real Laura. Fenton's victim. The woman who dared to get involved in a family and was killed for it. No wonder Fenton had been acting so strange when that book arrived. For him it must have been like seeing a ghost. *Good.* It's what he deserves.

This also explains the signature on the divorce papers. They're like Jack said, a forgery. Because Laura was already dead. And Lazarus covered it up.

Oh my God. What have I gotten myself into here? And how do I get out? All I know is my head is spinning with everything that's happened. I need refuge... a place to figure things out, determine my next move.

And unfortunately there's only one place I can think of.

But it's going to take some groveling.

THIRTY-SIX
WINTER

When I pull up and cut the car off, it's almost eight. Hopefully it's not too late. I park on the side of the road as not to appear too presumptuous. Cammie's dog-cleaning van sits in her driveway, beside Mike's truck. I make my way around the long fence and to the front door, knocking instead of ringing the bell.

I'm not sure anyone will answer, but I'm out of options. There are only so many hotels in this town and I'm sure Lazarus's people will check them all looking for me. And I'm so exhausted that if I try driving, I'm afraid I'll fall asleep. Honestly, if Cammie doesn't answer, I'm going to have to find a parking lot somewhere and sleep in my car. If sleep is even possible.

Just as I'm about to give up, something shuffles behind the door and the latch turns. The door opens to reveal Cammie, fully dressed in her new official "uniform." Though her slacks are peppered with water spots from a full day's work.

"I... Um." Suddenly, I've lost my nerve again. "I came by earlier... with coffee," I say. "Thought we could catch up."

"I was out all day working," she says, her voice cold and indifferent.

Nodding, I swallow hard. "How's it going? With the van?"

"Is that really what you came here to say?"

"No," I reply. "I came to say I'm sorry for not being there for you when you needed me. I know I've been a horrible friend this past week. You've always been the only person who was there for me, no matter what. It's hard for me to reciprocate that sometimes. I'm not the best with maintaining relationships."

"You can say that again. I really needed you this week, Win. This is a big deal for me, starting this business. I wanted my best friend with me to celebrate."

"I know. I've been selfish. And too wrapped up in my own shit. *Again.*"

Her mouth forms a thin line, and her face remains stern. She isn't going to forgive me this time; I've burned this bridge and there's no way back. I drop my eyes. "I just want you to know I love you. Because if I never get to talk to you again, I want it to be the last thing you remember about me. Not... not everything else." I take one last look at her, hoping for any kind of break in her stone façade. Seeing nothing, I head back down the steps.

"God, you can be so dramatic sometimes," Cammie says behind me. My heart springs because I know that voice. It's the voice of resigned indignation. "I'm not going to stop being your friend just because we had a fight. This is the thing you don't seem to get. One event isn't worth throwing everything away. At least it isn't to me."

I walk back up to the door. "It isn't to me either."

Cammie's face softens. "I know." She pauses. "You look like shit."

"A lot's happened." I glance down both sides of the neighborhood. "I know this is asking a lot considering I just said I wasn't going to make everything about me anymore, but... can I stay here tonight?"

"Of course you can," she says, stepping aside. "What happened? Did you meet up with that woman again?"

"Oh... no, it's a lot more than that."

· · ·

An hour later I've changed into a comfortable pair of Cammie's spare pajamas and am sitting at her kitchen table, holding a warm cup of tea in my hands while Cammie and Mike sit on opposite sides of the table, listening to my story.

In a way, relating everything to them after the book showed up is cathartic, more than it was when I tried to tell Detective Marsh, who kept questioning every little detail.

But Cammie and Mike just let me go with it, not interrupting the entire time.

I find it's more helpful than I realized to go over it all again, just for my own benefit. So much has happened I find myself taking a second to make sure I get the sequence of everything right. When I'm done Cammie just stares at me, processing.

Finally, she gets up and comes over, wrapping me in a hug. I tense at first but eventually relax, allowing some of the tension I've built up over the past few days to flow out of me.

"I am so sorry," she whispers. "If I had known—"

"I didn't want to burden you with it," I say. "I already felt bad enough."

She pulls back. "Win. This isn't the kind of thing you can handle on your own. You know that right? I'm—we're here for you." She turns to Mike who hasn't said a single word this entire time. "Right?"

He nods. "Absolutely." Mike is a big guy who gives off football-center vibes. He's the kind of man people hire to be the bouncer at a club as his biceps are about as thick as my neck. "We got your back."

"Thanks," I say, smiling.

"Okay. What do we need to do?" Cammie asks. "How can we help?"

"I'm not sure. I don't know what to do anymore. Part of me says I should just run... get out of town and start a new life somewhere." I clear my throat. "But then I think about Laura. And how she'll never have justice for what happened to her. I don't know... In some strange way I feel connected to her. Like I understand what she went through, living with Fenton. She didn't deserve to die for it."

"Do you think Lazarus killed her?" Cammie asks.

"Maybe. But he'd never get his own hands dirty. If he is behind it, he hired someone else to do it," I say. "He's ruthless. And he didn't have any trouble threatening me. The man is power-hungry. But really... I think Fenton did it."

"You think he's capable? He's always seemed so..." she trails off.

"So?"

"Well, wimpy," she finally says. "I mean, not in a bad way. But like in a sensitive way."

I nod. "I know what you mean. But I've seen these flashes lately... a temper I didn't know was there. He said he'd been in therapy a while, probably trying to deal with that. Eight years ago? He was probably much worse. He probably just lost control one night. And then he did what he always does... he called his family to come clean up his mess. Plus, he admitted to bruising her. He could have escalated."

"Wait," Mike says. "I'm confused. If the woman you met *isn't* Laura, how would she know about the bruises?"

"No idea," I say. "Honestly, everything about her is a mystery. I've been trying to get back in contact with her, but she's either ducking my calls or something's happened."

"Do you think Lazarus might have gotten to her?" Cammie asks.

"I don't know." I may not know who this mystery woman really is, but she very well could have saved my life. I owe her.

"Okay, so we know you can't go to the police," Cammie says. "What about your neighbor's FBI friend? Surely Lazarus doesn't have him in his pocket?"

I sit back and take a sip of the cooling tea. "That's true. He might have connections. Someone *outside* of town we could trust to investigate this." While I don't want to stay in the middle of this, I also don't want to be looking over my shoulder for the rest of my life. If we can somehow prove Fenton killed Laura and Lazarus helped cover it up, I'd be home free. They'd be in jail and I could finally get back to my life. I am done with this insane family and everything that comes with it.

"Yeah," I say. "I think that might work."

"Great," Mike says. "Problem solved."

Cammie glares at him. "That's right, honey. It's so simple." She gives him a little placating pat on the head.

He purses his lips. "I'm not one of your dogs."

"Yes, you are, you just don't know it." She turns back to me. "You know, if Hulk over here had this much baggage, I'd have left long ago."

"Hey!" Mike protests.

"Oh, don't worry, you big baby. I know all about your 'tawdry past.'" She uses air quotes.

Mike grimaces until it becomes a heavy frown.

"Tawdry past?" I ask.

Cammie turns back to me, an excited smile on her lips. "Oh yeah. He shadowed a male stripper for a few months. Didn't have the nerve for the stage, though."

"Jesus, Cams! That's private!" Mike sputters.

"I know, honey. But it's a good thing. See, Winter has more respect for you now that you abandoned the pole life." She motions to me, and whatever expression is plastered across my face makes her crack a huge grin. I can't imagine Mike as a stripper, but as soon as I think about it, I form a mental image and begin giggling. I guess I can imagine it after all. It feels good to laugh again. I can't remember the last time. Mike, for all the ribbing, has crossed his arms, but he's wearing a bit of a smirk behind his grimace.

I've missed this. I've missed my friends, a life outside of Fenton's family drama and everything else that's come along with it. There's no doubt in my mind. Tomorrow I'll contact Janet again and hopefully figure a way out of this mess.

For now, I'm just happy to have a place to sleep.

THIRTY-SEVEN

FENTON

"She thinks I'm a killer," Fenton said to no one in particular as he watched Winter's taillights disappear around the path of the driveway leading away from his family's house. He didn't dare chase her a second time—he'd already done enough damage. Both psychologically and physically. He hadn't been able to take his eyes off that cracked window on her car.

"Sir."

Warren's voice brings him back. He turned to see the man standing behind him at a close-enough distance. Fenton frowned. How had things gotten so out of control? First the book, then the break-in and now Brian fighting for his life in the medical wing. And on top of it, his fiancée thought he could have actually *killed* Laura.

"I need to speak to my father," Fenton said as he headed back to the house.

"I'm sure he's still downstairs with your brother," Warren said, accompanying him back to the house.

"He's not a surgeon," Fenton said. "He doesn't need to be there."

Warren stiffened. "I'll inform him you want to speak with him." The man who had worked for his father longer than Fenton had been alive headed off for the medical ward. This was getting out of control. Winter had met with... someone. Someone pretending to be Laura. Obviously, whoever it was, they were the one responsible for sending the books. And also most likely responsible for Brian's condition.

Fenton headed into his father's study. The room was more opulent than those owned by some kings. It was a disgusting display of wealth and power and Fenton wanted nothing to do with it. He'd turned away from this life long ago and he wasn't about to get sucked back into it. They needed to do something about this *woman*. First and foremost, finding her and putting a stop to all this.

What he couldn't figure out was if she was going to all this trouble, why had there been no demands? Obviously, she wasn't looking for money. So what was her motivation?

He tried racking his brain. There had to be something he'd missed eight years ago. Of course, he'd only been twenty-five at the time. His father and Brian had taken care of the dirty work. And that had been when Fenton had decided he could no longer be part of his family's business. Any of it.

A half-consumed glass of bourbon sat on his father's desk. Fenton grabbed it and downed the remainder of the liquid, the spicy notes burning all the way down.

"Make yourself right at home."

Fenton turned to see his father in the doorway, his normally immaculate white shirt unbuttoned at the collar and his hair frazzled. He hadn't seen his father like that in a long time.

"How's Brian?"

"They're working on him now. The doctor is hopeful the internal damage isn't too bad. You were right to bring him here."

"Wow. Was that actually a compliment?" Fenton said as his father walked over to the bar and poured himself another drink in a fresh glass.

"Merely stating facts." He downed the full drink. "Your fiancée came to see me."

"I saw," Fenton said. "There's a problem."

His father scoffed. "I told you that the day you began dating her."

"Not Winter," Fenton reiterated. "Someone approached her. Someone claiming to be Laura. That's how she found out about my first marriage."

His father had been about to pour himself another drink but stopped short, setting the glass and bottle down. "I know."

Fenton furrowed his brow. "Then what are we going to do about it?"

"We?" Lazarus turned to face him. "We aren't going to do anything. I'm handling it."

"Like you handled Laura?"

"Careful, boy," he growled. "You will not speak to me that way in my own house. I saved your ass. I can just as easily throw you to the wolves again."

Fenton shook his head. "I'm tired of being intimidated by you. I didn't do anything wrong."

"Those bruises on her arm say different. Or did you forget I have photographs of those?"

He paused. "You'd turn in your own son?"

Lazarus didn't answer. Instead he returned to his drink, making himself a fresh one before taking residence in his chair again, leaning back. "Don't worry about this woman. We will find her. And we'll put a stop to all this nonsense."

Fenton didn't need him to answer. He already knew what his father would do if his back was against the wall. It was one of the reasons he'd left in the first place. Still, the mystery woman wasn't their only problem. "But Winter... She thinks I killed her."

"Good." Lazarus took a sip.

"*Good?*"

"She isn't the woman for you, son. I tried telling you that before. She's bad stock. Comes from her upbringing. She's too emotionally charged and too unpredictable to be part of this family. As this incident shows."

"She's just a normal person," he reiterated. "*We're* the anomaly here. The family who doesn't go to the hospital and instead has their wounds treated by a private doctor in their own home as not to arouse suspicion. The family who has the resources to make *people disappear* and no one questions it. No. It's not her. It's us."

"Wouldn't you rather be a wolf than a lamb?" His father shot him a wicked grin.

"Not if it costs me my humanity," Fenton said. "I've already lied to her enough. And all it's done is push her away from me. I'm going to find her and tell her the truth. *All* of it."

"It's a waste of time," Lazarus replied. "She'll never believe you."

"At least I can say I tried," Fenton said. "At least my conscience will be clear." He headed for the door.

"Son."

Fenton stopped, looking over his shoulder.

"You do this, you don't come back, understand? I won't sacrifice everything we've built here because you're having a bout of puppy love."

"She deserves to know."

"All you're doing is putting a target on her back," the older man replied.

"Yeah, and you're the one holding the gun," Fenton said, and headed out of the study and down the long corridor to the front room. Warren stood near the doors, his hands clasped in front of him.

"Any update on Brian?"

He shook his head. "Nothing yet."

"Will you call me if there are any developments? I can't count of my family to keep me in the loop."

Warren nodded. "Of course. Where are you headed?"

"I need to find Winter. See if I can try to explain this mess."

Warren hesitated, his eyes glancing in the direction of Lazarus's study.

"I know," Fenton added. "He's already warned me of the

consequences. But I have to try and fix this. Before I completely lose her forever."

Warren pressed his lips together. "Good luck, sir."

Fenton headed outside and hopped in his car, backing out of the group of other cars. He then followed Winter's tracks all the way to the front gate. He couldn't help but smile. Resetting the gravel on the drive would cost Dad a good five figures when it was all said and done. It wasn't much, but he'd appreciate the little victories where he could.

It was unlikely she'd gone back home, given her state of mind. And he knew trying to call or text would only result in pushing her farther away. He needed to talk to her face to face. Explain what he should have explained from the beginning. Why hadn't he just told her the truth? Why had he been so adamant about keeping his father's secrets? His future was with Winter, not his family. But he'd been keeping them so long he'd forgotten there was another way.

And it had taken Winter practically accusing him of being a murderer before he saw it.

It was possible she could have returned to the hotel, or a different hotel in the city. Or she might have even gone to her mother's house, though that was a good two-to-three-hour drive.

He'd check the hotels around town first, make sure she hadn't shown up at any of those first before he went traipsing all the way to Boston.

But there was another possibility. Cammie.

Fenton only really knew Cammie through Winter. They'd met and hung out a handful of times, but because Winter was so bad at keeping up with her friends, those times were few and far between. Cammie hadn't even seen the house after he'd finished it. Were they still on close terms? It pained him to realize he didn't even know.

But it was worth checking out.

As he drove he found her address by looking up that new business she stared—the dog grooming thing. It listed her home address as the primary business address, and it wasn't very far away. Only a twenty-minute drive.

However, as Fenton turned on Pierce Highway, he noticed a pair of headlights growing larger in his rearview. He thought they'd pass him, but they got all the way up on his tail, to the point where he couldn't see anything else in the rearview and had to shield his eyes from the brightness.

"Just go around," he yelled, though it would have been impossible for them to hear him.

If they weren't going around, then he'd just have to get away from this psycho. He stepped on the gas, speeding to ten, fifteen, and finally twenty over the speed limit.

And the other car kept up with him the whole way.

All of a sudden, he didn't think they were just an asshole driver anymore. And as he was about to step on the brake, his car lurched forward as he was struck from behind.

Fenton kept both hands on the wheel, trying to keep himself on the road. *What the hell?*

His car lurched again, and his seat belt tightened, pulling him tight against the leather seats.

Whoever this was, they were going to run him off the road. Maybe even kill him.

He hit the gas again, hoping to get away from them at whatever speed it took. But he was rammed a third time as he did, this time from the driver's side corner.

The back of the Mercedes fishtailed and he tried to overcorrect, but it ended up only causing him to skid in the other direction.

The next thing Fenton knew, he was airborne.

THIRTY-EIGHT

WINTER

I manage to get better sleep on Cammie's sofa than I have had for the past week. And I'm awoken by the smell of fresh coffee brewing. When I sit up and look over the edge of the couch, Cammie stands in the kitchen in her sweats, running the pot.

"Sorry, didn't mean to wake you."

I run my hand through my hair. "It's no problem. Smells good."

"Colombian frap," she says. "Want one?"

"I'd love one."

She finishes brewing and brings over a pair of mugs, sitting across from me in the only other chair in her living room. Their home is modest, but it's warm... comfortable. I don't feel like if I move something out of place here that it will upset the balance.

"Have you ever thought about getting a dog of your own?" I ask.

"Pretty much every one I wash," she says. "Are you looking to adopt?"

"Maybe one day," I say. "If Fenton and I are done... really done. Then, yeah. He never wanted one. Always said it was too much to deal with."

"Obviously he's never had a pet."

"Considering how he grew up, are you surprised?"

She chuckles. "Hey, I washed your clothes, just in case. I wasn't sure if you were going back to the house."

I shake my head. "He's probably waiting there. I don't want to risk it. I can just buy new clothes."

"You're not ever going back?"

"I'll send someone for my things, eventually," I say. "Right now I just want to focus on getting the spotlight on that whole family."

She nods, but I can see a sadness in her features. "What?"

"I just hate that it didn't work out." She takes a sip. "After everything you went through with Thomas."

"I might have judged Thomas too harshly," I admit. "But I was young and stupid. With Fenton... I really tried to make it work. I wanted to trust him... and I did. And then..."

"Yeah."

"Morning," Mike says, trudging into the kitchen.

"Morning," we both say in unison. I smile. It's been a long time since Cammie and I have spent this much time together. We need to do it more often.

"You mind if I take a quick shower?" I ask. "I may have to go back over to Jack's place, and I don't want to smell like day-old Winter if I do."

Cammie chuckles. "Sure. Just don't use all the hot water."

I take my mug with me to the bathroom. As I stare at myself in the mirror, it's not hard to tell this has taken its toll on me. There are bags the size of pillows under my eyes and my skin is a sallow color. I haven't been eating enough the past few days. Maybe Cammie and Mike will let me take them out for breakfast... Only I remember that I'm probably being hunted. No, the first thing I need to do is contact Janet. Given how she was looking at Jack the other day, I have no doubt he'd be willing to pick up the phone at a moment's notice for her. And once we get a plan in place, *then* maybe I can start to relax. But not before.

It feels good to take a shower without worrying Fenton is around. I wish I could stay under the water all day. But by the time I emerge, I feel energized and the smell of sizzling bacon and eggs reaches my nose. I return to the kitchen to find Mike has crafted a hearty breakfast for everyone.

"Help yourself," he says.

"Just don't get between Mike and the waffles," Cammie replies. "He'll bite your hand off."

"I'll be careful." I laugh, as I fill up a plate. It all looks delicious. And it turns out Mike can cook. It's some of the best food I've had in a long time.

"Careful, babe. She's gonna give you a run for your money on how much she can eat."

"Sorry," I say with my mouth full of eggs. "I guess I'm hungrier than I thought."

By the time we're done, their kitchen looks like a warzone.

"I can help clean up," I say.

"Nonsense." Cammie pushes me back to the living room. "Get on the phone. We'll take care of this."

"Are you sure?"

She looks at me like I'm crazy. "Haven't you ever been a guest at someone's house before? We don't make guests clean."

Wow, I really have been out of the social scene for a while.

Grateful that Cammie opened the door for me last night and I didn't have to sleep in my car, I head back into the living room and ring Janet. She picks up on the first call.

"Winter?"

"Hi, Janet. Yeah. Good morning. Is this a bad time?"

"Of course not. Are you okay? What happened with the records?"

"Well, that's actually why I'm calling," I say. "I... I tried going to the police... but it didn't work out so well."

"Oh, no."

"So I was hoping I could talk to Jack—Mr. Keever—again about my options. Things have gotten... complicated."

"Of course," she says. "I'm sure he'd be thrilled to help. I think he misses it, you know? The investigations."

I give Cammie the thumbs-up and she shoots one back to me. "Well, that's good to hear. Because I really could use some advice."

Half an hour later I'm back at Mr. Keever's house. Cammie volunteered to come along, but that would have meant canceling on the clients she had booked for today and I wasn't about to let her do that. She's already done more than enough for me, she's not going to sacrifice her business because of me too. Plus, this is just a strategizing meeting.

Mr. Keever welcomes me into his house for the second time, and I go through the entire story, start to finish. From the minute the book showed up on my doorstep to my final escape from Fenton last night, including Lazarus's not-so-veiled threats against me.

Janet sits nearby, listening to the entire story. I feel like the more people I can talk to about this, the less scary it becomes. The Byrneses derive their power from isolating and intimidating. And they're not going to do that to me any longer.

"Then the only people who can corroborate the story work for Lazarus Byrnes," Mr. Keever finally says once I've finished.

"Pretty much. I don't have any other witnesses, if that's what you're asking."

"Damn." He gets up, pacing the room. "I know Detective Marsh. She's a good cop. I can't believe she's in Byrnes's pocket."

"It seems like everyone in this town is," I say. "No one would be crazy enough to go against him."

"Except you, apparently."

"Yeah. I guess."

"Winter," Janet says, leaning forward. "I know this is a lot. But... what if you just left? Surely they wouldn't hold that against you."

"You don't know Lazarus Byrnes," I say. "He made that apparent in not so many words. Especially now that I know his secrets."

"She's right," Keever says. "She's a potential witness against him now. But you, by yourself, isn't enough. We need solid proof. Phone records. Documentation. A statement from Laura would be the clincher, but obviously that's impossible."

"No, it isn't," I say, remembering. "Before Brian came over to the house, I stashed a couple of her manuscripts in my closet at the house. They had handwritten notes in them. Almost like a manifesto."

He pinches his features. "I'm afraid a couple of manuscripts won't be enough to prosecute for murder. The defense would just argue they were meant to be fiction."

"I don't think they were," I say. "I think they were a record... of Fenton's actions towards Laura. Of how trapped she felt." Now that I think about it, given everything she was going through, it makes perfect sense. What I thought had been nothing more than an inventive story was actually a woman making a record of everything she was witnessing. Everything happening to her. And maybe even making plans for a way out. I got the distinct impression the protagonist wasn't just about to accept her situation in those books. She was going to get out, no matter what it took. It's part of what made them so compelling.

Keever's face is still pulled in consternation.

"Let me at least get them for you. Then you can make a determination."

"But wouldn't you have to go back to the house to do that?" Janet asks.

I nod. "I can wait until Fenton is gone. His brother is still critical. My bet is, if he's there now, he won't be for long. And if he's already gone, he'll probably stay gone for a while. He'll want to be with the family."

"You can use my driveway to keep watch if you want," Janet says. "You can see part of the front of your home from there. It's not perfect, but it'll be better than sitting out on the street where he'll spot your car."

"In fact," Keever says, "why don't I go with you? Just in case."

"Oh, no, I couldn't let you do that," I say. "I know exactly where they are. It will take me two minutes to get in and out. I can be back here in twenty if he's not there." Not that I don't think Mr. Keever can hold his own. But he has to be in his early seventies. And I don't want him risking anything for me.

"Okay," the man says. "At least take my car. That way no one will be suspicious." He grabs a set of keys from the kitchen and tosses them to me.

"Are you sure?"

He nods. "Just bring the manuscripts back and we can take a look. I have a few friends who live out of Byrnes's reach. I'll see what they think. But it will be tough. No murder weapon, no witnesses. There will have to be something ironclad in those notes."

I nod. "Like her saying she based a scene off Fenton threatening to kill her."

"Exactly. I won't make any promises. But if we can find something like that, it'll be a start."

Janet reaches out as I head for the door. "Winter. Are you sure you want to do this?"

I nod. "Someone needs to stop them. And I feel like I owe it to Laura. She never made it out. He needs to pay for that."

She pats my arm. "Be careful. And good luck."

THIRTY-NINE
FENTON

"Good moooorning!" The singsong voice permeated the air, rousing Fenton from sleep. He was groggy, heavy. His entire body felt like it was full of lead. He tried lifting his head, finding it more difficult than normal. Where was he?

The crash.

His head snapped up. What felt like dried blood cracked on his forehead. But he couldn't move anything else. His arms were bound behind him. And so were his feet. He had been tied to a chair.

Spots danced in his eyes as he struggled to make sense of everything through the pounding headache. What was going on? But as he looked down at the chair and then his bindings, he realized he recognized the floor.

He was back home.

"Fenton? Honey, are you there?" He turned his head towards the voice. The quick movement caused his entire world to swim, and for a brief second he thought he might throw up and pass out at the same time.

He had a concussion. He needed a hospital. And not his father's fancy medical wing. A regular hospital where he could be seen by a *real* doctor.

Light flooded his eyes and he shut his eyelids reflexively, crying out at the sudden change as the curtains revealed it was much later than he thought.

"Oh, sorry. Guess I should have warned you." That voice. It was both familiar and strange at the same time.

"Who..." he asked, trying to squint at her, but his eyes wouldn't focus. All he could see was a dark outline against a bright white room.

"Don't you recognize me, my love? I came back. I couldn't bear being away too long. The divorce just isn't working for me." She ran her manicured fingers along his cheek. A soft, sensual motion that sent a tingle through him, despite the injuries. Finally, his vision began to focus. Her hair was dark and long down her back. And she wore the same glasses she always did. Was it her?

Impossible. Laura was dead.

"I don't understand," Fenton said, trying to move. But the more he did, the tighter his bonds felt.

"Now, don't move too much. I don't want you getting away from me," the woman said.

Fenton's vision finally cleared and she came into focus. Her face was familiar, similar to his wife, but it wasn't her. Not by a long shot. Maybe if he'd been a hundred yards away and only seen her from the back. She had a similar build, but everything else was wrong. Her hands, her nose, her eyes. And yet he'd seen her somewhere else before. But his head hurt so badly he couldn't figure out where.

"Who are you?" he said with more conviction. "And what are you doing in my house?" He'd been positioned in the living room, which itself had been rearranged. The couch was moved back and the rug had been rolled up again. The trap door was exposed but remained closed beside him.

"Not doing it for you, huh?" the woman said, facing him. "It was worth a shot." She removed her glasses and stuck them in a small bag. She extracted the book he and Winter had received last week. *The Last Man I'd Marry*. Funny title. Maybe 'funny' is the wrong word. Ironic title? What do you think?"

"Who the hell are you?" Fenton asked.

"Oh," the woman said, placing her hand on her chest and feigning a shocked expression. "You don't recognize me? You don't remember me at all? That really hurts."

"Should I?"

"I work for your father, you moron," she said, deadpan.

Now that she said it, he thought he remembered seeing her around his father's house a few times.

"I barely have any contact with my father's employees. Or him, for that matter."

"I know," the woman said. "I just thought you might remember the person who helped you clean up your mess the *first* time around." She raised the book up and brought it down hard on his thighs, creating a slapping sound that echoed throughout the house.

"Ow! Dammit, what was that for?"

"Just testing it out." She smiled. "The funny thing about you, Fenton, is you don't see the obvious. Now, I can't figure out if it's because you're dumb, or if it's because you're just naïve. Either way, it's probably not good for you." She tossed the book onto one of the couches. "Being an observant person is a skill everyone needs, and I'm afraid you just don't have it. Which is probably why you're in that chair, and why I'm standing here explaining this to you."

Fenton shook his head. "I still don't understand. What do you want? Why are you here? Are you looking to impress my father? Bring me in like I'm a bounty?"

The woman threw her head back and cackled. "You wish! No, no, my dear, blind Fenton Byrnes. My employment with your father officially terminated at nine forty-two p.m. last night, when I ran you off the road and carted your unconscious body back here. I have never cared about your father's business or his shortsighted attempts to rein control over this small corner of the northeast. I don't care about the work he hired me for, nor do I have any loyalty to him. What I care about... is you. It's always been about you." She leaned down and stared him directly in the eyes.

"Me? Why?"

She shot back up. "See, there it is, right there. You can't see what's staring you in the face. You just don't have it, honey." The woman tapped her lips with one finger. "Which is kind of distressing, knowing what you do for a living. I mean... isn't being detail-oriented kind of the defining characteristic of an architect?" She gave him a mirthless chuckle.

"Just tell me what you want from me," Fenton said, staring her in the eyes. At least she hadn't captured Winter too. But this must have been the woman pretending to be Laura. The one who told Winter everything.

"You are so frustrating!" the woman said, storming from the room. "Don't go anywhere. I'm coming right back," she called from the office. Fenton managed to turn his head so he could see the clock mounted in the kitchen. The time read 8:55.

She stormed back in with another book in her hands. But this one was thinner, with a glossy cover.

"What is... Is that *my* yearbook? How did you know where that was?"

"Oh, baby, I know where everything is. I spend a lot of time in this house."

"What?"

The woman clicked her tongue against her teeth a few times. "I mean, I tried to put everything back as I'd found it, but sometimes you just forget." She slapped herself upside the head. "Silly Rene."

"Rene?" That's right. She was here that morning, helping them with Laura's body. Lazarus had instructed her and Brian to take the body to be incinerated. He hadn't thought much of it at the time, he'd been in shock having come home to find his wife dead. "Now I remember you. You were here the night Laura died. You helped destroy her belongings."

"That's what I was supposed to do, yes."

"But you looked... different then. What happened to you?"

"Really? You're going to give me grief over a little plastic surgery? I'm not allowed to get a little work done? Men." She opened the yearbook and flipped a few of the pages. "I don't look *that* different."

She dropped the yearbook in his lap, pointing to one photograph. "Rene Lawson," he read. "We went to school together?"

"Sure did, dummy. But you wouldn't remember. We never crossed paths. In fact, I loathed you for most of my school career. You and your easy money, your easy life. But I watched you. I thought, *Rene, what makes him deserving of so much and me of so little? What has he done that makes him better than me?* And you know what I discovered?"

Fenton shook his head.

"Absolutely nothing! You were no better or worse than me. Maybe a little stuck-up, but overall you did what most kids did. It wasn't until I found out about your family I became really interested." She leaned in close to him. "And then I thought, *Maybe if I get close enough to his world, maybe then I'll figure it out.* There had to be something that made the universe choose you to have this privileged life, and not me." She paused. "Now," she said, her voice like a middle school teacher's, "I already know the answer to this, so don't bother lying. But I want to hear it from you. What is the most important thing in your life?"

"Winter," he said, not even hesitating.

Her hand moved faster than he thought possible, striking his cheek and sending spittle flying from his mouth.

"Try again."

"It's true. She is. More than anything."

SMACK!

"One more time. Think now."

He furrowed his brow. His cheek ached and was probably swelling. He'd never been hit by a woman before, but Rene packed one hell of a punch. "Freedom," he finally said, hanging his head.

"Ding! Winner!" Rene smiled wide. "The only thing you've

ever wanted was to get away from those shackles you call a family. And I couldn't quite understand it. I started working for your father right out of college. I'm sure he thinks he recruited me, but I made sure all the pertinent information fell right into his lap at the right time. I'm good at organizing. But as I continued to work my way deeper and deeper into your home life, all I saw from the shadows was you shunning it, pushing it all away. And maybe I'm just a fool, but I needed to understand it. Your family was what I'd been looking for my entire life. And you wanted to throw it away!"

"Because they're toxic!" Fenton yelled. "Can't you see that?"

Rene grew quiet for a moment. "Maybe." She flipped through the yearbook again. Coming to another page, she held it up for him. "Look familiar?"

Fenton squinted. It was a picture of the band practicing, the black-and-white grain of the photo blurring some of the details in the distance. He'd probably seen the photo before, but never thought anything of it. He hadn't been in band as a student and neither had anyone he'd known.

"Right here, hotshot," she said, tapping the page. Off to the side were two girls, laughing at something, but only one of them was turned towards the camera enough to capture her face.

"Is that... Laura?"

"That," Rene said slowly, "was my best friend." She sighed. "That's where you first met. In high school. Of course, you didn't date then because Laura wasn't interested in you. The boy with the stuck-up family and all the secrets. But as I observed you, I caught you sneaking glances at her. Trying to build up the courage to ask her out. I watched you waste three years and never acting on that impulse, not once." Rene turned around and sat on the couch opposite Fenton, her forearms on her knees and her hands hanging down.

"So it's a jealousy thing, then? I never paid any attention to you, and you're getting revenge for it."

Rene reared back, laughter erupting from her lungs. "You think I'm attracted to *you*?" she asked as soon as she caught her breath.

"It makes sense."

"No, it doesn't. Because I'm not interested in your kind."

"Guys?"

"*Toxicity*," she spat.

"What the hell are you talking about?" Fenton could feel the heat rising in his chest. This woman was crazy and this had gone on long enough. He wasn't about to be tortured by some high school crush gone awry.

"It was that chance meeting in college that did it. You found the woman you'd been gaga over for years and had never made a move on. And she was everything you hoped she'd be and more. And you were charming and sociable and loving. The only problem was, that wasn't the real you. Was it?"

Rene picked up the discarded book on the couch, flipping through its pages. "Do you know why she wrote these?" she asked. Fenton didn't feel like giving her the dignity of a response. "She wrote them because she realized a life with you was a prison sentence. But you never read them. Did you support her at all?"

He dropped his gaze. "I knew what they were about." As much as he'd tried to ignore them or pretend that her books didn't exist, Fenton knew she'd been writing as a way to excise her demons. Demons that had come from their... troubled relationship. There had been a reason she'd chosen those titles. *The Last Man I'd Marry. Undesirable. What He Did.*

The other woman was quiet for a moment. "And yet you still didn't let her go. Even when she asked you to."

"I couldn't," he admitted. "My father—"

"Your father wasn't married to her. He wasn't here, day after day, watching a woman disappear into herself as she sank under the weight of your ego. Of your desire to build your business, to create something bigger and better than your father ever could. You were killing her day by day and you didn't even see it."

Fenton winced. How many times had she asked for a divorce? And how many times had he convinced her to stay? That things would be different *this* time? And yet, everything between them only deteriorated.

It was why he'd been so careful with Winter. Why he'd barely ever raised his voice at her, why he'd gotten control of his anger and had learned to be a better, more supportive partner. He couldn't bear to see another woman wilt away right in front of him.

Then there had been that night. *The fight.* When she'd told him she was leaving, no matter what he said. He'd been so *angry.* He'd grabbed her and he hadn't realized how hard until he pulled away and both her arms were purple. But he'd seen a fire in her eyes he'd never seen before. And for the first time, he'd been afraid.

"You were never going to let her leave, were you?"

Fenton dropped his gaze. He thought they could work it out. That he could convince her staying was best. He loved her. He couldn't lose her. "No."

Rene nodded, as if confirming it for herself. "Yeah. I didn't think so. You know what the problem with the rich and powerful is? You have enough money to do almost anything. Even if I could have gotten her away from here, you or your father would have found her again. You would have tracked her down, and dragged her back to this prison you call a life. And I couldn't let that happen."

His eyes went wide as the realization surged through him. "It was you. You killed her that night."

"No. I *saved* her."

I keep my eyes glued to the road the whole way from Mr. Keever's house back to the place I called home up until a few days ago. I'm so paranoid I'll pass Fenton on his way back to his parents' house that I'm staring at every car that drives past on the other side.

But really, I don't even know that he went home last night. For whatever reason, he didn't seem as intent on chasing me down as he had the other day. Maybe it was because his brother was still in surgery or maybe he didn't want to make a scene. But it's very possible he stayed at his parents' house last night. And even if he didn't, there's no way he'd recognize me in this car.

I turn down our street, a sickly feeling filling my stomach as I catch sight of the house at the end of the road. Seeing that house used to fill me with joy and pride. Now all it does is make me want to puke.

I pull into Janet's driveway as instructed and kill the engine. From here I don't see Fenton's car anywhere. But it could be in the garage. I'm going to have to check before I venture into the house.

Moving slowly and methodically, I get out of the car and quietly close the door behind me, before making my way across Janet's driveway and the green space which separates our houses from each other. As soon as I'm in our driveway, I jog up to the garage door and stand on my tiptoes to look inside the windows that run along the top of the door.

It's empty.

I breathe a sigh of relief. I can get in and out in no time.

Keys in hand, I head for the front door. But when I put them in the lock, it's already unlocked. That's odd. Did he accidentally leave it unlocked for some reason? I'm still thinking about it as I open the door before I freeze in place.

"Hey there."

It takes me a second to take stock of the scene in front of me. Fenton, tied to a chair in the middle of the living room. The woman I know as Laura, who apparently isn't Laura, standing beside him, her face drawn in frustration.

"Close the door behind you, and walk forward," she says, removing a revolver from the back of her waistband. She doesn't point it at me, but the meaning is clear enough. She's not wearing her glasses, but otherwise looks the same as the last time I saw her at the café. My feet feel like lead bricks as I take in the scene before me. But I manage to follow her instructions.

"Well, shit," she says. "You're not supposed to be here."

I open my mouth to say something, but nothing comes out at first. What's going on here? Why is Fenton tied to one of the dining room chairs? What is she trying to do?

"What...?"

"What indeed," she says. "I was just having a nice little discussion with Fenton here. May I ask what you're doing?"

My heart is all the way in my throat. My eyes search the place. There is dried blood on Fenton's forehead. And his arms are bruised, his shirt torn. What happened to him?

"I... I came for my things."

She *tsks*. "I thought I made it clear that you needed to stay away from here. From *him*," she replies. "I thought you were smarter than this, Winter."

"Who... are you?"

"Her name is Rene," Fenton says. "She works for my father."

"Correction, *worked*," she says. She grins at me. "I'm recently unemployed. Who else knows you're here?"

"No one," I lie. Maybe too quickly.

"You sure about that?" she asks. "Not your friend Cammie? Or maybe nice ol' Janet next door?"

I shake my head.

"Toss me your phone."

I hesitate until she presses the barrel of the gun to Fenton's ear. I pull it from my pocket and toss it over.

Rene catches it one-handed, the gun still on Fenton. "Passcode?"

"One-zero-two-one-eight-five."

"Thanks. Let's see here, recent texts... recent calls... hmm. Been calling your mother, no answer. No big surprise there. And wait, what's this? A call this morning to Janet. What was that about?"

"Nothing," I say. "Just... checking in on her. She helped me find your documents. *Laura's* documents."

She nods. "I see. So recluse Winter, who barely reaches out to her friends, just calls to check on her neighbor for fun. Is that right?"

I don't reply.

"I mean, it's not like I don't know where she lives. After I'm done here I can just go over and ask her when she gets home."

"I called asking for help," I stammer. "I was trying to get dirt on him." I nod to Fenton. "And his father. For what they did to Laura."

She smiles, turning to Fenton. "Well, well, well. Isn't that interesting? Looks like you can't *keep* people from looking into your dirty business, can you?"

"Go to hell," Fenton says through his teeth. "I didn't do anything wrong."

Rene holds out her hand with my phone in it. "Winter, come on over here and take a seat. I don't like you so close to the door."

I follow her instructions and take a seat on the couch, where a copy of *The Last Man I'd Marry* sits, having been tossed here haphazardly.

"Turned out pretty good, didn't it?" Rene asks, following my gaze. "Laura always wanted her books published. But she never got the chance. But it's surprisingly easy. All she needed was a cover and some basic formatting. And in an afternoon I had this. Just like she wanted."

"So it was you. You did all of this." I look directly into her eyes. "Why?"

"Because you were about to make the same mistake as Laura." Rene glances down to my ring finger where Fenton's engagement ring had recently lived. There's a light band noting the ring's absence.

"What mistake?" I ask.

"Marrying him. Into this family. I tried to warn her too, but she wouldn't listen. And after the wedding, things only got worse and worse. It would have been the same for you in time."

"That's a lie," Fenton says. "Winter is nothing like Laura."

"Is it?" She turns to me. "Has he been physically violent with you?"

I think to his hands pressing into my arms. The crack on my window.

"You know it was coming, don't you? And let me guess, you never had any idea until now."

I shake my head.

"That's because he's an exceptional liar."

"Winter," Fenton says. "You have to believe me. I never meant to hurt you. I *love* you. All I wanted was for us to be happy together."

Rene wiggles her eyebrows at me. "I bet he said he loved Laura too. And look what happened to her."

"*You* killed her, not me."

I stop breathing. "What? I thought you—"

"He *did*," Rene says, waving the gun back and forth. "He killed her emotionally, spiritually, transcendentally, in every way that mattered. He beat her down until there was nothing left but a husk of a person. I ended her suffering."

"That's not true," Fenton says. "We had our problems, yes. But she wasn't a *husk*."

"But she was, Fenton, dear. I saw the light go from her eyes. They were already dead."

"Why?" I ask, completely dumbfounded. "Why—"

"End her misery? Because I *loved* her!" Rene snaps her mouth shut and stares at the ceiling, taking deep breaths. "Do you know what it's like to watch the person you care about most in the world take beating after beating and not be able to do anything about it? To sit there, helpless as you watch the pain on their face, even as they try to tell you it's okay?"

She's practically yelling, her emotions right at the surface.

"You're not talking about Laura, are you?" I ask.

She winces, trying to reset herself. "Look, we're not going to get into it. We all have trauma. So my father was rough with my mother. Big deal, I'll go to therapy. The point is, I wasn't about to sit around and watch it happen again. Not when I knew I could do something about it."

I lean forward and she motions for me to lean back into the couch again. "But to *kill* her?"

"As I said, she was already dead. She'd tried to leave. And she was punished for it. Bruises on the arms turn into bruises on the cheek, which turn into split lips, which turn into black eyes. And it only gets worse from there."

"Winter, that's not true," Fenton yells. "She's lying!"

Rene whacks him with the body of the gun. "Shut up! You were the one who hurt her. You were the one who forced my hand!"

Blood runs from Fenton's mouth. "You didn't have to kill her."

She turns to me. "What would you have done? Hmm? If you see an animal that's been hit by a car, suffering on the side of the road. The humane thing to do is to shoot it."

"Why didn't you kill him?" I ask, nodding to Fenton.

"If there is one thing I learned while working for Lazarus Byrnes, it's that for every action against a Byrnes, there is a swift and brutal reaction. I was young, inexperienced. Killing Fenton would have brought with it too many questions, too many investigations and I wasn't convinced I could get away with it. The rich don't let their own dogs lie. The only way to save her was to remove her from the equation. And Laura left me the perfect tool after she died."

The pieces are coming together, slowly. "So then you sent the books to scare him."

She exhales, relief on her face. "Yes. To scare him. Torture him. Humiliate him, in your eyes, of course. But that was only step one. Step two was meeting you. And warning you off of him. I knew I couldn't come right out and say it. But a few carefully worded conversations, a few strategically placed props. And you were out of here."

"The box under the house. That was you." She nods. "And the person at the end of our driveway?"

She takes a little bow. "Thank my drama class for that one. I can be exceptionally creepy when I want to be."

"The mobile home?" Fenton asks, his words wet with blood. Some of it has stained his shirt.

"Purely for your brother's benefit," she says. "I didn't think you'd be man enough to actually go with him. Which is why I had to warn you. I couldn't have you dying in an explosion before I was ready, could I?" She turns to me, a smile on her face. "My skills have improved considerably in the past eight years."

She then gets right up in his face. "I'm going to do to you what you did to her. I am going to beat you down every single day until you wish someone would come along and kill you. And then, I'm not going to be so generous."

"Just get it over with," he says. "Let Winter go."

"Oh no. Into the hole you go. I'll keep you fed periodically. Just enough to keep you alive. But don't worry. You won't be alone down there."

Fenton looks at me, his eyes wild.

"No, you idiot," Rene says. "Not *her*. Laura. You can spend that time apologizing for what you did to her."

I look down into the open hatch that leads under the house and it clicks. "She's... down there. You buried her."

Rene smiles. "Sure did. Managed to switch the bodies when Brian wasn't looking. But here's a fun fact. Men and women are pretty hard to tell apart when they're wrapped up in sheets headed for the incinerator."

"Who?" I ask.

"Some nobody crackhead I popped the same night," she says. "Doesn't matter."

"She's... been down there this whole time?" Fenton says, his voice barely above a whisper.

"Just waiting for you," Rene says.

Everything coalesces for me. It all makes sense. "You're not letting me go."

Rene shakes her head in disappointment. "I tried to warn you. You were free of him; all you had to do was stay away. I never wanted to harm you, Winter. I genuinely like you. If you'd never walked back through that door, you probably could have had a nice, long, happy life. And I hate that you've lost that now."

"Me too." The words escaped my mouth before I can stop them.

"Rene," Fenton says. "This is between you and me. Let her go. She doesn't need to be a part of this."

"Can't do that, boo," she says. "See, our little Winter here wouldn't be able to keep our secret. She'd have to do something about it. Which was one of the reasons I wanted her out of the way before I 'caught' you." She turns back to me. "What you want is impossible. No one will ever be perfect."

"I don't—" But the words die in my mouth.

"But you do," Rene says. "Otherwise, why keep using your little tests?"

"Tests? What tests?" Fenton asks.

"She pre-screened you. She keeps a list... It's in one of your apps, right? A list of undesirable behaviors or actions or past instances. Anyone she dates has to make sure not to earn a check on the list before she proceeds with the next phase of the relationship."

"Winter?" Fenton asks, his eyes watering.

I can't bring myself to admit it. The list was for my eyes only. No one is supposed to know about it. Plus, it didn't work. Fenton passed and look what happened.

Maybe that was the whole problem. What if I never had a list? What if I'd just let things develop naturally, instead of trying to control every little thing? Maybe there were no relationships that didn't hurt... at least sometimes. My eyes meet Rene's.

Rene makes a comical grin. "Guess you both have a few secrets." She takes a breath. "Okay, Winter. Would you mind getting in the hole? It will be much easier if I don't have to drag your lifeless body down there. Do a friend a solid, huh?"

One thing eludes me. "How did you do it? Get Laura's body in here? This house wasn't even on Fenton's radar when she died." Laura had been gone eight years and Fenton only finished the house last year.

"Oh, she stayed with me, most of the time." Rene shrugs, pulling the gun back out. "Gave me someone to talk to. And it helped develop my embalming skills. She had been my best friend, after all, and I needed to make sure she was properly taken care of. Unlike some people." She turns and kicks Fenton in the ribs, the move swift and hard. He cries out in pain as the momentum knocks him over again and he hits the ground with a thud.

"He's just not a fighter," Rene says, bending over to pick him up. "All it takes is a little bribery and you can get on to any construction site you want. Even one run by the great Fenton Byrnes."

Before I can think about what I'm doing, I'm on my feet, rushing the woman. Rene has one hand on Fenton's chair before turning her head in time. She tries raising the gun, but I get to her first, grabbing her and knocking her over. We both hit the ground behind Fenton.

"Winter, no! Run! Get out of here!" Fenton cries.

I punch and kick as hard as I can, not knowing if I'm doing any damage. But I remember from that one self-defense class I took that when in danger, you should make yourself as much of a pain in the ass as possible. Punch, kick, bite, scratch, whatever it takes. Rene still has the gun in her hand, but she's flailing back and forth with it. I grab for it, but it goes off. Rene grunts and it goes off again. Finally, she manages to get her knee between us and pushes me off, throwing me back into the couch.

"You should have stayed away," she says, pushing herself up and training the gun on me. "Gotta make everything difficult." I have one arm on the couch and the tips of my fingers brush the edge of the book. It's the only chance I have. I grab it and throw it as hard as I can at her as she fires the gun at the same time.

Without really understanding what happens, Rene's head snaps back and she falls in the direction of the open hatch, the gun flying from her hand. Her body disappears down the hole and I hear a sickening *crunch* as she hits the ground.

Breathing hard, I crawl over to the open hatch, peering over the edge.

At the bottom, Rene is lying with all her weight on her neck, which is bent at a very strange angle. Her eyes are still open, staring up at me, and it takes me a second to realize she's no longer breathing.

"Win..." Fenton's voice is weak. I turn to him and see blood pooling in two places on his chest.

"Oh my God," I say, scrambling up and over to him.

"Win... I'm so sorry," he says, more blood coming from his mouth.

"Don't say anything," I say. "I'll get help. You'll be okay."

He smiles. "You're a terrible liar."

I get up, patting my pants for my phone only to realize it's at the bottom of the hole with Rene. I dash to the kitchen, grabbing the landline and dialing 911. I give the operator the situation and run back to Fenton, the phone in my hand.

He reaches for my hand and I take it as the operator tells me to stay on the line, that help is on the way.

But all I can do is stare into the eyes of the man I promised to marry. This man who had made so many mistakes and who had tried to make up for them. Who had wanted nothing more than a better life. A simple life... with the woman he loved.

"Fen, I'm sorry," I say.

He shakes his head as sirens wail in the distance from the nearby firehouse. "You don't have anything to be sorry about." His voice is so weak. "I never stopped loving you."

"Fen..." Tears prickle my eyes as I watch the light fade from his.

And by the time the firemen break the door down, he's already gone.

"From what the coroner can tell, the fall broke her neck instantly."

I'm sitting back in the police station, across from Detective Marsh while Mr. Keever sits on one side of me and Cammie sits on the other. Marsh has a large file folder beside her, along with some evidence from the case.

"Then there won't be any charges," Keever says.

Marsh shakes her head. "None." She reaches over and grabs the item that sits in an evidence bag, opening the bag and pulling it out. It's Rene's second copy of *The Last Man I'd Marry*. The one I threw at Rene.

Marsh turns the spine to face us. "Bullet hit it right here, causing the book to ricochet and hit Ms. Lawson in the head at the exact right angle to knock her off-balance. Had she not fired that gun at that exact moment, it probably would have just smacked her harmlessly." She pins her stare at me. "And the bullet would have gone right through you. It missed you by inches, according to the ballistics report."

The book saved me.

"What about the body?" Keever asks. "Under the house."

"Still undergoing DNA testing," Marsh says. "So far the coroner has confirmed the victim was strangled and was a female.

And from the level of decay, even with the... embalming... puts her between five and fifteen years dead. But if it does turn out to be Laura Blackwell... we're going to have some serious questions for the Byrnes family."

"Are you sure about that?" I ask. "You're not going to just cover it up?"

Marsh glares at me. "I told you. Bring me something solid and I'll do something about it."

"Doesn't get much more solid than a body," Keever says.

"No. But if Rene Lawson was the original perpetrator, it'll make things more difficult. Still, covering up a murder and then conspiring to hide the body isn't exactly peanuts. I just wish we still had Ms. Lawson around to testify against the Byrnes family."

"Someone over there might talk," I say. "Warren. Or one of the others. If they were given immunity. He knows all the family's secrets."

She nods. "We're bringing them all in. Don't worry."

"What about the house?" Keever asks.

"After taking a close look, we determined Ms. Lawson copied the key at some point from the brother. She probably got the security code from the father; he was the one paying for the security at the house." She pulls out another file. "We also determined the body was probably embalmed at that mobile home. There were trace amounts of embalming fluid found among the wreckage. We suspect Ms. Lawson kept the body there until she was ready or had the opportunity to bury it on the property."

"I still don't understand why she wanted to do it. Any of it," Cammie says.

"We'll never know for sure," Marsh replies. "But according to your testimony"—she nods at me—"Ms. Lawson was convinced Fenton was the cause of all her problems. He was rich, she was poor. And apparently, she couldn't stand her best friend being with her worst enemy. Perhaps when she found out he'd hurt Laura, something in her snapped. And when she realized he'd never let her go, she figured the only way to keep her 'safe' was to make sure he couldn't hurt her anymore."

"That's so twisted," Cammie says.

Keever clears his throat: "That's not what I was referring to. The *other* house matter."

I turn to him. "What other house matter?"

"Right," Marsh says, pulling out another file from her folder. "On a hunch..." She glares at Keever. "I pulled the property records for the home. The house on Maiden Lane was registered in both yours and Fenton Byrnes's names. Given he is now deceased, the house belongs to you. Of course, currently it is a crime scene. So until—"

"I don't want it," I say.

She nods. "We can take it to auction. Provide you with the proceeds as soon as it sells."

"You really think it will sell?" Cammie asks. "Considering someone died there and another person was buried?"

"That's exactly what will make it sell," Marsh replies. "A lot of weirdos out there. There's also a sizable life insurance policy. Winter, you were named the beneficiary, but the family is fighting it."

"I don't care," I say. "I don't want anything else to do with that family or their money."

She nods. "Well, I'll leave it to the lawyers. I'm sure they'll be in contact."

Keever inhales deeply. "That it?"

Marsh nods. "I believe so. We'll be in touch regarding the outcome of the investigation but at this point, we're not expecting any more surprises."

Keever stands, shaking Marsh's hand. Cammie and I follow suit. "Thanks for your help, Katy."

"I'm just sorry it's under these circumstances," she says. She nods to me. "Miss Southerland. Miss Tucker."

Cammie and I follow Keever out to where Janet and Mike sit, waiting. "Well?" Janet asks as soon as she sees us.

"No charges, like I said," Keever replies.

Mike wraps Cammie in a hug. "You keep her straight in there?"

"She just needed a little moral support," Cammie says. "That's all."

"Oh, I'm so relieved. When they said they'd be bringing you in—"

Keever gives Janet a big grin. "Don't worry. I made sure they played it straight."

"Thank you," I say to Mr. Keever and Janet. "None of this would have been possible without you."

"We're just so glad you weren't hurt," Janet says, pulling me into a hug. "Things will be better from here on out. I promise."

I smile, hugging her back. "Thank you."

"Ready to go home?" Cammie asks.

"Yeah, I am."

There's a knock at my door.

"Come in."

It opens to reveal Cammie. "Hey."

"Hey," I reply. It turned out Cammie's house has a spare bedroom after all, though before it was being used more as a storage closet. After everything that happened, she and Mike cleaned it out and even got a bed in here so I had a place to stay while I worked everything out with the police, the insurance companies, the real estate broker and everyone else that needs my attention.

"You're sure you're not going?"

I shake my head. "They'll all be there. I don't want to see them. And I know they don't want to see *me*."

Fenton's funeral is today. I seriously thought about going, but considering I technically broke off our engagement before he died, I didn't think it was right. Not only that, but I didn't want to sit under the stare of Lazarus Byrnes, considering he's now under investigation and has been ordered not to leave the state. I'm sure he'll find some way to wriggle out of it; men like him always do.

Keever has been feeding me nuggets of information as he gets them. He's kind of like my spy on the inside I never knew I needed. But so far, the case is stalled until the town appoints a new DA. Apparently, the first one quit under mysterious circumstances. But he assures me he'll keep doing everything he can from his side to make sure Byrnes is prosecuted. He says he'll call in favors from Washington, if he has to.

He also told me Brian is slowly recovering from his injuries, but he'll be permanently scarred from the burns. I try to imagine how Fenton's mother, Abagail, feels. She was never the warmest person towards me, but I can't imagine losing one son and almost losing another has been good for her. I also wonder how much she blames Lazarus for it.

"What are you working on?" Cammie asks, taking a seat on the edge of the bed. I only plan to be here another week or so, having already relinquished my partnership stake. While I thought maybe I could stay, after some soul searching I decided it was better to start over somewhere else. Sidhara asked me to reconsider, but after what happened with Fenton, I can't stay here. Not anymore.

"Oh, just a little project," I say, shuffling the papers into a folder and setting it to the side.

"Does it have to do with those manuscripts we pulled out of your closet for you?" She gives me a sly smile.

I give her a grin.

"Okay, okay, you don't have to tell me. When you're ready."

We hear the door open and close. "Babe!" Mike calls.

"In here," Cammie calls back.

"Come here a second," he yells.

She rolls her eyes and gets up. "Hang on a moment. He's needy." She heads out while I put the folder into one of my open suitcases. Ever since Detective Marsh showed me the book with the bullet nick in it, I couldn't stop thinking about it. And I—

"Surprise!" Cammie and Mike yell in unison as they come around the corner.

I'm so startled I jump, placing my hand over my chest until I see what Cammie has in her hands.

"Oh my God," I whisper.

It's a small, very wiggly dog. And his tail is whipping back and forth as quickly as possible.

"Is that...?"

She nods, handing him over to me. "He's yours. Mike got him from the humane society this morning."

The little dog begins licking my face immediately. He can't be more than fifteen pounds. "What's his name?" I ask.

"Whatever you want. But they were calling him Biscuit."

"Hi, Biscuit," I coo, causing him to lick my face even harder, his little nose going up in my nostrils. "Ah, gah." I wipe my nose with my sleeve.

"Yeah, forgot to mention he does that," Mike says.

"Thank you," I say, holding him tight to my chest. "Both of you. This is... It's—"

"It's the least we could do," Cammie says, pulling me into a hug. "Think of him as the start of a new life."

I look down at the little dog, his big brown eyes staring back up at me. I think she's right. I see something brand new there.

Something better.

EPILOGUE
SIX MONTHS LATER

I look out over the ocean from my window, the cool, salty breeze filtering in. My desk sits right up against the opening, giving me a perfectly unobstructed view of the sea. I rented this place specifically for this view and it doesn't disappoint. And so far, it's only stormed at night, which actually is very comforting, listening to the rain on the roof.

Biscuit lays at my feet in the little doggie bed I got for him. So far he's been the perfect traveler. We're now on our fourth Airbnb in as many months as I work on my new project. He loves the car *and* the beach. We take walks in the morning together and he always chases the seagulls.

He's filled a hole in my heart I didn't know was there. And he's become my best friend in such a short amount of time. I can't imagine my life without him and I'm so grateful to Cammie and Mike for giving me that last little push I needed. Without them, I might not have ever come around, because there was always something else to do.

But now, I've left Brighton back in Brighton. I'll answer the odd correspondence every now and again, and sometimes I get emails from Sidhara asking me to reconsider coming back to work, but I don't think I can go back to the life I had before. Everything about it seems too... foreign. Like it was someone else living that life.

Unsurprisingly, the Byrnes family managed to block the life insurance policy Fenton kept. But they couldn't block the house sale. And so far, the proceeds from that have been what I've been living on for the past few months. And there's more than enough to keep me going for at least a few more years. In some ways, I consider it a final gift from Fenton. There are days when I miss him so much it hurts, and others when I'm still so angry with him. And I think that's just how it will be for a while. He didn't deserve to die for what he did, even if he did make some very *poor* decisions.

Instead, I've been focusing more of my energy on Laura. The police managed to DNA match and confirm it *was* her buried under our house. And she was given a proper funeral for what few family members of hers that remained. Her father had already died by the time she met Fenton and her mother died a few years later. She also didn't have any brothers or sisters, so the service was mostly for friends and extended family.

That has been the only time I've been back to Brighton. Which was good. It gave me a chance to catch up with Cammie, who is now engaged to Mike with a wedding set for next year. I think I might suggest they come out here to the coast for a beach wedding. It's one of the most beautiful places I've ever seen.

But more than that, I couldn't stop thinking about Laura, and what she must have endured. I've read both the books I still have— the manuscripts that I stashed in secret. The police have everything else which is staying in evidence until the trial. I won't be going back for that either, not unless they need me to testify. But Keever is confident they won't, given the evidence they've amounted.

Laura—the wordsmith. Who poured herself into her books as an outlet for her grief. Once I finally had the time, I devoured them. And it's clear to me that neither Fenton nor Rene actually *read* them. If they had, things might have been different. Because at the end of each one, the protagonist *kills* her tormentor. And I can't help but draw the parallels between the protagonist and Laura and the tormentor and Fenton. I feel like I know Laura through her books. And I'm pretty sure she was planning on killing Fenton eventually. If only Rene had taken the time to understand her friend rather than jump to conclusions, Laura might still be alive now.

I decided the best way I could honor her was to make sure she got the recognition she deserved. Much in the way Rene did, I've taken Laura's manuscripts and I've fixed them up, formatted them and given them beautiful new covers. And I've published them... taken the final step that Rene never could. But of course, I didn't want to use Laura's real name. In a way, I feel like it's a collaboration between the two of us.

So I made one up.

I also needed to fix the titles. While they were good, I realized they needed a little more of a punch. Something that would both honor and respect her.

The doorbell rings and Biscuit's head pops up.

"Don't worry, bud, that's just the mailman," I say. He gets up and trots over to the door.

I grab the mail out of the little slot and pick up the box that has been left outside. "Perfect timing."

Taking it all inside, I set the box on the table and open it with a pair of scissors. I took the liberty of ordering a couple of copies of the new book for myself, to keep with me.

As I look at the cover, my heart fills with gratitude. This book saved my life. Literally. The least I can do is help it find a new one. For her.

I pick up the book, feeling it in my hands. *"The Forgotten Wife,"* I say.

Sounds like the perfect title.

A LETTER FROM THE AUTHOR

Dear reader,

Thank you for reading *The Forgotten Wife*. I hope you enjoyed Winter's story. If you'd like to hear about my new and upcoming releases, you can sign up for my author newsletter.

www.stormpublishing.co/alex-sigmore

If you enjoyed this book and could spare a few moments to leave a review, that would be greatly appreciated. Even a short review can make all the difference in encouraging a reader to discover my books for the first time. Thank you so much!

The idea for this book originally came about very early in my career, when I was just beginning my writing journey. In fact, the first version was only the fourth book I'd ever written. Since then it has gone through many, many revisions and was even previously published under the title *Forgotten*. However, thanks to Storm, we managed to take that original clay and mold it into a psychological thriller that is much more worthy of Winter's story.

As a new writer, I have to admit I was still very much in the experimental phase when I first penned this book. Fortunately, that very first version will never see the light of day. But it gave me a basis to work with. And now, after eight years and almost twenty-five books under my belt, I finally felt ready to give this book its due. And after rewriting the book from the ground up, we came back with the story you now hold in your hands. This idea is one that has been rumbling around in the back of my head for the better part of a decade, so to now finally see it come to life in the way I had always imagined is quite the dream come true.

Thanks again for being part of this amazing journey with me, and I hope you'll stay in touch—I have so many more stories and ideas to entertain you with!

facebook.com/AlexSigmoreBooks

instagram.com/alexsigmore

bookbub.com/authors/alex-sigmore

amazon.com/Alex-Sigmore/e/B0B1YXMZ7N

ACKNOWLEDGMENTS

Despite writing being a very solitary job, bringing a book to life is a team effort, and *The Forgotten Wife* is no exception. I want to take a moment to thank the people who made this journey possible.

First, to Storm Publishing, for believing in my stories and bringing them to readers around the world. To my editor, Kate Smith, thank you for your steady guidance and sharp insight—you make every draft stronger and really brought out the possibilities of what this book could be. Thank you for believing in it. To Alexandra, Jon, Oliver and everyone else at Storm, thank you for giving indie authors like me a space where we can deliver our books to more readers.

A special thanks as well to Anne McDonagh, whose skillful narration brings these characters to life in a way that still amazes me every time I listen.

On a personal note, I am endlessly grateful to my wife. Thank you for standing by me, for your patience, and for giving me the space I need to write. This book, like all the others, wouldn't exist without you.

Finally, to my author community—your encouragement, wisdom, and friendship keep me going even in the darkest moments. I am constantly inspired by your passion and persistence.

And most of all, to you, the reader holding this book in your hands, thank *you*. Here's to many more to come.